THE
PREDATOR
HUNTER

BY

PHIL M. WILLIAMS

Printed in the United States of America.
First Printing, 2018.

Phil W Books.
www.PhilWBooks.com

ISBN: 978-1-943894-48-2

Cover design and formatting by Tugboat Design

Dedicated to victims of child abuse: past, present, and future.

A NOTE FROM PHIL

Dear Reader,

If you're interested in receiving my novel *Against the Grain* for free, and/or reading my other titles for free or discounted, go to the following link: http://www.PhilWBooks.com.
You're probably thinking, *What's the catch?* There is no catch.

Sincerely,
Phil M. Williams

CONTENTS

CHAPTER 1

CROWDED LONELINESS

Kyle Summers stood in the waiting area, holding the restaurant pager, and watching the entrance. The revolving door bustled with well-to-do people coming and going. The three-story brick restaurant was busy as usual. He'd had to park across the street at the grocery store. He glanced at his outfit. *I need some new clothes.* He wore a button-down shirt, khakis, and work boots—his best ensemble, but obviously many years old, and a bit baggy for the current fashion trends. One of his phones buzzed in his pocket.

Lori: I just parked. Be there in a minute.

Kyle: See you soon!

Dumbass. Why did I text an exclamation point? I already look needy and desperate. I am needy and desperate. *Relax. Keep it together. It would be better if she didn't know that.*

She stepped from the revolving door, looking even better than her profile picture. Curves in the right places, round face, large brown eyes, and a button nose. He approached her, weaving in and out of the middle-aged clientele waiting for a table. She looked around, her shiny chestnut hair moving about her shoulders like a freaking shampoo commercial. *Beautiful—and out of my league.*

1

It wasn't that Kyle was ugly. He was actually fairly handsome underneath his outdated clothes. He had short dark hair, a square jaw, and a symmetrical face. He was fit and young, in his mid-twenties. But he wasn't exceptional in any way, and he felt deficient in many ways.

Moving closer, he smiled as he caught her eye. Her eyes narrowed for a split second, giving him a once-over, then a tight smile.

"Lori?" he asked, still smiling.

"Kyle?" she replied, her smile gone.

"Thank you for coming out." He held up the restaurant pager. "Hopefully our table will be ready soon. I did call-ahead seating, but they still make you wait."

"This place is crazy, especially on a Saturday night. I've waited two hours before."

"It shouldn't be too much longer. I've been here for forty-five minutes."

She furrowed her brows. "Did I get the time wrong?"

"Oh, no. I came early, so you wouldn't have to wait too long."

Lori smiled, the expression reaching her eyes. "That's really nice of you. Thank you."

"No problem."

The pager buzzed, and the red lights blazed. They'd been chosen. They were led upstairs by a hostess. He walked behind Lori, purposely diverting his eyes from her butt in those skinny jeans.

They sat in a cozy corner booth, perusing their menus. Her phone sat faceup on the table. They ordered beers and filet mignon with cauliflower mash, salad, and bread that tasted like doughnuts. Kyle grinned to himself. *Maybe she's the one. We ordered the same thing. Like an old married couple.* He handed his menu to the young waitress after she had taken their orders.

Lori's phone buzzed. She scrolled and tapped for a few minutes. Kyle watched, his optimism fading by the second. Finally, she looked up.

"So," Lori said, folding her hands in her lap. "You're in construction?"

He nodded. "Landscape construction ... and maintenance. That's why I don't have a lot of clothes. Everything gets dirty."

She scrunched her nose as if she'd smelled something foul.

Why did I say that?

"You like ... work outside? I thought you ran the company?"

His stomach tumbled. "No. I work for the company."

"Are you, like, a manager or something?"

He dipped his head as if being scolded. "No."

"So you, like, work on a crew or something?"

"Yes."

Lori sighed. "I didn't know white people did landscaping around here."

"They generally don't."

"Then why do you?" Her face was twisted in disgust.

"It pays the bills."

Her phone buzzed. She tapped and thumb-typed.

"You seem disappointed," Kyle said.

She still thumb-typed.

"You seem disappointed," he said louder.

She set down her phone. "I heard you the first time."

"Are you?"

"Disappointed?"

"Yes."

"No. I don't know you well enough to be disappointed. I'm annoyed but not disappointed."

"Why are you annoyed? Just because I work for a landscaping company?"

Lori blew out a breath. "You said you were *in* construction. That implies you, like, own the company or at least have a decent job. And your profile says you're six feet tall. I bet you're more like five-ten."

The waitress set their beers on the table.

"Thank you," Kyle said to the young waitress.

"Your salads will be out shortly," she replied and turned on her sneakers, leaving them alone again.

Kyle turned back to Lori. "Every guy on Match adds at least two inches to their height. If I put five-ten, people would think I was five-eight."

She shrugged and took a swig of her beer. "You asked why I'm annoyed, and I'm telling you."

Kyle rubbed his eyes with his thumb and index finger. "Working in landscaping isn't my main job. I do something else."

"And what's that?" While she had asked the question, she didn't seem to care about hearing his response.

"I hunt pedophiles." He drank a bit of beer.

She leaned forward, her eyes widening. "You what?"

"I hunt and expose pedophiles."

"Like, guys who like little girls?"

"And boys."

The waitress dropped off their salads.

After the waitress left, Lori asked, "Do you work for the police?"

"No. I work by myself. Well, mostly by myself. My friend Troy films for me."

"I don't understand. You don't work for the police, but you hunt and expose pedophiles?"

"Yes." Kyle took a bite of his salad and washed it down with some beer.

"But, how do you do it? You can't, like, arrest them?"

"I meet up with these guys and confront them on video. Then I give the evidence to the police."

"What evidence?" Lori dug into her salad.

"I pose as young girls and boys online. I chat on Whisper and Kik and Grindr, and I have fake profiles on a bunch of dating sites. I chat with these guys until they wanna meet."

"You have to be eighteen on dating sites."

"My profiles say nineteen, but I tell the guys I'm thirteen or twelve when they contact me, and my profile pictures are of people who look very young. Then I meet and confront them about why they wanted to meet a twelve-year-old girl or whatever."

She narrowed her eyes. "Where do you get the profile pictures?"

"When I started, I bought images from Shutterstock. I'm not sure if that was legal, but now my audience sends me pictures to use. The pictures are of people who are adults now but from when they were kids."

"What about the police?"

"I give the evidence to the police and then post everything online, so everyone knows who these pedophiles are."

Lori set down her fork and scrunched her face. "You, like, *talk* to these pervs?"

He nodded.

"What do they say?"

"All sorts of things. Sometimes the conversations are nonsexual, but sometimes they're not. I get a lot of penis pictures. It's awful." Kyle shook his head. "But, if they're talking to me, that's one less child they're talking to. And, when I confront them, everyone knows who they are, so they're less likely to hurt a child in the future."

"How many guys have you gotten the police to arrest?"

Kyle cleared his throat. "None, but I just gave this detective a bunch of evidence."

"Where do you post the videos?"

"YouTube and Facebook mainly, plus my website."

"Do you have a lot of followers?"

"Not yet, but it's growing."

Lori frowned. "How are people gonna, like, see that these guys are pedophiles if nobody watches your videos?"

"Like I said, I'm getting more followers, and the police are gonna make arrests."

"But they haven't made any arrests."

"Not yet."

"How can you even talk to these freaks?"

"It's not easy, but I guess I'm kind of numb to the stuff they say."

She pursed her lips. "Do you, like, get off on it?"

Kyle sat up straighter. "No. Why would you think that?"

"Because normal people wouldn't want anything to do with these pervs."

"What about cops and Chris Hansen?"

"They actually arrest these guys. They don't friend them online. It's weird." She crossed her arms over her chest.

"I'm not friending them. I don't ever bring up the sex stuff. I have a code."

She looked over her shoulder. "Where's the bathroom?"

"It's downstairs."

"I'll be right back."

Lori grabbed her purse, slid from the booth, stepped downstairs, and disappeared into the crowd. Kyle sat alone, feeling self-conscious, eating his salad. He glanced around at the tables of happy couples and groups. He thought about loneliness and how it's much worse in a crowd. His decoy phone buzzed in his pocket—a message on Whisper.

Hurricane Ron: Hey, baby. What are you doing?

Cuddly Kate: Jus eating dinner

Hurricane Ron: By yourself?

Cuddly Kate: Yeah ☹

Hurricane Ron: I could come pick you up and take you out.

Cuddly Kate: Can't my mom and her stupid bf will be back soon

Hurricane Ron: We're still on for next weekend, right?

Cuddly Kate: Yes ☺

Hurricane Ron: Did you get my pic?

Cuddly Kate: U have a nice body

Hurricane Ron: Thanks, baby. I bet you have a hot body. I wish you'd send me a naked pic. Please!

Cuddly Kate: U know I'm shy I'm only 13

Hurricane Ron: I wish I could kiss you right now.

Cuddly Kate: Where

Hurricane Ron: All over. ☺

The waitress approached with their entrees. She glanced at the empty seat across from Kyle and set the warm plates on the table. "Be careful. They're hot," she said.

"Can you, uh, bring me the check and some to-go boxes?" Kyle asked.

The waitress tilted her head. "Is something wrong?"

"My friend … had to leave. I'm sorry." Kyle looked away for a moment.

"Oh." Her face fell, then brightened. "It's no problem. I'll be right back with your check and containers for your food."

Kyle hung his head and rubbed his temples. He went back to Cuddly Kate's chat.

Hurricane Ron: You still there?

Cuddly Kate: Gotta go my moms home bfn

Hurricane Ron: See you soon. Love you, baby.

Cuddly Kate: ☺

CHAPTER 2

DEAR OLD DAD

Kyle paid for the meal and carried his food in two Styrofoam containers. He exited the crowded restaurant. Someone was probably thrilled at the shortened wait to take his table. *Dumbass. You just wasted a day's pay.* Outside, it was a cool April night—mid-fifties. He was comfortable in his long-sleeve shirt. He'd been working outside in cooler weather all winter.

He hustled across the lit street to the grocery store parking lot. He balanced the food in one hand as he opened the door to his old Hyundai. The odometer read 176,032. The cloth seats were stained with dirt and grass and meals eaten in the car. He drove across town, then through Crosspointe, a neighborhood of beautiful homes on acre lots with million-dollar price tags.

He exited Crosspointe and crossed Ox Road into a neighborhood of bigger and more beautiful homes on six-acre lots with even bigger price tags. Divided by large lots and mature forests, the Virginia homes afforded a privacy like no other this close to DC. He made the first right and followed the asphalt road to the end of the cul-de-sac. Lights emanated from the mansions, but no streetlights were here. Kyle parked just off the road, against the forest, his car pointed out for a quick getaway, if necessary.

Kyle grabbed one of the Styrofoam containers and exited his car. He walked through a small stretch of woods, the lights from the house in the distance beckoning him. He stopped just short of the manicured lawn, hiding behind a gigantic oak. The classic red brick colonial had black shutters, a massive front door, a four-car garage, and a Lincoln Town Car parked in the circular driveway.

Kyle sat against the oak, eating his dinner with a plastic fork and knife, occasionally glancing around the tree at the house and the man seated in the black town car. Kyle finished his dinner and found a better vantage point behind some brambles and a blooming redbud tree. His decoy phone buzzed—a direct message on Grindr.

Big Bad Wolf: What's going on, YM?

Cody12782: Why d u keep calling me ym?

Big Bad Wolf: YM stands for Young Man. That is how I think of you. You're a young man but still a man.

Cody12782: SMH I can't go to PG-13 movie. Being 12 suks

Big Bad Wolf: What movie do you want to see?

Cody12782: Ready player one its bout vid games in future

Big Bad Wolf: Sounds cool. What about X-rated movies?

Cody12782: Like porn?

Big Bad Wolf: Yeah. Have you ever seen porn?

Cody12782: Yes

Big Bad Wolf: What kind of porn do you watch?

Cody12782: Guys doing it

Big Bad Wolf: Do you touch yourself when you watch?

Cody12782: Sometimes

Big Bad Wolf: Does it feel good?

Cody12782: I guess

Big Bad Wolf: You guess? You must not be doing it right.

Cody12782: Don't make fun me

Big Bad Wolf: I'm not making fun of you. I'd like to help you. Make it feel really good.

Cody12782: How?

Big Bad Wolf: I know all the tricks.

Cody12782: Lk what

Big Bad Wolf: All good things come to those who wait.

Cody12782: Huh?

Big Bad Wolf: Maybe someday I'll show you the tricks.

Cody12782: K

Big Bad Wolf: I made you a movie.

Cody12782: What movie

Big Bad Wolf: Check it out. **LINK**

Cody12782: K gotta go bed have church tomorrow

Big Bad Wolf: Sweet dreams, YM.

Kyle tapped on the link. The video featured a big hairy man, with dirty-blond hair and sunglasses, sitting naked in a chair, his hands around his erection. He looked like a Norse pedophile. *Thor the pedo.* The masturbation wasn't the most disturbing part of the video. It was the coarse grunts, the hard-set jaw, the gritted teeth, and the reflection of the computer screen in his sunglasses. It was hard to tell for sure what he was watching, but it appeared to be a larger man having anal sex with a much smaller man. Kyle shut his eyes, but he couldn't shake the images burned into his retina. He turned off the video. *I really hope the smaller guy is older than he looks.*

Movement at the house caught his attention. The front door to the mansion opened, and a tall blonde tottered out on heels, wearing a fitted silver dress—no pantyhose or tights. Her limbs were gangly, her hair straight, and her face young—very young. A middle-aged man with silver hair waved and shut the front door behind her. The man in the town car stepped out and opened the passenger door. He looked like a secret service agent with his broad shoulders and dark suit.

Kyle hurried back to his car. He drove away, before the town car made it around the driveway. Kyle waited near the community intersection, parked at the bottom of someone's driveway, his lights off. The black town car turned left, headed for the community exit. Kyle followed.

The black car drove across town, the surroundings becoming more and more crowded and less and less affluent. Fifteen minutes later, the car turned into an apartment complex in Lorton, stopped in front of a five-story building, and the girl hopped out. She now wore a long sweatshirt and leggings, with a small backpack on her back. The town car turned around and exited the apartment complex. The girl watched the car for a moment, then started toward the building.

Kyle parked his car in a visitor's spot and jogged toward the building and the girl. Four flights of covered but outdoor stairs snaked up the middle of the building. She trudged up the steps, Kyle hot on her heels. She walked to an apartment on the third-floor landing.

"Excuse me," Kyle said as he crested the third floor.

She turned, her straight blond hair whipping around, her eyes narrowing at Kyle. She had the high cheekbones and tall thin frame of a model, but her too-small and too-wide-set eyes would never work.

"Hi, I just wanted to tell you something you should know about Robert—"

"Who are you?"

"I'm Kyle Summers."

"Did you follow me from his house?"

"Yes."

Her eyes widened.

Kyle showed his palms. "But—"

"He told me to stay away from you. That you're crazy." She back-pedaled toward an apartment door.

"He lies to girls like you. Tells them he's gonna get them a modeling contract."

She unlocked the apartment door, glancing over her shoulder at Kyle. "Stay away from me."

"He's just using you. That's what he does."

"Go away." She stomped inside, slamming the door behind her.

Kyle hung his head and pinched the bridge of his nose. He knocked on the apartment door, and a frumpy woman with dirty-blond hair answered the door.

"You need to get the hell away from my daughter," she said.

"You don't understand. Robert's using her," Kyle said. "He's a child predator."

She pointed to Kyle. Her eyebrows were thin lines, running upward at a forty-five-degree angle, accentuating her angry expression. "Robert told us who you are. I'm calling the police." She slammed the door in Kyle's face.

Through the apartment door, he heard a deep voice, "You want me to talk to him? I'll beat his fuckin' ass."

Hearing that, Kyle hustled back to his car.

CHAPTER 3

VA GOLFER11

Kyle drove south on Route 1 toward Woodbridge, or *Hoodbridge* as the locals liked to call it. He turned into the Harborview Apartments. There was no view of a harbor, a river, an ocean, a bay, a lake, or even a pond. There were plenty of parking lot views, where you could admire the work trucks, vans, and Japanese cars with shiny chrome rims. The four-story buildings each housed sixteen units. The buildings were faced with doodoo-brown brick and dingy vinyl siding.

He parked and carried the Styrofoam container with Lori's uneaten meal. He opened the shared front door and trudged to the fourth floor. He knocked on an apartment door. The door opened, and a young man with short hair and a neatly trimmed beard stood in his socks and sweats. Troy was gangly and a little goofy, all arms and legs. Even without shoes he was six-three.

"You want some food?" Kyle asked, holding up the Styrofoam container.

Troy stepped aside, allowing Kyle to enter. "How'd it go?"

"This is her dinner, so …"

Troy took the container. "Where's this from?"

"Mike's."

"Nice."

"It's been sitting for about two hours."

"So?"

"So, it's meat, … medium-rare meat."

"I'll put it in the microwave."

"I'm not sure that makes it any safer."

Troy shrugged, walked to the kitchen, and nuked the dinner. Kyle plopped down on Troy's black leather couch. A crowded futuristic city was paused on the flat-screen television.

"You wanna beer?" Troy called out from the kitchen.

"No, I'm good," Kyle replied.

The microwave dinged. A minute later, Troy set his beer on the coffee table and sat down beside Kyle, balancing a warm plate in his lap.

"What are you watching?"

"*Blade Runner 2049*." He took a bite of filet mignon.

Kyle nodded.

"Man, this is good," Troy said, his mouth full.

Kyle smirked. "I'm glad you like it." He glanced at the shoes by the door—Troy's black boots and small pink sneakers fit for a six-year-old. "Sophie's here?"

"She's asleep in my bed."

"What about the bed you got her?"

"It's in my room, but she still sleeps in *my* bed. Says she's scared the clown's coming to get her."

Kyle tilted his head with raised eyebrows. "The clown?"

"Heather's douchebag boyfriend let her watch *It*. Now Sophie's freaked about that clown." Troy gulped his beer.

"Does she sleep with Heather?"

"Heather won't let her. Or maybe douchebag Darby won't let her. I don't know. Sophie told me that she sleeps in the hallway outside Heather's bedroom door."

"That's awful. Did you say anything to Heather about it?"

"Yeah, she blamed it on me. Thinks I caused this because I don't have a room for her. Like I made her needy. I wasn't the genius who let her watch a movie about a psychopathic clown. ... Don't ever get divorced." He took a bite of cauliflower mash.

"No chance of that. I can't even get a second date."

"What happened to what's-her-face?"

"Lori."

"Right, Lori. She looked pretty hot in her profile pic."

"She was attractive, but shallow and not interested in me. Wasn't jacked to be going out with a landscaper, and I wasn't quite tall enough. She didn't buy that I was six-feet-tall."

"I'm tall enough to get on that ride." Troy grinned, his beard stretching across his face and his small eyes tightening to mere slits.

"I doubt she'd date a security guard either."

"Who said anything about dating?"

Kyle shook his head.

"What?" Troy ate some more steak.

"Your love life is almost as pathetic as mine."

Troy shrugged. "As soon as I get into the police academy, things'll be different. Chicks dig cops."

Little feet padded from the hallway to the living room. Sophie appeared, rubbing her eyes, her dark hair disheveled.

"Hey, peanut," Troy said.

Sophie climbed up on the couch and leaned on Troy, her little legs pulled to her chest. Troy put his arm around her and squeezed.

"Hi, Sophie," Kyle said.

"The clown's under the bed again," she said to Troy.

"Did you say hello to Kyle?" Troy asked Sophie.

She waved at Kyle, then looked up at her dad again. "He keeps coming back."

"You wanna snuggle with me on the couch?"

Sophie nodded her head.

"Go get your blankie."

She snuggled tighter to Troy. "Not by myself."

Troy's hands were full with his daughter and his dinner.

"I'll get it," Kyle said, standing from the couch.

"Thanks," Troy said.

Kyle returned with Sophie's blanket.

"What do you say?" Troy asked.

"Thank you, Kyle." She flashed him a grin.

"You're very welcome, sweet pea," Kyle replied, draping the little blanket over Sophie.

Kyle's decoy phone buzzed in his pocket. He checked the message from a Whisper user.

VA Golfer11: Hey, girl. I love your picture. It says your location is in Woodbridge. I'm in Alexandria, VA. You like to party?

"Got a live one?" Troy asked.

"Yeah, I should get going. I'm wiped out," Kyle replied. "I'm gonna message this guy and go to bed."

"That meeting still on for next Friday night?"

"As of now. We'll see if he gets cold feet. You'll still be there, right?"

"I got your back."

"Thanks. Good night, Sophie. Don't let the bedbugs bite."

She giggled. "*Eww*, we don't have bugs."

Kyle walked next door to his apartment. The living room housed a ratty recliner and an old television on milk crates. The walls were empty and eggshell white, the carpet worn and beige. He went to the kitchen and tossed his keys on the counter. He opened the fridge. Bread, lunch meat, expired condiments, and not much else. He closed the door and stepped to his bedroom, housing a wooden desk, dresser, and a twin-size bed shoved against the wall. He set his phones on his desk, plugging one into the charger. He changed into sweats, grabbed the decoy phone, and sat on his bed. He stared at the message from VA Golfer11. The guy's profile picture was a grainy image of a redheaded guy at a pool with his shirt off. The guy in the picture was average-looking, with a decent build, but probably headed for a sunburn. Kyle shook his head. *This picture must be twenty years old.*

Cuddly Kate: Thx

VA Golfer11: You really are very beautiful.

Cuddly Kate: ☺

VA Golfer11: You look like a girl who likes to party.

Cuddly Kate: K

VA Golfer11: Do you have a boyfriend?

Cuddly Kate: No

VA Golfer11: I'm surprised.

Cuddly Kate: I'm only 13

VA Golfer11: Wow, you look older. Don't you have to be 17 to be on Whisper?

Cuddly Kate: No r u mad?

VA Golfer11: No, I'm not mad, but we can only be friends.

Cuddly Kate: K kewl. How old r u?

VA Golfer11: 35

Cuddly Kate: So old!!!

VA Golfer11: Now you've hurt my feelings.

Cuddly Kate: J/k

VA Golfer11: It's OK. Have you ever kissed a boy?

Cuddly Kate: Have u?

VA Golfer11: Haha. No I haven't, but I'd like to kiss you.

Cuddly Kate: Why

VA Golfer11: Because you're beautiful.

Cuddly Kate: But I'm 13

VA Golfer11: I think age only matters if you're immature. You seem mature. Are you?

Cuddly Kate: Yes.

VA Golfer11: That's good. Have you ever been interested in an older guy?

Cuddly Kate: No

VA Golfer11: Maybe you haven't met the right one.

Cuddly Kate: Maybe. But he wd have to be hot lk Ryan Gosling

VA Golfer11: Haha. What do you think of my profile pic?

Cuddly Kate: Is that u?

VA Golfer11: Yes. What do you think?

Cuddly Kate: Cute but lks like old pic

VA Golfer11: It's not that old. People say I look like David Caruso.

Cuddly Kate: Who's that?

VA Golfer11: He's a famous actor. Look him up.

Cuddly Kate: K

VA Golfer11: Do you think I'm cute enough for you?

Cuddly Kate: Maybe

VA Golfer11: You're a heartbreaker.

Cuddly Kate: Lol

VA Golfer11: Is Kate your real name?

Cuddly Kate: Yes what's ur name

VA Golfer11: Dylan

That can't be his real name.

Cuddly Kate: Kewl name

VA Golfer11: Thank you! So, what do you like to do?

Cuddly Kate: Hang w friends, shop, go beach

VA Golfer11: I bet you look great in a swimsuit.

Cuddly Kate: Idk

VA Golfer11: Don't sell yourself short. You're a beautiful girl.

Cuddly Kate: K

VA Golfer11: Don't talk like that. I can tell you're beautiful on the inside and the outside.

Cuddly Kate: Thx I'm gonna go to bed

VA Golfer11: Can I message you again sometime?

Cuddly Kate: K

VA Golfer11: Good night beautiful Kate.

Cuddly Kate: Bfn Dylan

Kyle checked that the iDrive app was functioning, backing up his photos and videos. He took screenshots of the chat with VA Golfer11 and created a new folder to keep the images organized. If he lost his phone, or it crashed, he'd still have the screenshots of the chats.

After the tech maintenance, he brushed his teeth, peed, and stripped to his boxer briefs. He climbed into bed and pulled his comforter tight over his body. He lay in silence, replaying the day's events. Lori. … VA Golfer11, Hurricane Ron, Big Bad Wolf, … Robert. His chest tightened. Tears welled and overflowed.

CHAPTER 4

HURRICANE RON'S COMING

Kyle drove a pickup truck, pulling a trailer full of lawn mowers. Hector and Julio spoke Spanish in the cab, their faces agitated. Kyle drove into an industrial park with roll-up garages and warehouses. He parked in front of the open garage door of Creative Touch Landscaping. Kyle and Julio unloaded the equipment, while Hector headed inside. Kyle then parked the truck and walked into the office with his clipboard in hand. Hector exited the boss's office, not making eye contact with Kyle. Sam Irwin emerged from his office, making a beeline for Kyle. Sam was in his mid-forties, with salt-and-pepper hair and a goatee.

"Hector said you guys still have eight lawns left," Sam said, his hands on his hips, his chest puffed out like Superman.

"I have to be somewhere at eight," Kyle said. "I'll come in tomorrow and do them."

Sam glanced at his wristwatch. "It's only six, and your crew is pissed because they want the hours."

"I'm sorry, Sam. Those last eight lawns are far away. If we got caught in Friday traffic on the way back, I'd never make my appointment."

Sam frowned and shook his head.

"I'll do the lawns tomorrow on my own. You don't have to pay me.

Give the money to the guys."

"All right. But don't be makin' this a regular occurrence. You know what the spring's like. We work sunup to sundown."

* * *

Kyle sat in traffic for nearly an hour to drive the eleven miles to his apartment. Troy's car wasn't in the parking lot. Kyle bounded up the stairs to his apartment. He used the bathroom, his khaki pants shedding grass clippings on the tile. He washed his hands and glanced at himself in the mirror. His gray T-shirt was dirt- and grass-stained. His face was covered in dark stubble. His blue eyes were bloodshot from chatting with the Big Bad Wolf, Hurricane Ron, and VA Golfer11 the night before. He had a strong jawline and proportional facial features. If he cleaned himself up and got a good night's sleep, he'd pass for handsome.

He slapped together a turkey-and-mayo sandwich and ate standing over the kitchen counter. He checked his decoy phone.

Hurricane Ron: I'm worried, baby. I haven't heard from you all day. Maybe we should meet another day.

Cuddly Kate: Sorry left my phone home I had track practice. My mom late pick me up and traffic soooo bad.

Hurricane Ron: I was worried about you. I'm glad you're OK. I don't know what I'd do if something happened to you.

Cuddly Kate: Awwww u r sweet! U still want meet?

Hurricane Ron: I'm worried. I've never even heard your voice. Are you really who you say you are?

Shit, he's gonna wanna talk.

Cuddly Kate: R u?

Hurricane Ron: You know I am, baby. But I have a lot to lose.

Cuddly Kate: If u don't want to whatever. I'm not feeling good anyway. I have cold

Hurricane Ron: I'm sorry, baby. Are you OK?

Cuddly Kate: Just cold w/ scratchy throte. I'm OK to meet but u can't kiss me. U might get sick lol

Hurricane Ron: For you I'd risk it.

Cuddly Kate: U always know what say. R we meeting?

Hurricane Ron: I want to hear your voice first. Call me. 571-555-0899

Cuddly Kate: U don't trust me? ☹

Hurricane Ron: Of course I do. You're a dream come true, but I need to know you're real. Please call me.

Kyle set his decoy phone to record the conversation. He grabbed his camera and tripod and recorded himself. Kyle thought of the last time he had tried to imitate a girl. That guy had hung up on him, and Kyle had never heard from him again. Kyle had been practicing since then, but he still needed work, hence the "cold" gambit. He took a deep breath, cleared his throat, and tapped "Hurricane Ron's" icon. "Ron" picked up on the first ring.

"Hello, Kate?" he said.

"It's me," Kyle said in a babyish high voice, with an impossible-to-hide hint of manliness.

Hurricane Ron was dead silent.

"Are you there?"

"I'm here."

"You, um, don't like my voice, do you? Everybody says I sound like a little girl, and, um, with this cold …"

"You sound just like your picture, baby."

"For real?"

"Yes."

"Are you sure you still … like me?" Kyle as Cuddly Kate asked.

"I more than like you," Hurricane Ron replied.

"What does that mean?"

"I think I'm falling in love with you."

"For real?"

"Yes. For real." Hurricane Ron paused. "What do you think of *my* voice?"

"I love it. You still wanna, like, meet?"

"More than anything. Eight o' clock at the Woodbridge 7-Eleven. It's on Route 1, right?"

"Yep. It's right by my house. I can walk there."

"I can pick you up at your house."

"My neighbors are so nosy. They might, like, tell my mom."

"I don't want you to get into trouble," Hurricane Ron said.

"You either," Kyle replied, his Cuddly Kate voice holding. "Are we still, um, going to the hotel?"

"I got us a really nice room. We can order room service for dinner, watch a movie. Then we can explore each other, maybe take a bath."

"I've never, um, done it before. I'm a little scared."

"Don't worry, baby. I'll be gentle. You're gonna feel so good. I promise."

"You promise?"

"I promise."

"I should, like, get ready," Kyle/Cuddly Kate said. "See you at eight?"

"See you at eight. Bye, baby."

"Bye."

Kyle hung up the phone with a relieved breath. *I think he bought it.* He grabbed his camera and wireless mike, walked next door, and knocked on Troy's apartment. No answer. He called Troy's cell.

"I'll be home in five minutes," Troy said in lieu of a greeting.

"I'll wait for you in the parking lot," Kyle said. "I wanna get there early, so we can go over the plan and get a good parking space.

"I have to change."

"Who cares what you wear? We're meeting a pedophile, not a hot date."

"I can't wear my uniform. I could get in trouble. This guy could find out where I work and cause problems."

Kyle sighed. "He's not gonna do shit."

"Still."

"Hurry up." Kyle disconnected the call and waited in the hall.

A few minutes later, Troy showed up and changed into jeans and a hoodie. A few minutes after that, they drove Kyle's Hyundai to the nearby 7-Eleven. They parked alongside the building, near the ice machines. Kyle glanced at his phone—*7:33. No new messages from Hurricane Ron.* They stepped out of the Hyundai and looked around. The last gasps of sunlight bathed them in a golden glow. Patrons hustled in and out of the store, the parking spaces directly in front of the building like musical chairs.

"It should be dark by eight. And we can see everyone coming and going from the car." Kyle pointed. "Those ice machines and the building and the fence near the back of the property make a nice bottleneck, if we can lure him there."

"He'll have a tough time getting away from us back there," Troy said with a crooked grin.

"We'll hide behind the ice machines, and, when he comes out, you can film by the building, blocking his exit on the sidewalk, and I'll stand between him and the parking lot. He'll be cornered. We can't physically restrain him, so if he moves, we move with him."

"Sounds like a plan."

Kyle nodded. "I'll message him when he gets here and say Kate's by the ice machines."

"You should type it now, so you can just hit Send when he gets here."

"Good idea." Kyle thumb-typed the message but didn't send it.

"You know what this piece of shit looks like?" Troy asked.

"Yeah, but he's never sent me a really good picture of his face. It's blurry, or he has on a hat or sunglasses. His dick pics were crystal clear though."

Troy mimed throwing up. "I don't know how you can even talk to these creeps, much less look at their junk."

"Better me than a kid."

"Better you than me."

"He has blond hair, the front kind of flipped up."

"What a douche."

"He has a cleft chin, good teeth, and a slightly large nose. He's probably in his early-forties. Not a bad-looking guy."

"Seriously, dude?"

"I'm just making an honest observation."

"I think you get in a little too deep."

"Maybe." Kyle walked toward the car. "Let's get back to the car. I don't like being out here in the open. You never know. He might be the type to stake out the place first."

CHAPTER 5

THE CONFRONTATION

The sun was gone, replaced by a nearly full moon. The parking lot of the 7-Eleven was well lit by post lights throughout and lights on the building. Kyle sat in the driver's seat, watching the parking lot for signs of Hurricane Ron. Troy sat in the passenger seat, doing the same thing, the video camera in his lap. Kyle checked his phone again—*7:59 p.m. No new messages.* "One minute to eight," Kyle said.

"You think he'll show?" Troy asked.

"I don't know. He wanted to talk to me before meeting. On the phone."

Troy turned to Kyle. "Did you talk to him?"

Kyle nodded. "I did my impression of a thirteen-year-old girl with a cold, but he was a bit hesitant. I do think he bought it."

"I hope so."

"We'll see. It's still early. There's lots of traffic."

They sat in silence, watching the cars and people come in and out of the convenience store. Kyle's nervous energy manifested with the constant tapping of his foot on the floor mat.

A BMW 5 Series sedan parked in front of the 7-Eleven. Kyle and Troy sat up straight. A white man, about six-feet tall, stepped from the vehicle. He wore a baseball cap pulled low over his eyes. He had a cleft chin, wide mouth, and a slightly large nose.

"I think that's him," Kyle said, turning on his wireless mike.

Hurricane Ron looked around the parking lot, then entered the convenience store.

"Let's get into position," Kyle said, exiting the car.

They hid behind the ice machine, and Kyle sent the message telling Hurricane Ron that Cuddly Kate was outside by the ice machines. Kyle's heart thumped in his chest, his palms and pits sweaty.

"Kate?" Hurricane Ron said around the corner.

Kyle held up one hand to Troy as a stop sign. He wanted Hurricane Ron to come a little farther.

"Kate?" Hurricane Ron said again, walking past the ice machine.

Kyle and Troy sprang into action, cornering Hurricane Ron between the fence, the building, and the ice machine.

"You looking for Kate?" Kyle asked.

Troy stood silent, filming.

"Who are you?" Hurricane Ron asked.

"I'm Kyle Summers. I hunt piece-of-shit predators, like you."

Ron backed up against the wall, his eyes wide. "I don't know what you're talking about."

Kyle moved closer, his jaw set tight. "Really?" Kyle removed his phone from his pocket and tapped Ron's number.

The phone chimed in Hurricane Ron's pocket, startling him.

"Why did you come here to meet a thirteen-year-old girl?" Kyle asked.

"I don't know what you're talking about," Ron replied. "This is a mistake. I just came to get a coffee … and some ice."

"Bullshit. Why were you calling out for Kate?"

"I, I wasn't." Ron turned to the camera. "Are you filming me?"

"Smile for the camera," Troy said.

Ron turned back to Kyle. "I do *not* give you permission to film me. If you use any of this footage, I'll sue you for everything you have. I will ruin you."

Kyle laughed. "This is a public place. I can film you if I want. Even if you could sue me, I'm broke as shit."

Troy laughed.

"I have the chat logs and even our phone call." Kyle tapped the naked picture of Hurricane Ron holding his erect penis and showed it to him. "Why'd you send this disgusting picture to a thirteen-year-old girl? Why?"

"That's not me."

"You're a fucking liar, and you're starting to piss me off. Tell the truth or this video's going up on Facebook, YouTube, everywhere. Everyone's gonna know exactly what you are."

Hurricane Ron removed his phone from his pocket. "You can't threaten me like that. You can't hold me here. I'm calling the police."

Kyle and Troy laughed again.

"That'll save me the trip," Kyle said. "I'm meeting with the police about you on Monday."

Hurricane Ron's hand shook as he put his phone back in his pocket. "You can't keep me here."

"I just wanna ask you a few questions. Why did you solicit sex from a thirteen-year-old girl online?"

"I told you. I don't know what you're talking about."

"You sure about that?" Kyle tapped his phone and played the recorded clip he'd isolated for this occasion.

"I got us a really nice room," Hurricane Ron said through Kyle's phone. "We can order room service for dinner, watch a movie. Then we can explore each other, maybe take a bath."

"I've never done it before," Cuddly Kate replied through the phone's speaker. "I'm a little scared."

"Don't worry, baby," recorded Hurricane Ron said. "I'll be gentle. You're gonna feel so good. I promise."

Kyle slipped his phone back in his pocket. "That's definitely you, and you know it. Every guy I confront tries to lie their way out of it, but I have all the evidence. Your life is over."

Hurricane Ron pushed past Troy, toward his BMW. Kyle and Troy followed, nipping at his heels.

"You said you were falling in love with Kate," Kyle said. "She's thirteen. Explain yourself, you piece of shit. How many underaged girls have you coerced into having sex with you? How many?"

Hurricane Ron hurried into his BMW. Kyle lay on the hood, his face near the windshield.

Ron stepped out of the BMW. "Get off my car."

A middle-aged woman approached the scene and Hurricane Ron. "You're Aaron Wells, the weatherman! I'm such a big fan."

Kyle smiled wide.

"No, I'm not," said Aaron Wells aka Hurricane Ron.

"Yes, you are. I watch you every night. I'm sorry to be a bother, but could I have your autograph? I have a pen and paper somewhere." She riffled through her purse.

"Go away."

"You don't have to be rude," the woman said, with a frown. "And why is that man on your car?"

"Because Aaron Wells tried to solicit a thirteen-year-old girl for sex," Kyle said, turning to address the woman.

The woman twisted her face, as if she'd eaten a lemon. "Why would you do that?"

"I didn't do anything," Aaron said, then turned back to Kyle. "Get off my car before I call the police."

"Not until you tell the truth," Kyle said.

"Maybe he is telling the truth," the woman said.

"I *am* telling the truth," Aaron said.

Kyle grabbed his phone and tapped the naked picture of Aaron and held it out for the woman to see. "This is what he sent the girl."

The woman glanced at the picture and put her hand to her chest, sucking in a breath. She turned to Aaron Wells. "That's you!"

Aaron ducked into his car and started the engine.

"Hold my phone," Kyle said to Troy.

Troy grabbed Kyle's phone as Aaron reversed slowly, with Kyle still on the hood. Troy shoved the phone in his pocket and continued to film, following the BMW. Aaron turned the vehicle around, and started and stopped a few times to shake Kyle from the hood, but Kyle held firm, his hands gripping the top edge of the hood.

"Tell the fucking truth!" Kyle said.

"Get off my car!" Aaron replied.

"Not until you tell the truth."

Aaron turned onto Route 1, traffic whizzing past on the left lane. The BMW accelerated to thirty miles per hour, Kyle facedown, hanging on for dear life, with wind blowing up his T-shirt. Drivers pointed and honked at the BMW with a 175-pound hood ornament. Aaron slammed on the brakes at the first traffic light, and Kyle flew from the vehicle onto the asphalt. Aaron drove around Kyle and ran the red light, disappearing into the distance.

A fortysomething man exited his car and stood over Kyle. "Are you OK?" the man asked.

Troy approached, out of breath, running with the camera in hand. "Are you all right?"

"I think so," Kyle said.

Troy and the man helped Kyle to his feet. Kyle moved his stinging arm in a circular motion, his forearm red with blood from the fall to the asphalt.

"What the hell were you doin' on that guy's car?" the man asked.

"Trying to stop a child predator."

CHAPTER 6

SWEET DREAMS, YOUNG MAN

"Did you get the accident?" Kyle asked as they staggered back to the 7-Eleven.

"You need to go to the hospital," Troy said.

"I'm fine. Did you get the accident or not?"

"No, I didn't get it." Troy frowned. "I'm not Usain Bolt. I'm not gonna catch a car."

"What did you get?"

"I got the beginning of your ride and the end with you on the ground."

Kyle blew out a breath. "The accident would've gotten a ton of views."

"You could've died."

"I didn't."

Troy shook his head.

"Still, this is gonna be huge," Kyle said. "That scumbag's a weatherman. Have you ever heard of Aaron Wells?"

"I don't watch the news."

"Me neither, but a lot of people do. The guy's at least a local celebrity."

Troy drove Kyle and his Hyundai back to their apartment building. They trudged upstairs to their fourth-floor apartments.

"You want some help fixing up your arm?" Troy asked, standing in front of Kyle's apartment.

"I got it," Kyle replied. "But thanks."

"You know where to find me if you need help." Troy handed the video camera to Kyle and walked toward his apartment next door.

"Thanks for being there tonight."

Troy turned to Kyle. "You know I always got your back."

Kyle entered his apartment. He set the video camera and his decoy phone on his desk next to his laptop. He went to the bathroom and leaned against the sink, looking in the mirror. He ran his hand through his short dark hair. A knot was developing on the side of his head, and his right ear had dried blood. He removed his T-shirt, his right shoulder barking in pain as he did so. His right forearm was bright red with road rash, tiny pebbles mixed with the blood. He took off his pants and boxer briefs and turned to the side. His right hip was tender, a black-and-blue bruise brewing.

Kyle showered, cleaning his wounds and grunting through the pain. He dried himself, added a healthy dose of Neosporin to his road rash, and dressed in sweats and a T-shirt. He made ice packs from Ziploc bags, shoving one ice pack in his boxer briefs against his hip, the other wrapped around his shoulder with the help of an Ace bandage.

He sat at his desk, adjusted the ice on his hip, and attached the camera to his laptop. He did a little research into Aaron Wells. The woman was right; he was a local weatherman. Kyle went through the video, watching the confrontation and his ride on the hood of Aaron Wells's BMW. He added earlier footage of their text chats and phone conversation to the video, followed by the confrontation and dramatic conclusion.

A few hours later, Kyle uploaded the video to YouTube and Facebook with the title, "Weatherman Aaron Wells Tries to Meet 13-Year-Old Girl for Sex." Kyle wondered if he was spitting into the ocean. He didn't know if his audience was big enough. *I do have sixty thousand YouTube subscribers. People send me thank-you messages all the time.*

This guy's a sort-of celebrity. Maybe it'll go viral. That'll be a ton of shame raining down on him. But that's not enough. The police need to do something. But they still haven't done anything with the information I gave them weeks ago. At least I don't think they've done anything. I am meeting with a detective on Monday. Maybe they'll do something then. He glanced at the time—11:27 p.m.—and shut his laptop. Kyle took off his sweatpants and climbed into bed.

His decoy phone buzzed on his desk. A minute later it buzzed again. *The freaks come out at night.* He pulled his pillow over his head. His phone buzzed again. He yanked the pillow off his head, staggered to his desk, grabbed his phone, and returned to bed.

Big Bad Wolf: You awake, YM?

Big Bad Wolf: I haven't heard from you since I sent my movie.

Big Bad Wolf: Did you like it?

Cody 12782: Was that u?

Big Bad Wolf: The one and only. Did you like it?

Cody 12782: Scary

Big Bad Wolf: What scared you?

Cody 12782: You know

Big Bad Wolf: My big dick?

Cody 12782: Yes

Big Bad Wolf: Hahaha. It is pretty scary. Don't worry. It won't hurt you … too much.

Cody 12782: Not funny

Big Bad Wolf: Sorry, YM. I thought you were a man. A man can handle a big dick.

Cody 12782: I'm 12

Big Bad Wolf: Don't worry. I'll make a man out of you.

Cody 12782: How?

Big Bad Wolf: By teaching you how to handle my package. There are ways to do it so it doesn't hurt. It feels really good.

Cody 12782: Like how?

Big Bad Wolf: Is this a setup? Are you a police officer?

Shit, I asked too many "how" questions.

Cody 12782: ??? R u crazy

Big Bad Wolf: Do you know what a setup is?

Cody 12782: No

Big Bad Wolf: If this is a setup, I'll kill you.

Cody 12782: ??? Why say that? Don't want tk to u anymore

Big Bad Wolf: I'm just kidding. You passed the test though.

Cody 12782: Going back bed u woke me up

Big Bad Wolf: Sweet dreams, YM.

CHAPTER 7

PROTECT AND SERVE

Kyle watched his speed and made a full stop at the stop sign, before parking his Hyundai in the back of the lot. He marched toward the brick building with a manila folder in hand. He wore khaki pants and a T-shirt that read Creative Touch Landscaping. The afternoon sun blazed overhead, a light spring breeze cooling him. He had rushed through his mowing route, marking the last few as done, even though they weren't. He had written down the addresses, so he could mow them tomorrow. His crew's silence had cost him forty bucks.

Near the three-story building, he passed a few light-blue police cruisers. The sign over the glass doors read Prince William County Police Department. Inside, an officer sat at a large reception desk.

"How can I help you?" he asked.

"I'm Kyle Summers. I have an appointment to see Detective Fitzgerald."

The officer handed him a clipboard with the sign-in sheet attached. "Fill in your information, and I'll need to see your ID."

Kyle gave his driver's license to the officer and filled out the sign-in sheet.

"Have a seat," the officer said, handing Kyle his license back. "I'll let Detective Fitzgerald know you're here."

Kyle sat in the waiting room, which was just a bank of chairs near the front door. He checked his phone. Two messages from VA Golfer11.

VA Golfer11: I've been thinking about you.

VA Golfer11: How was school, beautiful Kate?

Cuddly Kate: SSDD

VA Golfer11: What does that mean?

Cuddly Kate: Same stuff different day

VA Golfer11: That's a good one!

Cuddly Kate: K

VA Golfer11: You remember my name?

Cuddly Kate: Dylan

VA Golfer11: I'm happy! Did you ever look up David Caruso?

Cuddly Kate: Who???

VA Golfer11: Remember the actor that I look like.

Cuddly Kate: BRB

VA Golfer11: What does that mean?

Kyle waited for a few minutes.

VA Golfer11: Be right back! I looked it up.

Cuddly Kate: CSI Miami?

VA Golfer11: Yes! He was in that.

Cuddly Kate: He's kinda cute but old

VA Golfer11: Ouch!

Cuddly Kate: Sorry have 2 keep it rl

VA Golfer11: It's OK. I'm only crying a little.

Cuddly Kate: Aww

VA Golfer11: Do you have a lot of friends at school?

Cuddly Kate: Not rly

VA Golfer11: Why not? As beautiful and smart as you are, you should be the most popular girl at school.

Cuddly Kate: I'm not bful or smart

VA Golfer11: That's not true. I've seen your picture, and, texting you, I can tell you're smart.

Cuddly Kate: Whatever I jus want schl over

VA Golfer11: I'm sorry to hear that, beautiful. I was like you, when I was your age. I hated school. I think we would've been great friends ... maybe more.

Cuddly Kate: Why u hate schl

VA Golfer11: I was really skinny when I was young and guys picked on me.

Cuddly Kate: I don't lk bullies

VA Golfer11: Neither do I. Is someone bullying you?

Cuddly Kate: Not rly I jus feel invisble

VA Golfer11: I see you, beautiful Kate. You're not invisible to me.

Kyle heard footsteps. He looked up to see a tall man approaching with a bald head, ruddy complexion, and a paunch.

Cuddly Kate: Thx gotta go bfn

Kyle grabbed his manila folder, stood, and shoved his phone in his pocket.

"Kyle Summers?" the bald man asked.

"Yes, sir," Kyle replied.

"I'm Detective Fitzgerald."

They shook hands.

"It's nice to meet you," Kyle said with a smile.

The detective nodded, his mouth a straight line. "Let's go upstairs to my office."

Detective Fitzgerald was tight-lipped and expressionless as they rode the elevator to the third floor. The detective ushered Kyle into an office with a placard on the door that read Detective Sean Fitzgerald, Special Victims Bureau. The detective shut the door behind them, the small office suddenly feeling cramped. It was filled with two filing cabinets, a bookcase, and a wooden desk.

"Have a seat," the detective said, motioning to the two chairs in front of his desk.

Kyle sat down, a sinking feeling in the pit of his stomach.

Detective Fitzgerald sat behind his desk, opposite Kyle. He tapped the stack of papers in front of him with one jagged finger. "I read your … *information* that you dropped off."

"What did you think?" Kyle asked, sitting up straight.

The detective narrowed his beady eyes. "What you're doing is dangerous. You're likely to get yourself sued, hurt, or worse. *And* you're breaking the law by interfering with ongoing investigations."

Kyle's eyes widened. "How am I interfering?"

Detective Fitzgerald frowned and blew out a breath. "When we investigate a suspect, we collect evidence by the book, in anticipation of a trial. What if you spook a guy who we're investigating? Blow our whole case because you wanna play cop? We have no way of knowing exactly how your information was collected." He pointed to the stack of papers again. "These printouts could've been forged."

Kyle clenched his jaw. "I have all the original texts and recorded phone messages and video. Your tech guys should be able to tell that everything's legit."

"You're not hearing me, Kyle. I'm telling you to stop this, or I'll send you to prison."

"For what?"

"Keep going and you'll find out."

"There are seven child predators in that stack of evidence, plus I have two more." Kyle held up his manila folder for a moment. "You could arrest them for obscene internet contact with a child." Kyle pointed to his fingers as he named each potential charge. "Attempting to entice a minor by computer, attempted unlawful sexual conduct with a minor, intent to commit a felony. Don't you wanna arrest these guys?"

Detective Fitzgerald's face flashed fire-engine red. "Why do you do this, Kyle? You get your rocks off talking to perverts? Posing as little kids online? Is that what it is?"

Kyle was silent, glowering at the detective.

"What's gonna happen when one of these guys pulls a gun on you?"

"That'll be my problem."

The detective shook his head. "No, it'll be *my* problem. What happens when the guy misses you and hits an innocent bystander? What happens when you scare the guy, and he speeds off into traffic and kills someone?"

"I don't know."

"That's right. You *don't* know. Look, I'd like to think your intentions are good, so I'm gonna ignore what you've done, but I better not hear about you ever doing this again. You got me?"

Kyle nodded, his mouth turned down.

"I didn't hear you."

"Yes."

"Good."

"Are you gonna arrest these guys?" Kyle held up the manila folder again.

"No. Didn't you hear what I said?" The detective paused, glaring at Kyle. "We make our own cases. Cases that can stand up in court."

CHAPTER 8

JEWEL'S BIG DREAM

Kyle punched the time clock and hurried from Creative Touch Landscaping to his Hyundai. His car interior was still warm from the afternoon sun. He sat in Friday traffic for fifteen minutes to go two miles down Route 1. He turned into the apartment complex where the wannabe model lived. *Robert's going down. He's not getting away with this shit anymore.* Kyle backed his car into a visitor space across from the girl's building.

His car windows were down, so he could hear cars and people coming and going. He grabbed his phone and checked his messages, alternately looking at his phone and watching for the girl.

Big Bad Wolf: What's up, YM?

Big Bad Wolf: You there?

Big Bad Wolf: You still scared?

Cody 12782: A little

Big Bad Wolf: Don't be. I'm the Big Bad Wolf, but I don't bite.

Cody 12782: K

Big Bad Wolf: You get to see that movie yet? Ready Player One

Cody 12782: No

Big Bad Wolf: Your mom won't take you?

Cody 12782: She's always working

Big Bad Wolf: You need an older friend to take you, act like your parent.

Cody 12782: Idk

Big Bad Wolf: Kids do it all the time. It's not a big deal.

Cody 12782: K

Big Bad Wolf: But you're not ready for that yet.

Cody 12782: How do u know

Big Bad Wolf: There you go, YM. Now you sound like a man.

Cody 12782: K???

Big Bad Wolf: I'd like for you to do me a small favor.

Cody 12782: What?

Big Bad Wolf: Send me a picture of you naked. You don't have to put your face in the pic, so nobody will ever know.

Cody 12782: Idk

Big Bad Wolf: What don't you know? I sent you a very private movie, but you haven't sent me anything.

Cody 12782: Idk

Big Bad Wolf: I'm trying to help you grow up, be a man.

Cody 12782: K

Big Bad Wolf: You need to be more appreciative. I'm trying to help you.

Cody 12782: I don't need do nothing

Big Bad Wolf: There you go, YM. I like that you got some fight in you. I don't like it to be too easy. At least think about the pic.

Cody 12782: K bye

Big Bad Wolf: Later, YM.

Kyle closed Grindr and navigated to his YouTube page, The Predator Hunter. His eyes widened. *Holy shit.* His latest video with Aaron Wells, the weatherman, already had nearly half-a-million views. Kyle scanned the comments.

Ducati Biker: Great job, Kyle! I'm from NOVA. I saw that douchebag on the local news last night. I wonder how long til he gets fired.

View all 17 replies

Clairebear: Kyle should wear a cape. My hero!

View all 20 replies

Scrapper919: Kyles hot AF

View all 35 replies

Plinker333: LMAO when he got on the car. A BMW too. So fucking funny.

View all 13 replies

Joytotheworld: Kyle, r u OK? Worried about you. You shouldn't get on cars. Too dangerous.

View all 8 replies

Truedat: That ladies face when Kyle showed him Aaron Wells naked pic. Priceless.

View all 4 replies

Kyle closed YouTube, his stomach in knots. He thought about Detective Fitzgerald's threat. *Hopefully he won't see it. The guy's old. Maybe he's not on the internet that much.* He placed his phone in the center console and continued to wait for the girl.

An hour later, with the sun nearly vanquished, a Ford Taurus missing a wheel cover parked in front of the building. The girl's mother stepped from the car with two McDonald's bags in hand. Kyle exited his car, following her at a safe distance. From the stairwell, he saw the mother enter her third-floor apartment. Kyle ran upstairs, stopping at her door. He cupped his hand against the door, listening.

"Jewel?" the mother said. "Jewel?"

"She ain't here," a man said.

"She with Robert?"

"She said she was goin' to that girl's downstairs."

"Brittany's?"

"Yeah."

"Can you go down and tell her dinner's here?"

"Text her."

"She don't answer my texts."

"My back's killin' me," the man said.

"I have to do everything around here," the mother said, her voice getting louder.

Kyle hustled down the stairs. Above him the mother exited her apartment and descended the stairs. Kyle hid at the bottom of the stairwell, behind the building. He peered around the corner. The mother approached a ground-floor apartment. She was probably only in her early thirties, but her face was haggard, her hair straggly. She knocked. A short teen girl answered the door.

"Have you seen Jewel?" the woman asked, her voice carrying through the stairwell.

"No, I haven't," the girl replied, not making eye contact.

"Could you text her for me, hon? She don't answer me."

"OK."

"Tell her dinner's gettin' cold."

"OK, Mrs. Holloway."

Mrs. Holloway went back upstairs.

Kyle knocked on Brittany's door. The girl answered again, this time with narrowed eyes.

"I need to find Jewel," Kyle said.

"Who are you?" the girl asked.

"A friend."

"I just told her mom that I haven't seen her."

"And you and I both know you were lying."

She crossed her arms over her chest. "Was not."

"Do you want me to tell Mrs. Holloway that you were lying, or do you wanna tell me where Jewel is?"

She frowned. "I *really* don't know for sure."

"But you have an idea," Kyle said.

"We were by the playground, and I had to come home, but she didn't wanna come home. She told me not to tell her mom, but I really don't know if she's still there."

Kyle glanced at the nicotine stains on her fingertips. "Where's this playground?"

"In the back of the apartments."

"You shouldn't smoke."

"Whatever." The girl shut the door.

Kyle walked back to his car. He drove to the back of the complex and parked near the rundown playground. There were swings with rusty chains, a jungle gym, and a seesaw missing a seat on one end. Jewel sat alone on one of the swings, her sneakers touching the weeds underneath, her head down.

Kyle approached, stopping fifteen feet away from her. "Jewel?"

She looked up and stood from the swing. "I told you to stay away from me."

Kyle showed his palms. "I'll give you twenty dollars if you talk to me for five minutes."

Jewel furrowed her brows. "Just talk?"

"Yes, and I'll stay right here."

She searched Kyle's face. She wore jeans and sneakers and a tiny T-shirt that showed a sliver of midriff. Her straight blond hair flowed past her shoulders. Her face was almost catlike, if not for her small, wide-set eyes.

"OK, but I want the money now," she said.

Kyle removed his wallet, grabbed a twenty, and moved a little closer to hand her the bill. She snatched it from his hand and took a step back.

"Did Robert tell you who I am?" Kyle asked.

"Yeah." She had a crooked smile. "You're his crazy son who ran away, got into drugs. Now you're trying to blackmail him for money."

"Do I look like I'm hooked on drugs?"

"You look kinda dirty, like a homeless person."

"I'm not homeless. I work for a landscaping company."

"Why'd you run away?"

"Because Robert's a piece of shit. Takes advantage of underaged girls. I called the cops."

Jewel looked away for a moment.

"Did he tell you that you're the only one?" Kyle asked.

She glared at Kyle. "If you went to the police, why isn't he in jail?"

"Because the girl lied."

Jewel crossed her arms over her thin body. "Maybe you lied."

"The girl lied because Robert promised to get her a modeling contract."

"How old was she?"

"Fifteen. How old are you?"

"Fourteen." She bit her lower lip.

"I think we should go back to your apartment and talk to your parents about this."

Jewel cackled, placing her hands on her cocked hips. "You think my mom's gonna believe you? She told me to tell her if I ever see you again. She's gonna call the cops on you for stalking."

That's the last thing I need. Kyle took a deep breath. "Why don't you wanna go home?"

"I'm done talking."

"I'll give you another twenty if you answer a few more questions."

She held out her hand. "Gimme the money."

Kyle removed another twenty from his wallet, and handed it over. She grabbed the bill and stuffed it in the tight pocket of her skinny jeans.

"Why you don't wanna go home," Kyle asked again.

"Because I hate my mother's boyfriend, Dale."

"Why do you hate Dale?"

"Because he's a creep. He sits on his fat ass all day. He's on disability, but it's bullshit."

"Does he touch you?"

She twisted her tiny nose. "No, gross. He's disgusting."

"Did Robert tell you that he's gonna get you a modeling contract?"

She put her hands on her hips. "He is. I'm going to L.A., New York, even Paris. I already have dates for my photo shoots. I'm leaving in May. I'm outta here in like three weeks, and I'm *never* coming back."

"Whatever date he gave you, I can guarantee he'll drop you right before."

"You don't know what you're talking about."

"I know my father very well. He's lying to you, using the promise of a modeling career as leverage against you, so you'll let him do whatever he wants."

She glowered at Kyle. "You don't know shit."

"I'm trying to help you."

"You don't even know me. You're the one who's prob'ly a creeper. He's the one with the modeling agency. What do you have?" She walked away from Kyle toward her apartment building.

Kyle followed. "Where are you going?"

"Home. I'd rather be around Dale than you."

CHAPTER 9

OBSESSED

Kyle drove through Crosspointe, passing McMansions on acre lots. It was sunny and clear and breezy, the temperature perfect, yet nobody was outside. He parked in front of a stone-faced colonial with a three-car garage. The lawn was freshly cut and deep green, with diagonal mowing stripes. His phone buzzed. Kyle checked his messages.

VA Golfer11: Hi, beautiful Kate. How are you?

VA Golfer11: How's school going? Still hate it?

VA Golfer11: It's been a long time since we chatted. I'd love to hear from you, beautiful.

VA Golfer11: I know you're busy, but please text me back.

VA Golfer11: I'm worried. Message me back.

VA Golfer11: Are you there? PLEASE text me back.

VA Golfer11: Now I'm REALLY worried. Even if you don't want to chat, text me so I know you're alive.

He's getting desperate. Time to reel him in.

Cuddly Kate: Hey Dylan

VA Golfer11: Thank God! I was so worried about you! Where have you been?

Cuddly Kate: Busy

VA Golfer11: I know you may not be used to people caring about you, but I really care about you. And when you disappear like that, it's scary and hurtful for me. Please don't do that.

Cuddly Kate: Sorry

VA Golfer11: It's OK, I understand. I'm here to talk anytime about anything.

Cuddly Kate: Thx

VA Golfer11: You're welcome. How's everything?

Cuddly Kate: SSDD

VA Golfer11: Same shit, different day.

Cuddly Kate: Stuff

VA Golfer11: Haha, right, sorry about the language.

Cuddly Kate: Its OK

VA Golfer11: I'm sorry you're going through a tough time. It'll get better. I promise.

Cuddly Kate: How do u know

VA Golfer11: Because I've been there myself. When I was your age, I was suicidal.

Cuddly Kate: Why didn't u do it

VA Golfer11: I don't know. But I'm glad I didn't because I wouldn't be here talking with you. ☺

Cuddly Kate: U r sweet

VA Golfer11: You're the sweet one. I could eat you up!

Cuddly Kate: Eww

VA Golfer11: Haha. It's just an expression if you really, really like someone.

Cuddly Kate: U lk me?

VA Golfer11: Of course I do. I'm in love with you, but that's for when you're older.

Cuddly Kate: Why me?

VA Golfer11: Because you're beautiful, sweet, smart, kind, and funny.

Cuddly Kate: Aww thx

VA Golfer11: You're welcome. How are things with boys at school? You'll probably find a great boyfriend and stop talking to me.

Cuddly Kate: Not lkly boys are dumb

VA Golfer11: That's because you're a mature young woman. When you start dating, it'll be with a mature man.

Cuddly Kate: Think so?

VA Golfer11: I know so. Are you still waiting for your first kiss?

Cuddly Kate: Its lame huh

VA Golfer11: It's not lame. I think it's hot. Virgins are a huge turn on. Virgins who have never even kissed are a huge turn on times a million.

Cuddly Kate: Don't U want a grl w exp

VA Golfer11: Exp is experience?

Cuddly Kate: Yes

VA Golfer11: No, I'd much rather have you than any porn star or Hollywood starlet.

Cuddly Kate: Starlet?

VA Golfer11: Like a movie star.

Cuddly Kate: U rather hve me than lk any movie star?

VA Golfer11: YES!

Cuddly Kate: Wow

VA Golfer11: You ever think about having me?

Cuddly Kate: Having u how?

VA Golfer11: Like being together and in love.

Cuddly Kate: I guess

VA Golfer11: I think you would grow to love me.

Cuddly Kate: Rly?

VA Golfer11: Yes! Too bad we have to wait five years.

Cuddly Kate: We can still b friends

VA Golfer11: Definitely. Do you ever think about what it would be like to make love to me?

Cuddly Kate: Not rly

VA Golfer11: Have you ever seen a man's penis?

Cuddly Kate: No

VA Golfer11: I could be your first.

Cuddly Kate: First what?

VA Golfer11: I could send you a picture of my penis, so I'll be your first. Then I can be your first love too.

Cuddly Kate: Idk

VA Golfer11 didn't respond for a few minutes.

VA Golfer11: I attached a picture of me naked. If you don't want to look at it, I understand. I hope you try because I think you are mature enough for love. This would be a great start. If not, it's OK. Either way, I love you very much.

Cuddly Kate: Will think bout it

VA Golfer11: What do you think about meeting?

Cuddly Kate: Like IRL?

VA Golfer11: I could come pick you up, and we could go somewhere and be together, just you and me.

Cuddly Kate: Idk what would we do?

VA Golfer11: Just talk. Maybe you could have your first kiss. If you're OK with it.

Cuddly Kate: Just kiss?

VA Golfer11: I'm up for anything, but I don't want to pressure you. I love you too much for that.

Cuddly Kate: K

VA Golfer11: We have to be careful though. I could get into big trouble.

Cuddly Kate: For kissing?

VA Golfer11: Yes. We probably shouldn't meet. We should wait, but I don't know if I can.

Cuddly Kate: K

VA Golfer11: What do you want to do?

Cuddly Kate: Up to u

VA Golfer11: I want to meet. I REALLY do. I'll have to think about it.

Cuddly Kate: K bfn

VA Golfer11: BFN. Bye for now! See? I'm learning.

Kyle clicked on the attachment. It was a grainy scanned picture of a stocky man with beady blue eyes, a blockhead, a sucked-in gut, and red pubic hair. One hand was on the camera, taking a picture in the mirror, the other hand around his erect penis. Kyle closed the picture and stowed his phone in the center console. He sighed and rubbed his temples.

Someone knocked on his driver's side window. Kyle turned and looked up.

"What are you doing?" Leigh asked. "You've been out here forever."

Kyle stepped from his car. Leigh's dark hair was pulled back in a bun, wisps framing her radiant face. She held hands with her three-year-old girl, Gwendolyn.

"*Unc Kye*," Gwen said, dropping her mother's hand and rushing to Kyle. She couldn't quite pronounce *uncle* or *Kyle*.

Kyle bent down, picked her up, and hugged her. "How's my favorite person in the whole world?"

She grinned. "Good."

He looked at Leigh and shifted Gwen to one arm, holding her against his side. "How are you doing?"

Leigh sighed. "The a-s-s-h-o-l-e didn't even see Gwen last weekend. Too busy with the w-h-o-r-e."

"House, I wanna go house," Gwen said, wiggling in Kyle's arm.

Kyle set her down. She wobbled toward the house "I think she wants to go inside."

"She wants to go to *her* house," Leigh said. "I had a playhouse built in the backyard."

"That's cool. I wanna see this thing."

Kyle and Leigh followed Gwen to the backyard. Leigh looked fit in yoga pants and a long sweater. The backyard was cordoned off by a wooden board-on-board fence. The grass was green, the flowerbeds freshly mulched, and the patio furniture looked nice enough to be inside. Gwen was already in her house—a small wooden cottage painted yellow and light blue. She stood by the open front window, in her make-believe kitchen, complete with plastic sink and plastic plates. She pretended to wash dishes.

"What are you doing?" Kyle asked, bending down to window level.

"The dishes," Gwen replied, not looking up from her work. She put a plate under the faucet and made a *whoosh* sound to represent the water.

"Do you need some help?"

"No. You sit with my mom. I gonna make lunch."

Kyle laughed. "All right." He looked at Leigh. "She's growing up so fast."

Leigh sat at the round table. "I know."

Kyle joined her at the table.

"You need to come over more often," Leigh said.

"I know. The spring is crazy-busy," Kyle replied.

"How long are you going to do this?"

"Do what?"

Leigh narrowed her dark eyes. "You know what. Be poor to prove a point."

Gwen approached the table with two plastic plates. "One for you and one for you," she said, placing a plate in front of Kyle and Leigh.

"What are we having?" Kyle asked.

"*Sammiches*. I go get the *dinks*." Gwen went back to her house.

"Money's not my focus," Kyle said, his attention back to Leigh.

"Then what's your focus? Talking to creeps on the internet?"

"I caught Aaron Wells."

"The weatherman?" Leigh asked.

"Yeah. His life's over."

"Why do you feel the need to be in this … seedy world?"

"Robert's seeing a fourteen-year old," Kyle said.

Leigh frowned. "How do you know that?"

"I saw the girl leaving his house in a skimpy dress."

"So you're spying on Dad now?"

"I'm gonna prove it this time."

"That doesn't prove anything. Dad's around young girls all the time. That's part of the business."

"It's part of his pattern. Just like with Kate."

"Jesus, Kyle, don't you ever stop? That was eleven years ago. The cops investigated. The girl said he never touched her."

"That's not what she told me."

"She lied to you."

"Then why did Mom leave?"

Leigh blew out a breath. "Don't even bring her into this. She was the one having an affair. Jesus, she married the guy and moved to France, never to be heard from again. You know that she's never even seen Gwen? Dad sees her every week."

"But her affair was with a man, not a *child*."

"How many times have we been over this?"

Kyle shook his head, his jaw set tight. "Kate was fifteen. He told her that she'd get a modeling contract if she kept her mouth shut."

"But she didn't get a contract, did she? She could've gone to the police then."

"Not after she had lied to them. Her credibility was ruined."

"No, Dad's credibility was almost ruined. The business could've gone under. Dad could've gone to prison."

"That's what should've happened."

Leigh shook her head. "I can't even talk to you when you get like this. You know, if you apologized to Dad, he'd give you a job."

"Like you?"

"What's so wrong with working for the agency? I've essentially been on maternity leave for over three years. Dad said I can stay home as long as I like. I can't imagine any other company would be this generous."

"How nice for you."

She raised both hands in disgust. "It's more-than-nice for me. If I didn't have that paycheck, what would I do? How would I take care of Gwendolyn? I'd have to depend on"—Leigh looked toward the playhouse, making sure Gwen was out of earshot—"the asshole."

"I could help."

She laughed. "You can't even take care of yourself. Remember that I've seen your apartment."

Gwen carried two cups, carefully, as if she didn't want to spill the contents. She set the plastic cups on the table. "Here's the *dinks*. Careful. Hot."

"What are we drinking?" Kyle asked.

"Hot cocoa," Gwen answered as if it were obvious. "I have to get dessert." She went back to her house.

"This has to stop," Leigh said. "I can't keep doing this."

"Doing what?"

"This. You badmouthing Dad and me defending him. Did you ever think you might be wrong? Did you ever think that maybe I know what I'm talking about?"

"It's hard to believe bad things about your parents. You're biased."

Leigh pursed her lips. "I think you're the one who's biased."

"You think I wanted to believe that shit about him? About Kate?"

She shook her head slowly. "No." Leigh took a deep breath. "But maybe it was easier to believe than the truth. It must've been awful to find out that she had a crush on Dad."

Kyle rubbed his eyes with his thumb and index finger. "I know what happened."

"That girl had problems, Kyle." Leigh reached over and put her hand on top of his. "She was your first love, but she didn't love you back. She loved Dad instead, and it messed you up. It made you see things and believe things that weren't true."

Kyle snatched his hand from his sister. "Dad preyed on her."

"It was the other way around."

He stood from his seat, turned, and marched to his car.

"Kyle, wait," Leigh said. "Kyle!"

He continued to his car and drove away.

CHAPTER 10

WJLA NEWS

Kyle reversed his Hyundai into the street and gunned the engine, leaving his sister's McMansion in the dust. He drove across town to his apartment complex and parked in front of his building. The sun streamed into his car, heating the interior. He sat with his head resting on the steering wheel, replaying his conversation with Leigh. His personal phone chimed in his pocket. He retrieved his phone, glanced at the unrecognized number, and swiped right.

"Hello," Kyle said.

"Hi, are you Kyle Summers?" the woman asked.

"Yes."

"I'm Rachel Franklin with WJLA News. We've picked up your YouTube video with Aaron Wells, and we'll be running a feature story on Monday. We'd like to interview you for the piece. I know it's short notice, but I'd like to interview you today or tomorrow. Are you available?"

"Is this a joke?"

"No, sir," Rachel replied.

Kyle thought of Detective Fitzgerald and his threat. "What's the angle of the story?"

"I'm not sure what you mean by *angle*?"

"How will I be portrayed?" Kyle asked.

"As truthfully as possible. We do our best to provide unbiased reporting to our viewers. This isn't a hit piece, if that's what you're worried about. What you do … luring and confronting child predators is very compelling."

"What if I refuse to be interviewed?"

"We'll still run the story with your YouTube video, but you won't be able to tell your side of the story."

Fitzgerald is gonna hear about this either way. "I'm available whenever."

"Are you at home?"

"Yes."

"I could be there in two hours or so."

"That's fine. Do you know where I live?"

"Harborview Apartments in Woodbridge."

"You must be a good reporter," Kyle said.

"Thanks. Oh, one more thing. I need the chat logs with Aaron Wells from your phone."

"That could be a problem. I'm using the same screen name for a couple of guys. I don't wanna blow my cover."

"That's not a problem. We can blur the name," Rachel said.

"OK, then you guys can have whatever you need."

"See you in a few hours."

"OK, bye." He disconnected the call. Kyle lifted his butt from the driver's seat and shoved his phone back in his pocket. He removed his decoy phone from the center console compartment. He sighed at the three new messages.

Big Bad Wolf: What's up, YM?

Big Bad Wolf: How's it hanging?

Big Bad Wolf: You man enough for that pic yet? I bet you look good.

Cody 12782: Idk I don't want naked pics of me on net

Big Bad Wolf: Don't include your face. Then you don't have to worry about it.

Cody 12782: Idk

Big Bad Wolf: I've never sent anyone that video I sent you. And you won't even send me one pic?

Kyle didn't respond.

Big Bad Wolf: You still there?

Cody 12782: Yes

Big Bad Wolf: I'll make a man out of you eventually.

Cody 12782: K???

Big Bad Wolf: You have pubic hair yet?

Cody 12782: Yes

Big Bad Wolf: Nice. You ever measured your dick?

Cody 12782: No

Big Bad Wolf: Come on. Don't lie. Every guy measures.

Cody 12782: Not me

Big Bad Wolf: Measure it for me.

Cody 12782: With a ruler?

Big Bad Wolf: A ruler would work. You have to take two measurements.

Cody 12782: ???

Big Bad Wolf: Measure with your dick soft, then make it hard and measure it again.

Cody 12782: K

Big Bad Wolf: Are you doing it?

Cody 12782: BRB

Kyle waited for a few minutes, rubbing his throbbing temples.

Big Bad Wolf: You still there?

Cody 12782: Done

Big Bad Wolf: What were the measurements?

Cody 12782: 2 and 4

Big Bad Wolf: That ain't bad for a kid. How thick around is your dick when it's hard?

Cody 12782: Idk

Big Bad Wolf: How did you get it hard?

Cody 12782: Touched it

Big Bad Wolf: What did you think about?

Cody 12782: Nothing

Big Bad Wolf: Come on. You had to be thinking about something. A boy at school? My video?

Cody 12782: No

Big Bad Wolf: Are you circumcised?

Cody 12782: ???

Big Bad Wolf: Do you have skin over the head of your dick or not?

Cody 12782: ???

Big Bad Wolf: Does your dick pop out like a dog's when you get hard?

Cody 12782: No

Big Bad Wolf: Then you're circumcised.

Cody 12782: K

Big Bad Wolf: I like little circumcised dicks like yours.

Kyle didn't respond.

Big Bad Wolf: You know what else I like?

Cody 12782: No

Big Bad Wolf: Hairless little assholes. I bet you don't have a single hair on that virgin ass of yours.

Cody 12782: Idk I have to go

Big Bad Wolf: Too bad. It was getting good. See you, YM.

* * *

A knock came at Kyle's door. Kyle turned off his television, rose from his ratty recliner, and padded across the carpet. He wiped his hands on his jeans and opened the door. A young woman with shiny dark hair stood next to a built guy in his forties.

"Hi, Kyle," Rachel Franklin said with a smile, holding out her hand.

"It's nice to meet you," Kyle said, shaking her hand.

"This is Rex, my cameraman," she said, motioning to the bearded man.

"Kyle," Rex said, extending his hand.

"Nice to meet you, Rex," Kyle replied, shaking his hand. Kyle stepped aside. "You guys can come in."

Rachel stepped across the threshold, looking around at the Spartan accommodation. She wore a pencil skirt, heels, and a silk blouse that showed a bit of cleavage. Her face was caked with makeup that she probably didn't need.

"Maybe we should do this outside," Rachel said, turning to Rex. "You think we have enough light?"

"We'll need to hurry," Rex replied.

"Is there a playground here?" Rachel asked, turning to Kyle.

"Yeah, but nobody uses it," Kyle said.

"Perfect."

They went to the WJLA News van, and Rex readied his equipment. Kyle showed them the playground, near the back of the apartment complex.

"This'll work," Rachel said.

Rachel and Kyle stood on the sidewalk, with the playground in the background, Rex and his camera in the foreground. Kyle's heart pounded; his mouth was dry. He felt faint.

"Don't worry," Rachel said, holding a microphone. "We can do more than one take. We aren't live. OK?"

Kyle nodded.

Rex gave the signal.

Rachel said, "I'm in Woodbridge, Virginia, in front of an empty playground. It's a beautiful afternoon. Why aren't any children playing? Is it too dangerous? Actually, your child might be in more danger in your own home. I'm here with Kyle Summers, the Predator Hunter. Mr. Summers poses as children online to lure child predators out into the open, where he videotapes and shames them online." Rachel turned to Kyle. "What made you decide to become a vigilante against child predators?"

Kyle swallowed. "I, um, I don't really think of myself as a vigilante. I just don't think enough is being done to protect children online. I, uh, wanna help with that problem."

"Isn't it the job of the police to find and arrest child predators?"

"Yes, but kids are still being preyed upon. No disrespect to the police, but they can't totally stop this. If I can stop one child from being abused, it's worth it."

"Your recent video with local weatherman Aaron Wells has gone viral. What do you think should happen to him?"

"It's not up to me to decide, but he could be arrested on charges of attempting to entice a minor by computer, attempted unlawful sexual conduct with a minor, and intent to commit a felony."

"Do you work with the police to ensure arrest?"

"I've tried."

Rachel raised her eyebrows. "But they don't want you luring child predators, do they?"

Kyle shook his head. "No, … they don't."

"How dangerous are these confrontations? You're meeting criminals without the help of police, without any protection. In your last video, you were thrown from a car. Are you concerned about your safety?"

"Of course, but what would be scarier? Me meeting these predators or a child?"

CHAPTER 11

PRIME TIME

VA Golfer11: How was school today, beautiful Kate?

VA Golfer11: Monday's are the worst, huh?

VA Golfer11: My job is so tedious sometimes. It does pay the bills though. Be thankful you don't have to worry about bills yet.

VA Golfer11: Are you there?

Kyle sat in his ratty recliner, wearing sweats, his decoy phone in hand. His personal phone sat faceup in his lap.

Cuddly Kate: Hi Dylan. I'm here had sucky day

VA Golfer11: I'm sorry to hear that, beautiful. I wish we could go away together.

Cuddly Kate: Where

VA Golfer11: Anywhere, as long as I'm with you.

Cuddly Kate: Aww ☺

VA Golfer11: I know this is weird, but I feel really close to you. Like we're meant to be together.

Cuddly Kate: Me 2

VA Golfer11: I'm so happy you said that.

Cuddly Kate: ☺

VA Golfer11: I think we should meet.

Cuddly Kate: When

VA Golfer11: This weekend. How about Saturday?

Cuddly Kate: K what time?

VA Golfer11: What time do you have to be home at night?

Cuddly Kate: When it gets dark

VA Golfer11: We should meet early then. What will you tell your mom?

Cuddly Kate: That I'm going to BFFs house

VA Golfer11: That's good. I could pick you up at 11:00 a.m.

Cuddly Kate: Where

VA Golfer11: I shouldn't come to your house. Maybe you could walk to a park or something that's close to your house.

Cuddly Kate: There is McDonalds by me

VA Golfer11: That would work.

Cuddly Kate: Where would we go

VA Golfer11: Someplace private. Where we can be together.

Cuddly Kate: Lk where

VA Golfer11: I'm not sure yet. I'll figure it out.

Cuddly Kate: K

VA Golfer11: Don't tell anyone about me, not even your friends. I could get in big trouble.

Cuddly Kate: I won't

VA Golfer11: I trust you.

Cuddly Kate: K

VA Golfer11: Can you message me the address of that McDonalds?

Cuddly Kate: I have to look it up. U want me to do it now

VA Golfer11: When we're done chatting. I can't wait to see you in person.

Cuddly Kate: IRL

VA Golfer11: In real life, right? Haha.

Cuddly Kate: Yes!

Kyle's personal phone chimed. He swiped right. "What's up, Troy?"
"You watching the news?" Troy asked.

Kyle glanced at the time on his phone—*6:08 p.m.* "Shit, I lost track of time."

"I'm recording it on my DVR."

"Cool, I'll call you back." Kyle disconnected the call.

VA Golfer11: I can't believe we're doing this.

Cuddly Kate: Mom alert bfn

VA Golfer11: BFN, Kate.

Kyle turned on his television and changed the channel to WJLA News. Rachel Franklin was on the screen with her shiny chestnut hair and pencil skirt, the playground in the background.

Rachel said, "I'm in Woodbridge, Virginia, in front of an empty playground. It's a beautiful afternoon. Why aren't any children playing? Is it too dangerous? Actually, your child might be in more danger in your own home."

The news cut to a shadowy figure typing on a keyboard. Rachel spoke over the images. "Child predators lurk in the dark corners of the internet, trying to lure children into offline sexual encounters. One man has had enough."

They showed Kyle standing next to Rachel in front of the playground. "I'm here with Kyle Summers, the Predator Hunter. Mr. Summers poses as children online to lure child predators out into the open, where he videotapes and shames them. Recently, Kyle posed as thirteen-year-old Kate and chatted with WDC11 weatherman, Aaron Wells."

"Shit," Kyle said, sitting up in his recliner.

The chat appeared on a black screen with white writing, a deep digitized voice for Hurricane Ron's messages, and a young girl's voice for Cuddly Kate.

Hurricane Ron: Did you get my pic?

Cuddly Kate: U have a nice body

Hurricane Ron: Thanks, baby. I bet you have a hot body. I wish you'd send me a naked pic. Please!

Cuddly Kate: U know I'm shy I'm only 13

Hurricane Ron: I wish I could kiss you right now.

Cuddly Kate: Where?

Hurricane Ron: All over. ☺

Kyle shook his head with gritted teeth. *They fucking blew my cover. I told Rachel not to show Cuddly Kate. If Dylan sees this, he won't meet.*

"Aaron Wells posing as Hurricane Ron lured Cuddly Kate to this Woodbridge convenience store," Rachel said over footage of the 7-Eleven. "The weatherman was quite surprised to find out Cuddly Kate's actually a twenty-seven-year-old man."

The news showed highlights from Kyle's confrontation with Hurricane Ron aka Aaron Wells. The clip ended with Kyle riding into traffic on the hood of Hurricane Ron's BMW. They cut to Rachel and Kyle.

Rachel said, "You're meeting criminals without the help of police, without any protection. Are you concerned about your safety?"

They showed Kyle in close-up. "Of course, but what would be scarier? Me meeting these predators or a child?"

The news desk appeared onscreen with a fortysomething male anchor. He said, "Thank you, Rachel. Very compelling and very scary. Kyle Summers may not be able to arrest these predators, but he is making an impact. We have confirmation from WDC11 that Aaron Wells has been dismissed."

CHAPTER 12

FAME HAS ITS DRAWBACKS

A hairy arm clapped Kyle on the back. Kyle punched the time clock and turned to his boss.

Sam Irwin smiled wide, his goatee stretching across his face. "The Predator Hunter."

Kyle shrugged, not sure where his boss was headed with this.

"Don't be shy. I saw you on the news last night. I like how you confronted that douchebag. How come you never told me?"

"I don't know. I, uh, figured it doesn't have anything to do with work."

"This is why you left early that Friday."

Kyle nodded. "Yeah."

Sam clapped him on the back again. "You have to leave early again, lemme know. It won't be a problem from now on."

"Thanks."

Sam stared at Kyle, serious as a heart attack. "No, thank you. I got two girls, you know." He pointed to his salt-and-pepper hair. "I didn't get this gray until they hit their teens. We were at Chili's a few weeks ago, and these old douchebags were starin' at my oldest like she was a goddamn piece of meat. I wanted to kill these guys. She's only fifteen."

Kyle nodded.

"Anyway, whatever you need. You keep doin' what you're doin'."

"Thanks."

* * *

Hector roared past, sitting atop the zero-turn mower, cutting a sixty-inch-wide strip of turf. Kyle squinted into the bright cloudless day, then slipped on his protective sunglasses. He yanked the pull-cord on the line trimmer, the two-cycle engine coming to life. Kyle started from the left corner of the house, holding the trimmer upside down and edging the flowerbeds. In the backyard, he trimmed along the fence, his khaki pants stained green from the knee down. Kyle returned to the truck. Hector parked the mower on the trailer. Julio blew clean the sidewalk and driveway, looking like a Ghostbuster with the blower attached to his back.

Kyle checked off the house as Done on his route sheet and started the truck as Hector and Julio hopped in. Kyle's work phone chimed. "Hello."

"Kyle, it's Sam. I need you to come back to the office."

Kyle glanced at his route sheet. "We only have three more houses. Can it wait an hour?"

"No. The police are here. They wanna talk to you."

Shit. "I'll be right there." Kyle disconnected the call and turned to his coworkers. "We have to go back. ... *Regresar,* ... uh, ... *oficina.*"

"*Porque? Tenemos tres mas,*" Hector replied.

"Uh, ... *policia.*"

Hector's and Julio's eyes widened.

Kyle touched his chest. "*Para me.*"

Hector and Julio relaxed.

Kyle drove them back to the shop, his stomach in knots, his mind racing for a defense. *Obviously, they saw the news report. They're gonna arrest me for interfering with an ongoing investigation or some shit. But technically that confrontation took place before Detective Fitzgerald told me to stop.*

At the shop, Hector and Julio unloaded the equipment, while Kyle walked into the office. Detective Shawn Fitzgerald talked with a female detective. Fitzgerald wore his usual suit and sour expression. The female detective looked to be in her thirties, fit, her hair pulled back in a bun.

Fitzgerald approached, his ruddy complexion a bit more red than usual. "We need to talk, now."

Kyle's heart pounded in his chest. "All right."

"Your boss said we can use the conference room," the female detective said. "I'm Detective Mitchell." She held out her hand to Kyle.

They shook hands, her grip firm. The company's receptionist and office manager stared at the trio as Kyle led the detectives to the conference room. Kyle shut the door behind them. The rectangular room was barely large enough for the oval-shaped table and ten chairs. Kyle smelled like sunshine, sweat, and freshly cut grass.

Kyle sat down, groaning, his legs worn out from the miles and miles of walking he'd done. The detectives sat across from him.

"Am I in trouble?" Kyle asked.

"What do you think?" Detective Fitzgerald said.

"Probably."

"Why do you think you're in trouble?"

Kyle shrugged. "Because you're here, and you look pissed."

Fitzgerald shook his head. "What did I tell you before?"

"Not to confront pedophiles."

"Exactly. And what do I see on the six-o'clock news? I see you luring Aaron Wells to a 7-Eleven, then jumping on his car and riding down the road on his hood. Have you lost your damn mind?"

"I haven't been confronting anyone. The video was taken before you told me to stop. Go to YouTube and check the upload date."

Fitzgerald nodded to Detective Mitchell. She removed her phone from her suit jacket pocket. It took her a minute to tap her way to You

Tube. "What's the name of your channel?" she asked.

"The Predator Hunter," Kyle replied.

She smirked and tapped a few more times.

"It's my most recent video. I haven't posted in over a week."

"The upload date is April 13," Mitchell said to Fitzgerald. "When did you two meet?"

Fitzgerald frowned. "The sixteenth." He glared at Kyle. "Are you still luring men on the internet?"

"No," Kyle replied, his head bowed.

"If you do, you'll be in for a world of hurt. You got me?"

"I understand."

Mitchell looked at Kyle, her gaze softening. "You seem like a nice guy. I know you think we're busting your balls, but what you're doing's dangerous. We don't want you to get hurt or to accidentally cause someone else to get hurt. Do you understand?"

"Yes."

The detectives stood from the table; Kyle remained seated.

"You have a girlfriend, Kyle?" Fitzgerald asked.

Kyle glanced at Detective Mitchell before answering. "No."

"Maybe you oughtta get one."

The detectives left the conference room, and Kyle breathed a sigh of relief. He turned in his route sheet, work phone, and clocked out. He made a notation on his time card that he'd stopped working fifteen minutes earlier. On his way to his Hyundai, his decoy phone buzzed in his pocket. He climbed into his car, his decoy phone buzzing again.

Kyle sat in forty-five-minutes' worth of traffic on the way home. He continued to ignore the incoming texts. He listened to the radio, his windows down. Thankfully, it was beautiful out, the temperature a perfect seventy-one. This trip home, without a working air conditioner, would be much less enjoyable come summer.

He rolled up his windows and parked in a shady spot near his apartment building. His personal phone chimed in the center console. Kyle answered this phone. "Hello?"

"Kyle, this is Detective Mitchell."

Kyle's stomach churned. *They know I'm still luring guys.* "What do you need, Detective?"

"I'm gonna tell you something off the record. Do you know what *off the record* means?"

"That I can't tell anyone, and, if I do, you'll deny ever saying it?"

"That's right, Kyle." She paused. "As a police officer, I have to follow procedures to the letter. I'd love to do a lot of things to get these predators off the streets, but I can't. The system often works against me. Off the record, I like what you're doing. And, technically, apart from you riding on the hood of a car, we can't cite you or arrest you for confronting these guys. We'd have to prove that you interfered with our investigation, but we weren't investigating Aaron Wells or anyone else in your videos. We had no idea what Wells was doing, and, the truth of the matter is, we don't know what most of these guys are doing. The problem is too big."

"What are you trying to tell me?"

"I'm not telling you anything. This is off the record, remember?"

"Right."

"I'm simply saying that, if you continue what you're doing, there's not much we can do about it. Fitzgerald's old school. He's probably never been on YouTube, and he doesn't even have a Facebook account. You're probably safe to post on the internet, but try to stay off the local news, and no more riding on the hoods of cars."

"OK."

"One more thing, Kyle. Please be careful. I'm sure you know this, but there are some seriously sick people out there."

"I know. Thank you, Detective."

She disconnected the call.

Kyle's decoy phone buzzed in his pocket again. He checked the messages.

Big Bad Wolf: You there, YM?

Big Bad Wolf: I got something for you.

Big Bad Wolf: Check out this video. **LINK**

Big Bad Wolf: What did you think? You think you're man enough?

Kyle clicked on the link. The video showed a large hairy man, standing, his pants around his ankles. A younger nearly hairless man choked while performing oral sex. Kyle tossed the decoy phone in the passenger seat and hung his head. Tears welled and spilled. After a few minutes, he wiped his face with his T-shirt and grabbed the decoy phone.

Cody 12782: Nasty don't send me that

Big Bad Wolf: Still being a little boy, huh?

Cody 12782: Don't call me that

Big Bad Wolf: You prefer YM?

Cody 12782: Yes

Big Bad Wolf: Then act like it.

Cody 12782: ???

Big Bad Wolf: Don't worry. I'll teach you.

Cody 12782: How

Big Bad Wolf: When we get together, you'll find out.

Cody 12782: U want to get together?

Big Bad Wolf: When the time is right.

Cody 12782: When?

Big Bad Wolf: When I say.

Cody 12782: K?

Big Bad Wolf: You have a problem with the dick sucking or the choking?

Cody 12782: Choking

Big Bad Wolf: You liked the dick sucking, didn't you?

Cody 12782: Yes

Big Bad Wolf: I was wrong. You are ready to be a man.

CHAPTER 13

SORRY? OR SORRY YOU GOT CAUGHT?

Contractors grabbing a coffee and families out for a late breakfast filtered in and out of McDonald's. Kyle sat in his Hyundai alongside Troy.

"I just can't catch a break," Troy said. "I've applied with forty-four departments over the past seven years. Forty-four fucking departments and nothing but rejection. It costs me money to apply. I have to take off work to interview and to take the tests. Gas to get there. You know? I really felt good about Prince William County. It woulda been perfect. I'd be close to Sophie. The pay's good. My boss used to work there. He even put in a good word for me."

"I don't understand," Kyle replied. "I thought you passed the written test. How can they already reject you?"

"Because there's a lot of competition. I passed but barely. Other people on the list aced the test."

"I'm sorry, man. That sucks."

"What am I supposed to do now? Keep trying for something that's never gonna happen? I'm literally Paul fucking Blart."

Kyle smiled. "Too bad you don't have Kevin James's salary."

Troy smirked. "Seriously. What am I supposed to do?"

"I don't know. I mow lawns for a living. It's not like I have it all figured out."

Troy blew out a breath. "And, to top it off, you know what Sophie told me on the phone last night?"

Kyle didn't respond.

"She said she liked Daddy Darby. Can you believe that shit? It's *Daddy Darby* now."

"It's good that he's nice to her."

Troy glared at Kyle.

"Would you rather he was mean to her?" Kyle asked.

"That's not the point."

"You're right. I get it. I'd be pissed too, if I was you, but you're her father, and nobody can change that. Let Darby be her friend."

"Let's talk about something else."

"The YouTube channel's been blowing up since Aaron Wells."

"I saw that. How many subscribers do you have now?"

"Last I checked, it was over 500,000."

"That's crazy. You must have a good cameraman." Troy grinned.

Kyle nodded and smiled at his friend. "I do. Thank you, Troy. You know? These police departments are missing out."

"It is what it is." Troy took a deep breath and looked out the windshield, slightly uncomfortable with Kyle's sincerity. "You think he'll show?" he asked, looking to change the subject.

Kyle glanced at his decoy phone. "I don't know. I'm worried that this guy saw Cuddly Kate on the news. I haven't heard from him since yesterday."

"That news report was on Monday. You've been talking to him all week."

"Yeah, but maybe he found it on the internet. Maybe someone at work was talking about it, and he looked it up."

"Message him again."

"I've already messaged him twice today, and he hasn't responded. I don't wanna scare him off. If I seem desperate, he might get scared." Kyle checked the time on his phone—*10:55 a.m.* "It's still early. Five minutes till. If he doesn't show, I'll message him again at ten after."

Troy gazed up at the sky, the clouds pregnant with rain. "You think it'll hold off?"

"It's not supposed to rain until this afternoon, around four. Of course, they might be wrong."

"It wouldn't be the first time the weatherman fucked up." Troy chuckled.

Kyle smiled and shook his head.

At 11:10 a.m., Kyle sent another message.

Cuddly Kate: Where r u? I'm going home

Thirty seconds later, he replied.

VA Golfer11: Don't go. I'm parked by the Giant. I'm sorry. I'm scared. Please tell me you're real.

Cuddly Kate: I'm rl

VA Golfer11: I want to talk to you first. Can I call you?

Kyle frowned at Troy. "He wants to talk to Kate on the phone."

Cuddly Kate: K

VA Golfer11: What's your phone number? I can't believe I don't have it after all this time.

Cuddly Kate: 703-555-8667

Kyle's decoy phone chimed. He cleared his throat and answered in a quiet, high pitched voice. "Hi."

"Kate?"

"It's me."

Troy shook his head, smiling at Kyle's spot-on rendition of a teen girl. Kyle had figured out that, if he spoke quietly, he could keep most of the bass out of his voice.

"It's so good to hear your voice. I'm sorry for putting you through this," VA Golfer aka Dylan said.

"You don't trust me?" Cuddly Kate replied.

"Of course I do, beautiful. But this is really dangerous for me. People might not understand, like we do."

"OK. Well, I'm here."

"I'll be there in a minute. I'll park in the back of the McDonald's. I'm driving a silver convertible, the top up. I'll wait for you in the car."

"See you soon. Bye."

"See you soon. I can't wait."

Kyle disconnected the call and turned to Troy. "I don't think he's gonna get out of his car."

"Shit, what do you wanna do?" Troy asked. "He'll drive away as soon as he sees us."

"He wants me to get in the car, so I'll get in the car."

A Chrysler Sebring convertible parked in the back of the lot near the Dumpsters. VA Golfer backed into the space, giving him a good view of the McDonald's and a good position to make a hasty retreat. Kyle and Troy were parked alongside the McDonald's, with a view of the rear parking lot.

"There he is," Kyle said. "We can't walk directly to him. Let's take a wide circle and come at him from the back by the Dumpsters."

The decoy phone buzzed.

VA Golfer11: I'm here.

Cuddly Kate: Getting drink b there in a min

"I messaged him that I'm getting a drink," Kyle said. "He'll be watching the McDonald's. He'll never see us coming."

They exited the Hyundai and initially walked away from the McDonald's and onto an adjacent sidewalk. They circled toward the back of the lot, the Dumpsters concealing their approach.

Kyle peered around the Dumpsters, catching a glimpse of the convertible, the engine idling. "I'm gonna run up there and get in the passenger seat."

"What if it's locked?" Troy asked.

"I don't know, but don't come out until you see me get in the car. I don't wanna spook him."

"All right."

They crept to the edge of the Dumpster. Kyle peered around the corner again. His decoy phone buzzed in his pocket. *He's getting antsy.* Kyle's palms were sweaty, his stomach queasy. Kyle took five quick steps and tried to open the passenger door. It was locked. He knocked on the window of the convertible. The chubby redhead in the driver's seat jerked upright, startled. The passenger window motored down halfway.

Kyle smiled wide. "Hi, sorry to bother you, but I was wondering if you could give me a jump. I left my lights on, and my car won't start."

VA Golfer aka Dylan wore an off-white sweater with a stripe of blue diamonds at chest level. His red hair was thinning and mixed with white. He had a fleshy fat neck, almost as wide as his blockhead. He definitely wasn't thirty-five. More like fifty-five.

The old redhead shook his head. "Sorry, buddy. I don't have jumper cables."

"I have cables. It'll just take a minute."

"No, I have to go."

With the speed of a cat, Kyle reached into the car, unlocked the door, and opened the passenger door. VA Golfer raised the window, but Kyle extracted his hand in time.

"What are you doing?" VA Golfer asked as Kyle slipped into the passenger seat. "Get out of my car, or I'll call the police."

Troy approached, the video rolling.

"What are you gonna tell 'em?" Kyle asked. "That you came here to meet a thirteen-year-old girl?"

VA Golfer's beady eyes widened. "I don't know what you're talking about. Get out of my car."

Kyle reached over, cut the ignition, and took the keys.

VA Golfer reached for the keys, but he was too slow. "Those are my keys. You can't take my keys." He sounded whiney.

"It's for your protection and mine. I'll give 'em back, but I have some questions you need to answer."

"I don't understand what this about." He looked at Troy. "Why is he filming me? He can't do that."

Troy kneeled next to the open passenger door, the camera pointed at VA Golfer.

"He's on public property. He can film you."

"I have to go. Give me my keys," VA Golfer said.

"My name's Kyle Summers, and I hunt piece-of-shit child predators, like you."

"What are you talking about?"

"You know exactly what I'm talking about. Why did you come here to meet a thirteen-year-old girl?"

"This is crazy. I don't know what you're talking about."

"Don't fucking lie to me."

"I'm not lying."

"Really? Your name's not Dylan?"

"No, my name's Fred."

"Can you prove it? Can I see your license?"

Fred paused, the wheels turning in his head. "I forgot my license at home, but I can send you proof."

"I actually believe that your name's Fred."

Fred let out a breath of relief. "This is all a misunderstanding. Can I please go?"

"You know why I believe your name's Fred?"

"I don't know anything about any of this."

"Because I knew you were lying when you told Cuddly Kate that your name's Dylan." Kyle removed the decoy phone from the front pocket of his jeans. "You're VA Golfer11, right?"

"I don't know what you're talking about."

Kyle leaned closer to Fred. "Don't fucking lie to me! You just told

Kate that you'd be here in a silver convertible, parked at the back of this McDonald's."

Fred reeled back, against the driver's side door.

"I'm *Cuddly Kate*, you fucking idiot. It was me talking to you the whole time. This is what I do. I catch child predators. You're a child predator."

Fred shook his head, his voice strained. "No, no, no. I didn't mean to."

"Oh, you didn't *mean to*?" Kyle tapped his phone, expanding the naked picture Fred had sent Cuddly Kate. Kyle showed his phone to Fred. "You didn't mean to send a child this picture of you holding your dick?"

Fred recoiled from the image. "I'm sorry. I'm sorry. I'm sorry. Please."

"Now you're sorry? No, you're sorry you got caught. You sent a naked picture of yourself to a thirteen-year-old. What the fuck is wrong with you?"

Fred hung his head, his eyes glassy. "I don't know what's wrong with me. I'm so sorry."

Kyle tapped the chat string between Cuddly Kate and VA Golfer11. "You messaged, 'Do you ever think about what it would be like to make love to me?' You texted this to a *child*. Then you asked, 'Have you ever seen a man's penis?'"

Tears slipped down Fred's face. "Stop. Please stop."

"You wrote, 'I could be your first.'"

"Please, no more."

"Then you wrote, 'I could send you a picture of my penis, so I'll be your first. Then I can be your first love too.' What kind of sick person sends this shit to a child?"

"I don't know. I don't know," Fred said through his tears.

"Get yourself together. Quit your crying." Kyle waited for Fred to compose himself.

Fred wiped his face with the sleeve of his sweater.

"How many times have you done this?"

"Never. I knew this was a bad idea. That's why I was late."

Kyle turned to his cameraman. "How many guys say, *It's the first time?*"

"All of 'em," Troy replied.

"What happens to me now?" Fred asked. "Are you going to call the police?"

Kyle shook his head. "No. I'm gonna put this video on the internet, so the world will know what you are."

"Please don't." Fred reached out and grabbed Kyle's arm.

"Get your *fucking* hands off me."

Fred let go. "I'm sorry. Please, you can't do this to me. I have four kids. I have grandkids. I'm married. My life's over if you do this." Fred's tears flowed again. "I have money. I can give you money. Please."

"This isn't about money."

"I'll get help. I promise." Fred clasped his hands, like he was praying. "Please. Please don't do this to me."

"I didn't do this. You did."

CHAPTER 14

SAVE 15 PERCENT OR MORE BY SWITCHING TO GEICO

The video featuring VA Golfer11 had only been up for six days, but there were nearly one million views. Kyle sat in his recliner, fresh from the shower, scanning the comments on his personal phone.

Dan the Man313: First time my ass. What a liar. Keep it up, Kyle!

View all 24 replies

Kaymayray: What a creep! And that sweater. What a freaking loser.

View all 31 replies

LT GOAT: It's super funny that the guy was driving a Chrysler Sebring convertible.

View all 6 replies

Youdontknowjack: U da man Kyle

View all 13 replies

Tinkerbell767: I love it when Kyle yells at them. He's so hot when he's mad.

View all 29 replies

Nationals fan44: That guy's my insurance agent. His real name is Fred Walters. His business is Walters Insurance Agency, located in Alexandria VA.

View all 57 replies

Kyle tapped on the replies.

The Real Slim Shady398: Look on the bright side. You could save 15% or more by switching to Geico.

Vera Wangless: You're in good hands with Walters Insurance ... provided you're under the age of 14.

The Real Deal12: This pedo lives close to Mount Vernon High School and Riverside Elementary School. 3560 Cherry Valley Court, Alexandria, VA 22309.

Terrible Toms: dudes life is ruined

Yolanda Escobar: I hope someone cuts his thing off.

Kyle's decoy phone chimed. He fished the phone from his sweatpants pocket. His eyes widened at the number. He swiped right.

"Fred?" Kyle asked.

"Kyle, please, you have to take down the video," Fred said. "Please. Someone sent it to my wife. She kicked me out. Please. I'll do anything. I'll go to therapy. Anything you want. You have to take it down."

"You *should* go to therapy."

"Will you take it down if I go to therapy?"

"No."

"Please, Kyle. I can't live like this. My life is over. There's no point in living." Fred sobbed into the phone. "Please, Kyle. I'll do anything."

"Get yourself some help, Fred."

"I'll kill myself. I swear, I will."

"I can't help you. I suggest you find someone who can." Kyle disconnected the call.

He powered off his phones and padded to his bedroom. He tossed the phones on the dresser and climbed under his comforter, wrapping himself like a cocoon. He shut his eyes and tried to sleep, but Fred's desperate begging haunted him. *Please, Kyle. I can't live like this. My life is over. There's no point in living. I'll kill myself. I swear, I will.*

CHAPTER 15

HUFF AND PUFF

Kyle parked in the grocery store parking lot, the sun low and orange in the distance. His decoy phone buzzed. Another text. *The Big Bad Wolf wants to blow my house down.*

He shoved the decoy phone into the side pocket of his windbreaker. He grabbed his camera with a long-range lens, strapped it around his neck, and stepped from his car. The parking lot was mostly empty. Saturday evening wasn't exactly prime time for grocery shopping. It was breezy, the temperature already dropping into the low sixties. Kyle hiked away from the lot toward Ox Road. He hustled across the four-lane highway into Roseland Estates.

He walked past massive mansions with perfectly manicured landscapes. The homes were concealed and separated from neighbors by five acres of mature trees. A herd of deer rustled in the woods, bounding away from Kyle. He made the first right and walked to the end of the cul-de-sac. He cut through the woods, approaching his dad's mansion. Leaves and twigs crunched under his work boots. He stopped at the edge of the wood line, hiding behind brambles.

The downstairs windows were lit, but the circular driveway was empty. *He must be home. The driver's gone though. Maybe picking up the girl?* Kyle found a comfortable spot, checked that he wasn't sitting on an ant hill, and waited. He alternately messaged with the Big Bad Wolf and watched the house for signs of life.

Big Bad Wolf: What's up, YM? You got big Saturday night plans?

Big Bad Wolf: You there?

Cody 12782: No plans

Big Bad Wolf: That sucks. No friends?

Cody 12782: Not rly

Big Bad Wolf: None?

Cody 12782: No

Big Bad Wolf: Not true. You have me. I'm your friend, right?

Cody 12782: I guess

Big Bad Wolf: What do you mean, you guess? We've been chatting for a long time. I tell you things I've never told anyone. We're more that friends.

Cody 12782: K

Big Bad Wolf: Than friends.

Cody 12782: I don't know ur name

Big Bad Wolf: Doug

Cody 12782: K

Big Bad Wolf: If these kids can't see what a cool guy you are, fuck them. They're assholes.

Cody 12782: U r rite

Big Bad Wolf: Damn right I'm right. Stick with me, YM. I got your back.

Cody 12782: Thx

Big Bad Wolf: Is Cody your real name?

Cody 12782: Yes

Big Bad Wolf: You been watching the videos I sent you?

Cody 12782: Sometimes

Big Bad Wolf: You like them, don't you?

Cody 12782: Make me feel wierd

Big Bad Wolf: It can be weird at first, but you'll get used to it.

Cody 12782: K

Big Bad Wolf: I want to talk to you on the phone. Texting is a pain in the ass.

Cody 12782: Idk I'm not allowed

Big Bad Wolf: You should be allowed to talk to your friend. We'll keep it a secret. Don't tell your mom.

Cody 12782: K but not now cause my mom will hear

Big Bad Wolf: When?

Cody 12782: When she goes to bed

Big Bad Wolf: How about 11:00 tonight? What's your number?

Cody 12782: K but I will call u

Big Bad Wolf: Talk to you later, YM. My number is 703-555-6521.

Cody 12782: Bye

The sun was nearly gone when the Lincoln Town Car drove into the circular driveway. Kyle grabbed his camera, moved a little closer, and watched the action through his long-range lens. The driver stepped from the Lincoln in a dark suit. He was a large man with thinning black hair. Even his facial features were large. Large ears, nose, mouth, chin. He looked like a caricature of a mobster.

The driver opened a rear door, and Jewel exited the Lincoln. Her long legs looked pencil thin in her stretchy pants. Kyle took pictures of the scene. Jewel sashayed to the front door. Robert opened the door before she had a chance to ring the bell. He smiled wide, looking her over. Robert shut the door, but Kyle still snapped images through the windowed door.

They were nearly identical height. Jewel's back was to Kyle, her long blond hair acting like a curtain. Robert was very close to her. *I think they're kissing.* Kyle continued to take pictures. *Shit. I don't think I got it from this angle.* Robert took her hand, turned, and led her up the spiral staircase. *To the bedrooms. Shit. Shit. Shit.*

Kyle grabbed his phone and dialed 9-1 and stopped. *I have no evidence. The cops will wanna know what I'm doing out here, spying. If Fitzgerald finds out, I'm screwed. I'll get busted for trespassing and being a Peeping Tom.*

He deleted the 9-1 and tapped Robert's cell phone. It went to voice mail. Kyle disconnected the call and tried the house phone. Voice mail again. He sent a text to Robert's cell.

703-555-8667: I have pics of you with Jewel. Send her home now or I will show the cops

Kyle called the cell again, this time leaving a message, his voice deep, mimicking a disguised voice. "I have pictures of you with Jewel. Send her home now, or I will show the cops. This is my final warning."

He left the same message on the house phone. Kyle tapped back to his text messages.

703-555-8667: You have one minute

Kyle looked up from his phone. Robert was at the front door, his face pressed to the glass. The driver's side door of the Lincoln was open. *Where's the driver?* Heavy steps approached—getting louder by the second. The driver ran toward Kyle, the light of Kyle's cell phone acting like a homing beacon. Kyle shoved the phone in his pocket and sprinted back the way he had come.

His work boots felt heavy as he ran through the small stretch of dark woods. Thin branches whipped him as he sprinted past. He spilled onto the cul-de-sac and ran down the asphalt road toward the community entrance. His breathing was labored, his legs like jelly. He turned to check his six, but there was nobody. The driver wasn't chasing him. The community was dark and dead. *I need to get to the grocery store. I can make an anonymous call to the police there.*

Kyle picked up the pace, running along the roadside, still in Roseland Estates, but Ox Road was only a few hundred yards in front of him. The dark road brightened, the roar of an engine behind him. Kyle turned to see the Lincoln Town Car speeding in his direction. He ran into the woods, feeling like he'd collapse from exhaustion. The car stopped with a *screech*, then heavy strides followed, with a flashlight bobbing in the darkness.

Kyle looked back. The driver was gaining on him. Kyle had nothing left, his sprint turning to a sporadic jog/run. The big man jumped on Kyle's back, tackling him to the ground. Kyle felt like he was beneath a compact car. The driver riffled through Kyle's pockets, removing the decoy phone. The driver snatched the camera and stood, pushing off Kyle as he did so. Kyle turned over and staggered to one knee, still breathing heavy.

"You're lucky he doesn't call the cops," the driver said.

"You don't care that he has sex with children?" Kyle asked.

"Give it a rest, Kyle."

Kyle's eyes were like saucers.

"Your dad told me all about you and your delusions." The driver took the SIM card from the camera and tossed the camera to the ground. He did the same for Kyle's decoy phone. "You need to get some help. You can't be takin' pictures of children without their consent."

Kyle stood and brushed off his jeans. "You don't know what the *fuck* you're talking about."

"Next time you wanna see your dad, come to the front door." He turned and walked back toward his car.

Kyle grabbed his camera and phone and ran to Ox Road. He hurried to the grocery store, putting his hood up as soon as he reached the parking lot. Inside, he kept his head down. He asked the young girl at customer service to use their phone. He called 9-1-1.

"Nine-one-one, what is your emergency?"

"A child is being raped at 4700 Cardinal Cove Court in Fairfax Station. Please send someone, quick." Kyle hung up, fast-walked to his car, and drove home.

CHAPTER 16

ESCALATION

Kyle exited the Verizon store with a new SIM card for his decoy phone. He sat in his car, the sun shining through the glass and heating the interior like a greenhouse. He installed the new SIM card, downloaded the Grindr app, and logged into his account. His chats with the Big Bad Wolf were gone, stored on his old SIM card, but he did have backed-up screenshots. Unfortunately, he hadn't taken screenshots from yesterday, so the chat containing Doug aka Big Bad Wolf's phone number was gone. Kyle found Big Bad Wolf's profile and sent him a message.

Cody 12782: Sorry I didn't call my phone crashed

Big Bad Wolf: Bullshit

Cody 12782: No rly just got my phone reset

Kyle attached a picture of his Verizon Wireless bag.

Big Bad Wolf: I hope for your sake that you're not playing me.

Cody 12782: ???

Big Bad Wolf: Fucking with me. Lying to me.

Cody 12782: No

Cody 12782: Can call now

Big Bad Wolf: Right now?

Cody 12782: My moms in grocery store I'm waiting in car

Big Bad Wolf: I got a little time. Go ahead and call me.

Cody 12782: I need ur number

Big Bad Wolf: 703-555-6521

Kyle cleared his throat and dialed the number.

"YM," Doug's voice boomed through the cell.

"Um, Big Bad Wolf?" Kyle spoke slowly, his voice high and shy. "Cody" was a slightly easier voice to portray than "Cuddly Kate" because he could allow a little masculinity into his speech.

The Big Bad Wolf laughed. "You can call me Doug. We're friends, right?"

"Yeah."

"It's good to hear from you. Put a name to the chat, so to speak."

"Yeah."

"What's going on, Cody? Stuck in the car waiting for your mom to finish grocery shopping?"

"Yeah."

"You live in Woodbridge, right?"

"Yeah."

"I don't live too far from there. Who knows? We might run into each other."

"But Woodbridge is pretty big."

"Not when the Big Bad Wolf has a scent." Doug chuckled to himself.

"OK?"

"What happened to your phone?"

"I don't know. It, um, just crashed."

"Downloading too much porn?"

"No! … I don't know."

Doug laughed. "Don't be ashamed. I wish I would've had access to the internet when I was your age. I would've spent all day jacking off."

"I, um, don't do that."

"What? Jack off?"

"Yeah."

"Come on. You've never jacked off?"

"Not like all day."

"But sometimes?"

"I guess."

"Feels good, doesn't it?"

"Um, yeah."

Doug's voice was lower, his breathing heavier. "Would you jack me off?"

"Um … I don't know."

"Would you let me jack *you* off?"

"As long as you, um, don't hurt me."

Doug's breathing was more ragged. "I'm jacking off … right now. You know what I'm thinking about?"

"No."

"You, Cody." He grunted. "Your hand on my dick, … stroking it. Your mouth, … sucking it. Your little asshole … bent over in front of me." He groaned. "Tell me it hurts."

"What? I should go."

"Tell me it hurts. Now!"

"It hurts."

The Big Bad Wolf bellowed, a deep primal shout, unlike anything Kyle had ever heard.

CHAPTER 17

HOOKED

Kyle disconnected the call and tossed his phone in the passenger seat of his Hyundai. He hung his head and pinched the bridge of his nose. His decoy phone chimed. It was the Big Bad Wolf again. *That sick fuck's hooked now. Let him pine for Cody. He'll call back.* Kyle let the call go to voice mail.

The decoy phone had a generic voice mail, with a Verizon-generated voice that said, "You've reached 703-555-8667. Please leave a message after the tone."

Kyle drove north on Route 1 toward Lorton. He turned into Jewel's apartment complex, parked, and hiked three flights of stairs to her apartment. A warm breeze blew through the open-air stairwell. He took a deep breath and knocked. After a minute he knocked again.

The door opened, and Jewel's mother stood behind the threshold. She wore sweats and a stained T-shirt that could double as a dress. Her brown hair was disheveled, her face puffy and blotchy.

She glowered at Kyle. "What the hell are you doin' here?"

"I'm sorry to bother you. I really need to talk to you about Jewel."

"I done told you, I ain't talkin' to you. You think I'm stupid?"

"No. I think kids are inexperienced, and adults sometimes take advantage of that."

"You need to go." She started to close the door.

"I have proof."

She opened the door wide again.

"I have proof that Robert is taking advantage of Jewel. It'll take five minutes to hear what I have to say. If you talk to me, I'll leave you and Jewel alone."

She scowled and sighed. "You got five minutes." She stepped aside and motioned for Kyle to come inside. "Well, come in. I don't wanna be airin' dirty laundry out here."

Kyle followed her into the apartment. They walked past a small kitchen on the way to the living room. A fancy coffee machine sat on the counter. In the living room, the white carpet was stained, the lighting dim, but the furniture looked new. A chubby bald man sat on the massive leather sectional, watching a seventy-two-inch plasma television. *I can guess who gave them money for the new stuff.*

The fat guy on the couch sat up straight as Kyle entered the room. *That must be Dale—the boyfriend.*

The man turned down the volume on the television. "Who's he?"

"This is Robert's son," the woman said.

"I'm Kyle," Kyle said, partly to the woman, partly to the man.

"I thought you weren't gonna talk to him," the man said as if Kyle wasn't in the room.

"He says he got proof that Robert's messin' with Jewel." The woman turned to Kyle. "Let's hear it then."

"I've been watching Robert's house. Last night I saw Jewel go into his house, and I saw them kiss. I called Robert's house to try to stop him, but his driver chased me off. I called the cops. I'm assuming the cops didn't talk to you since you don't know anything about this."

"I didn't hear nothin' from no cops," the woman said.

Kyle winced and shook his head. "Robert probably talked his way out of it. I'm sorry. ... I should've done more."

The man stood from the sectional and approached Kyle. "Who the hell do you think you are, gettin' into our business? If somethin' needs doin', I'll be doin' it."

Kyle showed his palms in surrender. "I'm just trying to help." Kyle turned to the woman. "Please, I'm telling you the truth."

"You ain't tryin' to help," the woman said. "What've you given us? Robert's helped us. You ain't done shit for us. You're tryin' to destroy your daddy 'cause you're crazy. I wasn't born yesterday."

"Where's the proof?" the man asked.

"Ask Jewel," Kyle said.

"You got pictures or video?"

Kyle dipped his head. "I have pictures of them kissing, but it's from a bad angle, so you can't tell."

"This is bullshit."

"Just ask her. I'll give you forty bucks ... for your time." Kyle removed forty dollars from his wallet.

The man snatched the bills from his hand and stomped to the hallway. "Jewel, get your ass out here," he called out.

There was no response.

The man walked down the hall and banged on a door. "Jewel, get your ass out here."

Jewel appeared with headphones around her neck. She narrowed her small eyes at Kyle. "What the hell's he doing here?"

"What happened at Robert's last night?"

Jewel looked away for a split second. "He was helping me with stuff."

The woman searched her daughter's face. "What kind of stuff?"

"Same stuff as usual. He's helping me get ready for my tour."

"Did he touch you?"

Jewel twisted her face. "Mom, no. Course not." She glared at Kyle. "Did he tell you that?"

"He said he saw you and Robert kiss."

"I saw you two," Kyle said. "Tell the truth."

Jewel frowned at Kyle and turned to her mother. "Robert, like, kissed me on the cheek to say hello, but it was just to show me what it's like in Paris. Everyone, like, kisses hello and goodbye there."

"Are you sure?" the woman asked.

"Yes, God," Jewel replied, exasperated.

"He doesn't know what he's talkin' about," the man said in reference to Kyle.

"I know what I saw," Kyle said. "Robert's using her. That's what he does—"

"You don't know anything," Jewel said.

"You're not gonna get that modeling contract."

"Get out," the woman said.

"I'm sorry. It's the truth," Kyle said.

Jewel cackled. "I'm leaving on Thursday for my tour."

The man crowded Kyle, close enough to smell his BO. "You best get the fuck outta here."

Kyle backpedaled, turned, and hurried for the door.

"You come back here again, and I'll kick your fuckin' ass," the man called out.

Kyle left Jewel's apartment and walked to his car. He drove south on Route 1, toward his apartment complex. He sat in Sunday traffic, weekend traffic now barely indistinguishable from rush-hour traffic. His decoy phone chimed. He glanced at the number and let it go to voice mail. *The Big Bad Wolf's worried that his prey's getting away.*

At home, in the comfort of his recliner, his decoy phone chimed again. He cleared his throat and answered in Cody's high, shy voice.

"Hello? Doug?"

"YM. I didn't think you were gonna pick up," Doug replied. "I thought maybe I scared you off."

"Yeah, maybe."

"Sorry 'bout that. I didn't mean to. I'm just showing you how much I care about you. You understand, don't you?"

"I guess. But, um, I don't think I'm ready for that."

"Don't worry. I'll help you get there."

"OK."

"Have you been to see that movie yet? Ready something?"

"*Ready Player One.*"

"Yeah, that one. Have you seen it yet?"

"No, I have to wait till I can stream it."

"I could take you."

"Like, in real life?"

Doug chuckled. "How else could I take you to the movies?"

"Um, … when?"

"What time does your mom get home from work?"

"Like seven."

"How about Tuesday afternoon, as soon as you get home from school? We'll go to a matinee."

"What's a matinee?"

CHAPTER 18

CONSEQUENCES

"What time are you gonna be back to the shop?" Sam Irwin asked through the cell phone.

Kyle glanced at his route sheet, his work phone to his ear. "I only have two more. Probably half an hour. What do you need?"

"A woman is here who wants to talk to you."

"Who is she?"

"Betsy. She wouldn't give a last name."

Hector finished the last strip of lawn and drove the sixty-inch mower toward the trailer.

Kyle stepped away from the truck to get away from the noise. "What does she want?"

"She just said she wanted to talk to you. Said she'd wait as long as it took. I put her in the conference room."

Kyle blew out a breath. "All right. I'll be back soon."

* * *

Hector and Julio unloaded the mowers as Kyle entered the office.

The receptionist looked up from her computer screen. "That lady's still in the conference room."

"Thanks, Judy," Kyle replied.

Kyle dropped off his route sheet, clocked out, and walked to the conference room. The door was open. A middle-aged woman sat at the head of the table, facing the door. She stood as Kyle knocked on the open door. She was short and portly, with curly hair and pale skin.

"You wanted to talk to me?" Kyle asked.

"Could you shut the door please?" the woman replied.

Kyle shut the door and approached the woman. "What's this about?"

Her eyes were puffy and red. "I'm Betsy Walters. You knew my husband, Fred."

Kyle nodded and looked away for a moment.

"He killed himself."

Kyle's eyes widened. He thought about Fred's desperate begging to take the video down, his threats of suicide. Kyle felt sick to his stomach.

The woman wiped the corners of her eyes with a scrunched-up ball of tissues. She sat back down.

Kyle sat kitty-cornered from her. "I'm sorry to hear that."

She stared at Kyle, her fist clenching over the ball of tissues. Her voice trembled. "Why did you do it? You trapped him. He made a mistake, and you ruined his life. You ruined my life, my kids' lives, my grandkids."

"I'm sorry, Mrs. Walters. My intention wasn't to hurt you or your family. Your husband met a thirteen-year-old girl on the internet and then decided to meet her in person with the intention of having a sexual relationship with her."

"But he didn't meet a thirteen-year-old girl." She narrowed her eyes. "He met you."

"Would you have rather it had been a thirteen-year-old girl?"

She shook her head. "You don't know what he would've done."

"I have a pretty good idea based on his chats. Would you like for me to read them to you?"

"It's just stupid talking. My husband said lots of stupid, stupid things, but he wasn't a child molester."

"How do you know?"

"Because he was my husband for thirty-two years!" Tears welled and slipped down her cheeks. "I knew my husband. This is *not* who he was. Now he's gone because of you. Why? Why did you do this to my family?"

"I'm sorry that this happened, but I didn't do this. He did."

She shook her head. "That's not true. You tricked him." She stood from the table and pointed a shaky finger at Kyle. "You killed him and ruined the lives of his family." She stomped from the conference room.

Kyle sat in the empty room. He hung his head and rubbed his temples.

CHAPTER 19

DOUG IRL

Kyle sat in the driver's seat of his Hyundai, bouncing his knee, the nervous energy too much to contain. Troy sat next to him, surveying the McDonald's parking lot. It was gray outside, the clouds heavy with rain. The parking lot was nearly empty this Tuesday afternoon between the lunch and dinner crowds.

"It's three," Kyle said, glancing at his phone. "If you wanna back out, I understand."

"Dude, come on. If he gets outta line, we can take him," Troy replied.

The video camera recorded Kyle from the dashboard.

"I got a bad feeling about this one," Kyle said. "This guy seriously creeps me out."

Troy chuckled, a nervous hitch in his laughter. "They're all fucking creepy. He's expecting a child, not two dudes who could fuck him up."

Kyle's decoy phone buzzed.

Big Bad Wolf: I'm here. I'm behind the Golds Gym across from the McDonalds.

"Shit," Kyle said. "He's behind the strip mall. He doesn't wanna be seen in public. Lemme see if I can get him over here."

Troy nodded and leaned over to watch Kyle thumb-type.

Cody 12782: ??? At Mcds waiting

Big Bad Wolf: Walk over here. It's not far.

Cody 12782: Y can't u come here?

Big Bad Wolf: You want me to get in trouble?

Cody 12782: No

Big Bad Wolf: Then come here.

Cody 12782: B there in 10

Big Bad Wolf: I'll be waiting, YM.

Kyle looked at Troy. "We gotta go to him."

Troy ran his hand through his beard. "We don't know what we're walking into."

"I know. Let's think about this." Kyle paused for a moment, the wheels turning in his mind. "We can split up and go around the back of the strip mall at opposite ends. I think we should both record, because we don't know who'll see the guy first."

"Good idea."

"He's probably ready to get the hell out of there at the first sign of danger, so we need to get his face on camera, even if we don't have any time for a confrontation."

"I agree. We should also do our best to sneak up on the guy."

"You're right. The longer it takes for him to figure out what's going on, the better."

Troy grabbed the camera from the dash. "Let's get this piece of shit."

Kyle and Troy stepped from the Hyundai and walked across the plaza parking lot to the strip mall. Near the strip mall, Kyle and Troy separated, circling the mall in opposite directions. Kyle walked past the storefronts—Gold's Gym, a Dollar Store, a florist, and a check-cashing place. He walked around the check-cashing place, keeping tight to the building. He stopped and peered around the corner to the back of the mall.

There was an alley four-car-lengths' wide, with a chain-link fence separating the plaza property from a medical building. Dumpsters were situated along the back of the strip mall, one blocking his view. He grabbed his decoy phone and started to record. Kyle slipped to the back of the strip mall, using the Dumpster for cover. He peered around the Dumpster. An old Chevy pickup truck with a cap was parked about thirty yards away, along the fence line. The front end faced away from Kyle, so he couldn't tell if Doug was inside.

Kyle crept around the Dumpster, hiding behind another and staying tight to the strip mall. Still no sign of Doug. Kyle moved as quietly as possible. *Good thing I wore sneakers.* Kyle continued like this, leap-frogging and using the Dumpsters as cover, counting off the businesses in reverse. *The check-cashing place. ... The florist. ... The Dollar Store. ... Gold's Gym.* He heard heavy footsteps and heavy breathing on the other side of the Gold's Gym Dumpster. *He's not in the truck.* The pickup with the camper was close now. The truck was white and dirty, but the camper shell was a faded-by-the-sun maroon. Kyle's heart thumped in his chest. His hand felt sweaty as he held up his recording phone.

Kyle hurried from behind the Dumpster to the other side, taking the turn wide in an effort to stand between Doug and his truck. Kyle stared at the man, his camera phone recording as he approached. Doug had a scraggly beard and dirty-blond hair spilling out of his trucker's hat. The hat was pulled low, shielding his eyes, and shading his face. He wore an old flannel shirt and acid-washed jeans for his big date.

"Hey, Doug," Kyle said.

"Who the hell are you?" Doug asked.

"I'm Cody."

Kyle had him cornered. Dumpsters on either side of Doug, the strip mall at his back.

"What the fuck is this?" Doug moved toward Kyle, his head tilted down, his eyes still obscured by the brim of his hat. He was a big guy, probably had four inches and fifty pounds on Kyle.

Kyle stood his ground, still videoing with his phone.

"You better back the fuck up," Troy said, arriving on the scene, also videoing.

Doug stopped in his tracks, Troy's arrival tilting the odds in their favor.

"Why did you come here to meet a twelve-year-old boy?" Kyle asked.

"I don't know what the *fuck* you're talking about," Doug said.

"I have the chat logs, *Big Bad Wolf.* You fucking idiot. I'm Kyle Summers. I hunt child predators like you."

Doug's face was blank.

Kyle tilted his camera to try to get a better view of his face. "I recorded our conversations. You sent disgusting pornography to a child, you piece of shit. I'm gonna broadcast your face all over the internet. Everyone's gonna know what you are. If you got something to say for yourself, now's your chance."

"You're fucking done," Troy said.

Doug reached behind his back, removed a Glock handgun, and pointed it at Kyle, then Troy, then back to Kyle. "Gimme that phone."

Kyle and Troy glanced at each other, their eyes like saucers.

"I said, gimme that fucking phone!"

Kyle handed Doug the phone, his heart pounding. Doug snatched it with his left hand, the gun still trained on Kyle. He shoved the phone in the front pocket of his jeans and turned the gun on Troy.

"Now the camera," Doug said.

Troy handed the camera to Doug, his hand shaky.

"Move outta my fucking way," Doug said, motioning to the right with his gun.

Kyle and Troy moved to the side, allowing Doug free access to his truck.

Doug glared at Kyle, the square barrel of the Glock pointed at Kyle's chest. "If you post those chats or our conversations, I'll kill you, … Kyle Summers." He grinned and turned his gun on Troy. "And you too."

Doug walked to his truck, the gun at his side. He screeched the rear tires as he gunned the engine, leaving the alley.

Troy leaned over, his hands on his knees. He shook his head. "I thought he was gonna kill us. I saw my life flash before my eyes."

Kyle blew out a breath of relief. "Me too."

Troy stood upright. "Fucker took the camera too. No footage."

Kyle smiled at Troy. "I got the footage."

"What do you mean, *you got the footage*?"

"He didn't turn off my phone. It's probably still recording."

Troy held out his hands. "So what? He's the one who has it."

"It's automatically backed up. Goes to the cloud. This piece of shit's going down."

Troy sucked air through his teeth. "You're not gonna post this, are you?"

"Why wouldn't I?"

"Because he said he'd murder us, and that motherfucker's crazy enough to do it."

"So we just let him get away with it?" Kyle asked.

"We could call the police. Let them handle it."

"Then I'd get arrested for interfering in police business or whatever stupid bullshit they decide to charge me with, and *you* can forget about the police academy. You think they'll give you a job when they find out you're a vigilante?"

Troy walked in a circle, his hands atop his head. "Goddamn it!" He returned to face Kyle. "Then we have to let it go."

"He has my name, not yours."

"I live right next door to you. You think he can't find me?"

"I told you that I thought he was dangerous. If you weren't up for it, you shouldn't have come."

"I have a kid to think about," Troy said through gritted teeth.

"What about all the kids this guy has abused?" Kyle replied.

"I'm asking you as your friend to let this one go."

"No."

Troy pointed at Kyle. "You're an asshole. I'm done with this shit."

CHAPTER 20

THE HUNTER BECOMES THE HUNTED

Kyle's alarm chimed from his phone. His eyes fluttered. His room and the barren white walls came into focus. He reached for the nightstand and swiped right, stopping the alarm. The time on his phone read 5:30 a.m. He went to the bathroom, peed, washed his hands, and brushed his teeth. He looked at his reflection in the mirror over the sink. His skin was tan from his work outside during this sunny spring. His eyes were bloodshot. A girl once told him that she was envious of his long eyelashes. He had a strong jaw and high cheekbones. He was handsome enough to attract women but why bother? It always fell apart when he told the truth. The truth that he could never fix. The truth that he could never change.

He returned to his room and opened his laptop. He powered up the computer and dressed in khaki pants and a Creative Touch Landscaping T-shirt. His new camera and decoy phone charged on his desktop. He'd bought replacements yesterday after Doug stole his gear. Kyle sat at his desk and navigated to his YouTube channel.

"Holy shit," Kyle said to himself.

His latest video featuring the Big Bad Wolf already had half-a-million views. His cloud backup didn't quite get everything. Apparently, he had it set to back up every fifteen minutes. The video showed the chats and conversations with Doug, followed by the rear of the strip mall as Kyle crept to the alternate meeting spot. It did show the Big Bad Wolf aka Doug in his trucker's hat and flannel, although his face was somewhat obscured by the hat.

The video footage ended after Troy arrived on the scene and said, "You better back the—"

That was it. Kyle didn't mention the gun in the video because the geniuses in the YouTube comment section would likely brand him a liar. Besides, Kyle didn't want police attention either.

Kyle scrolled through the comments, wondering if anyone recognized Doug. Nobody did. *What good is this if nobody knows who he is? I should've listened to Troy. Who knows if he'll ever film again. Give it some time ... for both. Troy won't stay mad, and the video's only been up for a day. Somebody will recognize this piece of shit.*

Kyle shut his laptop and padded toward the kitchen. On the way, he noticed a plain white envelope on the floor in front of his apartment door. It was labeled *Kyle* in all caps. He looked around, half-expecting someone to be in his apartment. He opened the envelope. Inside was a single sheet of trifolded white paper. Kyle unfolded the paper and read the message written in big fat marker letters.

You have until midnight to delete your YouTube channel, Facebook account, Twitter account, and all videos pertaining to your so-called predator hunting. If you don't, or if you ever try to do this again in the future, the hunter will become the hunted. Go to the police, and you will regret it. Tick-tock, Kyle.

CHAPTER 21

STAKEOUT

Kyle: I won't be at work today. I have an emergency. Hector can run the crew today. Wednesday's route is not too long.

Sam: You OK? Predator Hunter business?

Kyle: I'm fine. Yes, predator hunter business.

Sam: Be safe

Kyle: Thanks

Kyle stood from his kitchen table and shoved his personal phone in the front pocket of his khakis. He washed his cereal bowl and walked to Troy's apartment next door. Along the way, he looked up and down the stairwell, checking for signs of Doug or anybody nosing around. It was empty. He knocked on Troy's door. Nobody answered. The morning air was crisp and cool—mid-fifties. He knocked again, harder. Troy appeared in flannel pajama pants and a hoodie, his long angular body a bit wobbly.

"I worked the late shift last night," Troy said, rubbing his eyes. "I just got to sleep."

"I'm sorry about yesterday," Kyle said.

"You take down the video?"

"No."

Troy shook his head. "Then you're not sorry."

"I really am sorry. I just can't let this guy bully me. He's the worst kind of predator."

"So you wake me up to tell me that you're *not* taking down the video?"

"No. I got a death threat this morning."

Troy's posture stiffened, and his eyes widened. "Shit."

"Can I come in?"

Troy frowned and stepped aside. "I told you it was a bad idea to post that video."

"He's not gonna do anything." Kyle walked into Troy's apartment.

"How do you know?"

"I don't, but that's what I think."

"It's my life too, you know?"

"He didn't even mention you, so you're in the clear." Kyle reached into his back pocket and handed Troy the envelope.

They sat on the leather couch in the living room. Troy removed the trifolded death threat from the envelope and read the message. He handed it back to Kyle.

"You gotta go to the police," Troy said.

"What are they gonna do, except cite me for some bullshit? Doug didn't say he would do anything to me specifically."

"They might be able to find this guy. Watch him or something."

"They won't do shit."

Troy sighed. "What are you gonna do then?"

"I'm gonna pretend to go to work then stake out my apartment, see if he comes back, see if maybe he's watching me."

"Then what? What if you see him watching your apartment? What are you gonna do about it? He has a gun. You don't."

Kyle paused. "I don't know. Maybe get better footage of his face. Get his license plate."

"Really?" Troy wagged his head.

"Yes, really."

"Or do you just want good footage for the channel?"

Kyle blew out a breath. "That's part of it, but that's not the point."

"Then what's the point?"

"That this piece of shit's not gonna scare me."

"You can count me out on this one."

"I know. I'll do it alone."

"I should get back to bed." Troy stood from the couch with a groan. "I have the late shift again tonight."

Kyle stood. "I am sorry about yesterday. You're my best friend. I don't wanna ruin that."

Troy looked at the carpet for a moment. "We're good."

"Good." Kyle walked toward the apartment door.

Troy followed.

Kyle opened the door and stepped into the hall. "You're still gonna help me, right? I mean, I know you don't want anything to do with this guy, but other guys?"

"Man, you never quit." Troy chuckled, his hand on the doorknob. "Yeah, I'll still help you."

"Thanks, man."

"You need a new camera."

"Already taken care of." Kyle smiled, turned, and went to his apartment.

Troy shut his door.

Kyle pretended to leave for work. He drove to a nearby strip mall, constantly looking around and over his shoulder to see if he was being watched. He didn't notice anything out of the ordinary. He parked in a secluded space and walked back to his apartment complex.

The apartment tenants were waking up. People hurried off to work in Japanese compacts and work trucks. Kyle entered his apartment building from the rear. Inside his apartment, he moved his recliner near the door. He sat in the recliner—his new camera in his lap—ready to pounce if another note appeared. Periodically, he went to the window, parted a corner of the blinds, and scanned the parking lot for Doug's pickup truck. He direct-messaged with two new predators, Brandon4455 and Danny Boy MMA. There were always more predators.

The seconds and minutes and hours moved at a snail's pace. He fell asleep.

* * *

Kyle woke with a start. His eyes immediately checked the floor in front of the door. No note. He checked the time on his new decoy phone—*1:22 p.m. Shit, I've been asleep for three hours.* He went to the window to check the parking lot. It was mostly empty, the spring sun beating down on the asphalt. A postal truck approached the mailboxes.

Kyle sat back down in his recliner. He remained there for a few minutes, staring at the door. *This is a waste of time. If he's gonna deliver another note, it'll probably be really early again. School's almost out. I should go to Jewel's apartment complex and stake out the bus stop, ask her why she lied. She's supposed to leave tomorrow for her big tour. I wonder if Robert dropped her yet. Maybe she'll be willing to talk when he does.*

Kyle grabbed his keys, phones, wallet, and left his apartment. He hiked to the strip mall, picked up his car, and drove north on Route 1. Kyle parked in a visitor's spot near the entrance to Jewel's apartment complex, figuring the bus would drop the kids near there. Kyle sat in his car, the windows down, watching the sparse traffic in and out of the apartment complex.

Half an hour later, a yellow bus appeared, stopping just inside the complex, near the property manager's offices. A dozen or so high school kids trudged toward their homes, loaded down with backpacks. Jewel and a short girl separated from the pack, headed toward her apartment building. They wore short-shorts and carried small designer purses, no backpacks.

Kyle stepped from his car and approached the pair. Jewel narrowed her eyes at Kyle, then raised one side of her mouth in contempt.

"Can I talk to you for a minute?" Kyle asked.

"No," Jewel replied.

"This is the guy who came to my house asking about you," the other girl said.

"He's a creep," Jewel said, glaring at Kyle. "Leave me alone, or I'll call the police."

"Good. Maybe you can tell them what Robert's doing to you," Kyle said, stopping at the entrance to the apartment building stairwell.

The pair continued to the girl's ground-floor apartment.

"Why'd you lie to your mother?" Kyle asked.

No response.

"Robert's using you," Kyle said.

Jewel turned to Kyle at the threshold of her friend's apartment. "Get a life, asshole." She slammed the door behind her.

He pinched the bridge of his nose and shook his head.

Kyle returned home, parking at the strip mall again and walking to his apartment. Again, he entered his building from the rear. His stomach churned as he opened his door to find another white envelope on the floor. He opened the envelope and the trifolded note. The note contained one word in large capital letters.

Gwen.

CHAPTER 22

EMPTY THREATS OR LOADED PROMISES?

Kyle tapped the Leigh icon on his personal phone. His call went to voice mail. He tried again. Voice mail again. He ran back to the strip mall and his car. He tried his sister again. He left a message on her voice mail. "Call me when you get this. It's an emergency."

He disconnected the call and drove across town toward Crosspointe. He sat in rush-hour traffic on Lorton Road. It was only three, but rush hour started earlier and earlier. He tried Leigh again. No answer.

"Damn it!" Kyle smacked his steering wheel.

He drove on the shoulder to a chorus of beeps, shouts, and hand gestures. Once he passed the exit for I-95, traffic loosened, and Kyle gunned his engine, zipping past neighborhoods at highway speeds. Kyle and his Hyundai screeched to a halt in Leigh's empty driveway. He hustled to the garage window, checking to see if Leigh's car was there. It wasn't.

His phone chimed. Kyle swiped right. "Where are you?"

"On my way home … from Dad's." She said "Dad's" quietly as if she didn't want Kyle to hear. "I have like twelve calls from you. *What is going on?*"

"Is Gwen with you?"

"Yes. Why?"

Kyle breathed a sigh of relief. "I'll tell you when you get here."

A few minutes later, Leigh's BMW SUV parked in her three-car garage. Kyle followed on foot. He opened the rear passenger door. Gwen was in her car seat, fast asleep, her mouth slack-jawed, a puddle of drool on her shirt. Kyle carefully undid her seat belt and picked her up. Her little blue eyes opened just enough to recognize Kyle.

"*Unc Kye*," she slurred, her eyes falling shut again.

"Hey, sweet pea," Kyle whispered.

Kyle shut the door, Gwen on his hip.

Leigh shut the driver's side door and slung her purse over her shoulder. She was dressed suburban-mom-casual in yoga pants and a long lightweight sweater. Her dark hair was in a ponytail, her face radiant with minimal makeup. "*What* is going on?" Leigh whispered.

"Can we talk inside?" Kyle replied, also whispering.

"I thought you were mad at me." She turned and walked toward the door, not bothering to wait for a reply.

Kyle followed. "I'm not mad. You refuse to see what Robert really is."

Leigh smacked the garage door opener on the wall. The garage rumbled down. "You can go home if this is about Dad. I'm done with this conversation."

"It's not," Kyle whispered as he followed her inside.

They walked through the laundry room, past the living room, to the kitchen. The kitchen glistened with granite countertops and stainless-steel appliances.

Gwen yawned and rubbed her eyes with her tiny fists.

"She's ready for her nap," Leigh whispered, taking Gwen from Kyle. "I'll be right back."

Leigh went upstairs to put Gwen down for her nap. Kyle sat on a barstool at the center island. When Leigh returned, she stood on the opposite side of the island, her hands on her hips. "So?" she said.

"I got a death threat yesterday," Kyle said.

Leigh moved closer to the center island. "One of those … creeps?"

"I think so."

"Did you go to the police?"

Kyle shook his head. "No. It wasn't really specific. It just said that, if I don't delete all my videos by midnight, the hunter will become the hunted. The police and I don't exactly have a good relationship."

"Why not?"

"They don't like vigilantes."

Leigh sighed and shook her head. "You need to stop this. If you want to be a cop, apply. This vigilante nonsense will get you arrested or hurt or worse."

"I don't wanna be a cop. They can't do what I do. I mean, I guess they could, but they don't."

Leigh crossed her arms over her chest. "You're not going to stop, are you?"

"No."

"Then why are you here?"

"I got another note shoved under my door. This one said, … 'Gwen.'" Kyle winced.

Leigh stiffened and balled her hands into fists. "Jesus Christ, Kyle. You're bringing Gwen into your madness now?"

"I'm sorry. I've never once mentioned Gwen online. He must've done a background check on me."

She blew out a breath. "I can't believe you. We need to go to the police … *now.*"

"And tell them what? I got some vague letter that says the hunter will be the hunted and another one that says *Gwen.* What are they gonna do with that?"

"I don't know, but we have to do *something.*"

"I was thinking you and Gwen could go to the beach house for a few days until this blows over. If it doesn't, I'll go to the police. I promise."

She placed her hands on the center island. "I'm not prepared to go anywhere. I'm supposed to start work next week. I'll be working from home a few days a week."

"If you leave now, you can be at the beach by bedtime. You'll have all day Thursday and Friday to enjoy the beach. If you come back on Saturday, everything should be fine. This is just a precaution. This guy's just trying to scare me."

She narrowed her eyes at Kyle. "If anything else happens, you're going to the police, or I will."

CHAPTER 23

NOWHERE TO GO

A small sliver of light slipped under Kyle's apartment door. If not for the hall light, it would be pitch black. He sat near the door in his recliner, waiting for a sign, a note, a message, something to indicate his punishment for refusing to take down his videos by midnight. He glanced at his phone—*12:39 a.m.* Still nothing. No note under the door. No message on his decoy phone. He navigated to his YouTube channel on his phone, hopeful that someone had identified the Big Bad Wolf. Still no ID.

His eyelids were heavy. He set his phone on his lap. He shut his eyes for a few seconds, then opened them again. He shut them for a few more seconds and opened them again. Each time he did this, the pull toward sleep was harder to resist, until he finally relented, and everything melted away.

* * *

Kyle awoke with a start, his personal phone chiming. His gaze immediately fell to the floor in front of the door. Still no note. He searched for his phone, finding it in the recliner cushion. He silenced the alarm. The time read 5:30 a.m. He sent a text.

Kyle: I need another day off if possible. I'm sorry to be a pain.

Sam: No problem. Hector and Julio are happy for the extra hours. You OK?

Kyle: Yes. Thanks

Kyle spent the next six hours sitting in his recliner, wearing sweats and running shoes, watching the door, ready to pounce on the messenger, if and when a note appeared. By lunchtime, there was still no note. He tapped the Leigh icon on his personal phone.

"Yes, Kyle," she said.

"I was just checking on you and Gwen. Everything all right?"

"We're fine."

"Good. I haven't gotten another note or any messages."

"Well, we're coming home on Saturday. If it's not safe, you're calling the police, or I will."

"I know. I think the guy was just messing with me."

"Well, we're headed back to the beach. Gwen wants to play in the sand. I'll take my phone if you need to talk to me."

"OK, thanks, Leigh." Kyle paused for a moment. "I'm sorry about all this."

"I know." She disconnected the call.

Kyle changed into jeans and a T-shirt and made himself a lunch to-go. He hiked to the strip mall, grabbed his car, and drove across town to the shopping center across from Roseland Estates. He parked and hiked to his father's red brick mansion. The Lincoln Town Car was parked in the circular driveway, but the driver wasn't in the car. Kyle found a new spot in the woods behind an old hickory tree, with a good view of his father's front door.

It was warm and sunny but comfortable in the shade. He ate his lunch and sat for hours, alternately watching the house and messaging predators, constantly adjusting himself, his backside uncomfortable against the tree roots. Brandon4455 had already asked "Cody" for naked pictures and to meet. Danny Boy MMA sent "Bethany Beach Girl" a video of himself masturbating. The guy was huge and veiny. His muscles, not his penis. Kyle shuddered at the thought of a confrontation. *Maybe I need to take some self-defense classes.*

The front door to his dad's house opened, and the driver walked to the Lincoln. He wore slacks, a shirt, and a tie. His jacket was folded over his massive forearm. The driver entered the Lincoln and drove away. Kyle couldn't follow him. His car was too far away.

Kyle continued to surveil the house. Thirty minutes later, the driver returned. The rear tinted windows prevented Kyle from seeing if he had a passenger. But when the driver opened the rear passenger door, Jewel stepped out and bounded to the front door, almost skipping. She entered the house without knocking. The driver sat in the front seat of the Lincoln and opened a newspaper.

Shit. I can't call the police. That didn't work before. If I ring the doorbell, the driver will be all over me. If I call from either of my phones, they'll know I'm here. Maybe I can get in through the back.

Kyle moved through the woods, from the front to the back of the property. He hustled from the woods to the patio and the back door. It was locked. He tried a back window. Also locked. A wooden deck was to the left of the patio. It was twenty feet above him, with steps leading up from the patio. It connected to a sunroom. *I wonder if the sunroom door's open?*

A slamming of the front door echoed through the quiet. Kyle ran alongside the house. He peeked around the corner. Jewel climbed into the back seat of the Lincoln, her arms crossed over her chest, her face taut. *Robert finally broke the bad news to her.* The driver shut the door and drove her away.

Kyle ran from the woods, back to his car in the shopping center parking lot. His breathing was labored as he drove toward Lorton and Jewel's apartment. Once there, he saw no sign of the Lincoln at the apartment complex. *I'm too late. The driver's already come and gone. If she's in her apartment, I'll have to stake out the bus stop again.*

I can't knock on the door. They'll probably call the police. Maybe ... or she might be willing to talk, since she probably found out that her world modeling tour's bullshit. I should check the playground. That's where she was when she was upset last time.

He drove to the rear of the complex and parked by the playground. Jewel sat alone on a swing with rusty chains, gently swaying, her sneakers touching the weeds underneath. She wore designer jeans and a tiny overpriced T-shirt that showed a bit of her midriff. A purple suitcase stood nearby. Kyle approached. She looked up, her face tear-streaked and her blue eyes red-rimmed. He expected her to recoil, to shout, but she simply hung her head, staring at the ground.

"You all right?" Kyle asked.

She didn't respond.

"Mind if I sit?"

She shrugged. "Whatever."

Kyle sat in the swing next to her. He glanced at her. She was still so thin, but there was a tiny curve to her hips, accentuated by her seated position. *He used her up. Now he'll move on to someone else. Promise her the world. Then take everything away.*

"He lied to my friend Kate too," Kyle said. "Actually, she was more than a friend."

Jewel remained unresponsive.

"At the time, I was only sixteen. She was fifteen. I met her at the agency. I was working in the office that summer." Kyle blew out a breath. "It all went horribly wrong."

Jewel's gaze flicked to Kyle, her head still bowed. "What happened?"

"We became really good friends, but I fell in love with her. I think maybe she fell for me too, but"—Kyle shook his head—"I messed it up, and Robert preyed on her, just like he did you. Then he used her up and threw her away, like trash."

Jewel turned toward Kyle, the chains on the swing twisting. "What did you do?"

"I turned my dad into the police."

Jewel's eyes widened. "Did he get in trouble?"

Kyle shook his head. "No. Kate wouldn't back me up. She was too ashamed. And maybe she was mad at me."

"For what?"

"I told her that I didn't wanna be her boyfriend. Robert started with her after that. Maybe she was vulnerable because she was mad at me. Maybe she wanted to get back at me. I think it was partly my fault."

"But I thought you loved her. Why didn't you wanna be her boyfriend?"

"Because I'm messed up."

"Are you like your dad?"

"No."

"What happened to her?"

"She moved to California with her family."

"Didn't you, like, get into trouble for calling the cops?" Jewel asked.

"Not exactly. Robert acted all innocent and said I was delusional. Everyone thought it was a tragic misunderstanding and that I needed to get help. After I knew what he did, I couldn't live in that house with him, so I left. Dropped out of school. Got a job."

"That's what I have to do."

"No, you don't. If you tell your mother what happened, you guys can press charges. You can still go to school. Don't throw your life away when it's just beginning."

She shook her head, her eyes filling with tears. "I can't go home."

Kyle leaned forward and spoke almost in a whisper. "Why not?"

She shook her head.

"Jewel. Why not?"

"I just can't!"

Kyle recoiled, leaning back. *Her mother's piece-of-shit boyfriend.* "OK."

"The tour was like my chance to make a bunch of money and never come back. I can't go back there … *ever.*"

"Where are you gonna go then? Do you have some family you could stay with? I could give you a ride, if you need one."

"No."

"Friends? What about the girl I saw you with?"

She shook her head, her voice tinged with frustration. "That's not going away. She, like, lives in my same building."

"If something bad's happening at home, we could call the police. They have shelters."

"No. I'm not gonna be, like, locked up in some *fucking* shelter." She paused for a moment, then removed her phone from her pocket. "I'll just get on Craigslist and tell people I need a place to stay." She tapped on her phone.

"I don't think that's a good idea. You could get someone who might hurt you."

She glared at Kyle. "What other choice do I have?" She went back to her phone.

He paused. "I could help you."

Jewel looked up from her phone.

"Maybe give you some time to figure things out. But you'd have to tell your mom where you are and get her permission. Otherwise I could get arrested."

"Where would you, like, … take me?"

"Well, I was thinking you could stay with my sister for a few days. She has a big house, and it's just her and my three-year-old niece. But she won't be home until Saturday, so I could get you a hotel room for tonight and tomorrow."

Jewel pursed her lips. "OK."

"You have to call your mom and ask her though."

CHAPTER 24

VIRGIN TERRITORY

"You what?" Jewel's mother screamed through the Speakerphone. Jewel held her phone and her mother's hysteria at arm's length. "What the hell did you do?"

Jewel brought the phone near her lips. "I didn't do anything! Robert said it, like, wasn't my fault. He said, designers change what they want all the time. It's, like, trends and fashion. I can't control that."

"I'm gonna give him a piece of my mind."

Jewel frowned. "Don't, Mom. He said, if things, like, change, I might get another chance. Don't ruin this for me, like you do everything."

"Ruin this for you? What about me? We need that money. I spent a whole lot on your pictures and clothes and makeup and takin' you places. How you gonna pay me back now?"

"You don't have to pay for me anymore. I'm not coming home."

"What do you mean, *you're not comin' home*?"

"I'm staying in a hotel tonight. Then I'm, like, going to Kyle's sister's house to stay for a few days."

"Kyle? Robert's son?"

"Yes."

"Are you seein' him?"

"Mom, no. He offered to help me."

"You don't need no help. Where are you? You need to come home right now."

"No."

"No? You've lost your goddamn mind. Get your ass home now."

Jewel clenched her jaw. "I said, no."

"Then I'm callin' the police on this Kyle person. He'll be arrested for kidnappin'."

Jewel glanced at Kyle, then turned her back to him. "If you call the police, I'll tell them about Dale."

"What are you talkin' about?"

"You know what I'm talking about."

"He didn't do nothin'." Her mom sounded shrill and unconfident. "I have to go."

"You little bitch. You think you can do whatever you want, but you'll be back. You'll find out it ain't so easy livin' on your—"

Jewel disconnected the call and turned to Kyle, her blue eyes glassy. "Can we go now?"

"Yeah," Kyle replied, picking up her purple suitcase.

He stowed her suitcase in his trunk and climbed into his Hyundai. Jewel sat in the passenger seat.

"I'm gonna look up a hotel near my apartment," Kyle said, retrieving his phone, "so I can be close by if you need food or something."

Jewel glared at Kyle tapping on his phone. "Can you do that someplace else? I don't wanna be here."

"All right."

Kyle drove from Jewel's apartment complex onto Route 1 south. They sat in stop-and-go traffic, the windows down. The sun was orange and falling in the distance, but it was still warm.

"Don't you have air-conditioning?" Jewel said with a scowl.

"No," Kyle replied.

She blew out an exasperated breath and stared out the open window.

Kyle pulled into a 7-Eleven and parked.

"Can I have some money?" Jewel asked.

"For what?" Kyle replied.

"I'm thirsty. God."

Kyle gave her a five-dollar bill.

"That's it?"

"That should be enough to get a drink."

She slammed the door and went into the convenience store. Kyle did a search on his phone for hotels in Woodbridge near his apartment. Jewel returned with a fancy tea and a candy bar.

"Was there any change?" Kyle asked.

She frowned, removed a few coins from her pocket, and slammed them into the cupholder on the center console. "A whole thirty-five cents."

"I'm not rich."

"Obviously." She opened her candy bar and took a big bite.

Kyle took a deep breath. "A Sleep Inn's not too far from my apartment. It has breakfast. It's not too expensive."

"Whatever," she said, her mouth full. "It's probably a dump if it's cheap."

"I didn't say it was cheap. It'll be over a hundred dollars a night." Kyle started his car. "You ever heard the saying, beggars can't be choosers?"

"That's stupid."

Kyle left the 7-Eleven and continued south on Route 1 toward Woodbridge. The Sleep Inn was a beige-bricked building of two stories. He parked in the expansive lot. It was mostly empty on a Thursday evening.

"Stay here," Kyle said.

"Where am I gonna go?" Jewel replied.

Kyle walked into the lobby and booked a room with a king-size bed. He returned to his car with two credit-card-style keys. "You ready?" Kyle asked.

Kyle used the key to enter the back door of the hotel. They trekked upstairs and down the hall, Kyle leading the way. He stopped at room number 212. "You know how to use these?" he asked, holding up the key.

"I'm not stupid," Jewel replied.

Kyle sighed and slid the key into the slot. "Nobody said you were." The little light turned green and Kyle opened the door.

Inside the room, the bed was crisp with five fluffy pillows. A flat screen hung on the wall. There was a desk and a small fridge. Kyle stood her suitcase next to the dresser. Jewel grabbed the remote, slipped off her sneakers, and lounged on the bed. She flipped on the television and channel-surfed.

Kyle stepped in front of the television. "Don't order any movies. They're expensive. And don't talk to anyone if you go down to break-fast tomorrow."

"I'm not stupid." She turned up the volume on the television.

"You said that already."

"Whatever."

Reality television blared.

"Can you turn that down?" Kyle asked.

She ignored his request.

Kyle reached behind the television and disconnected the HDMI cable. The television went to a blue screen, the sound vanquished.

"Hey!" she said with a furrowed brow.

"I need you to listen to me for a minute."

She sat up cross-legged on the bed. "Fine."

"I have to go to work tomorrow, but, after work, I can come by, and we can go get something to eat. You need to stay in this room during the day. If some cop sees you and wants to know why you're by yourself and not in school, you and especially me will be in an assload of trouble."

She pursed her lips.

"Do you understand me?"

"I got it."

Kyle nodded. "We should probably go to the grocery store and get you some food for lunch tomorrow, and I don't know if you're hungry, but I don't think a candy bar is a good dinner. Are you hungry?"

She looked away for a moment. "I guess."

* * *

Kyle threw away the remnants of their dinner at Chick-Fil-A. He returned to the corner booth, where Jewel sat, finishing off her chocolate sundae. He sat across from her. His decoy phone chimed in his pocket. He checked the message.

Danny Boy MMA: Where u at girl what u think of my video?

Kyle sighed and shoved his phone into the front pocket of his jeans. He looked at Jewel. "You about ready?"

She spooned a bit of chocolate and melty ice cream from the bottom of the plastic container and sucked it off her spoon. "Who was texting you?" She had a crooked grin.

"Nobody."

"I looked you up on the internet."

"Yeah?"

"Yeah. *The Predator Hunter.*" She giggled. "Was that a creeper?"

"We should go. I have some things to do tonight, and I have to get up early tomorrow."

"What kinda things? Are you meeting some creep?"

"It's none of your business."

"I'm just asking." She put down her plastic spoon. "Don't you get scared? I mean, these guys could be, like, total serial killers."

"The chances of that are slim. But I do get scared. I actually don't like confrontations."

"Then why do you do it?"

Kyle shrugged. "Maybe because of my dad."

"You know, he's really not like those guys in your videos. Those guys are gross. Your dad never made me do anything. I was the one crushing on him."

"You're not old enough to make that decision."

She crossed her arms over her chest. "Who the hell are you to say?"

Kyle shook his head. "Nobody, Jewel. I'm nobody."

"I can make my own decisions."

Kyle didn't reply.

"You don't think I can make my own decisions, do you?"

"Not when it comes to a romantic relationship with an adult."

"Whatever. How would you even know? You, like, turned down the girl you loved. You don't have a wedding ring. Do you even have a girlfriend?"

"No."

"I've prob'ly had more experience than you."

Kyle clenched his jaw. "I'm not having this conversation with you."

"Whatever. It's OK to be all up in my business, but you don't want me to know anything about you. That's fucked up."

Kyle exhaled. "What do you wanna know?"

"How old are you?"

"Twenty-seven."

"How come you don't have a girlfriend?"

"I haven't met the right girl."

"Are you gay?"

"No."

"Bi?"

Kyle frowned. "No."

"How many girlfriends have you had?"

"What do you mean by that?"

"You know what I mean. A girl you text and go places with and kiss and, um, do it with."

Kyle rubbed the back of his neck. "None."

Jewel erupted with laughter.

Kyle sat, his face stoic, waiting for her laughing fit to subside.

"Oh, my God. *None*?"

Kyle glowered at Jewel.

She let out one last giggle. "I'm sorry. I'm not laughing at you. It's just, like, the situation. Are you, like, … a virgin?"

"It's time to go." Kyle stood. "I'll be in the car." He walked away.

CHAPTER 25

HOME SWEET SISTER

"What time do you think you'll be home?" Kyle asked, holding his phone to his ear.

"According to the GPS, in fifty-six minutes," Leigh replied.

"Is it OK if I come by? I need to talk to you."

"We're talking now."

"I'd rather talk to you about this in person."

"Did that psychopath contact you again?"

"No. It's not about that."

"Why can't you just tell me over the phone?"

"I'll see you in an hour."

"Kyle?"

He disconnected the call and stepped from his car. Kyle shoved his phone in the front pocket of his jeans. The sun played peekaboo with the clouds, the climate alternating from cool to warm and back again. He checked the time on his phone—11:54 a.m. He hustled up the back stairwell to Jewel's hotel room. He knocked on the door before entering.

Jewel lay on the bed, simultaneously watching talk-show nonsense and surfing Instagram on her phone. Her hair was shiny and blond and brushed straight. She wore leggings and a tiny T-shirt. She didn't acknowledge Kyle as he approached.

"We have to go," Kyle said. "Checkout's at noon."

Jewel continued to thumb-swipe.

"Did you hear me?"

She exhaled and set her phone on the bedside table. "I have to pack."

"I told you to be ready by 11:30."

"Gimme, like, ten minutes. God," Jewel replied with a scowl.

She shoved clothes into her purple suitcase. The bed was disheveled. The television still blared with her talk show. Kyle turned off the television and grabbed the room key from the dresser.

"I'm gonna check out. Meet me in the car in ten minutes."

"Fine."

Kyle went downstairs to the front desk. He handed the keys to the middle-aged woman, and she printed out his receipt. Kyle glanced at the charges. With tax and the pay-per view charges, the bill was nearly three hundred dollars for two nights. He shook his head and blew out a breath.

"Is everything OK?" the woman asked.

"Yeah," Kyle replied.

She plastered on a big smile. "I hope you enjoyed your stay."

He nodded. "Thanks."

Kyle waited for Jewel in his car. His decoy phone buzzed.

Brandon4455: Hey Cody. Been thinking about you.

Cody12782: Y

Brandon4455: Cuz I think your cool and cute

Cody12782: Thx

Brandon4455: Did you decide about the pic?

Cody12782: Idk its weird

Brandon4455: Will be a secret

Cody12782: Idk

Brandon4455: Come on! Please ☺

Cody12782: Maybe

Brandon4455: What about meeting?

Cody12782: Idk I'm only 12

Brandon4455: Its OK just meeting as friends

Cody12782: Can I thk about it?

Brandon4455: Course

Kyle flinched as his rear passenger door opened. It was Jewel.

Cody12782: Have to go moms home

She shoved her suitcase haphazardly onto the back seat. "I could, like, use some help."

"Looks like you got it," Kyle replied, returning to his phone.

Brandon4455: Later gator

Cody12782: Bye

Kyle set his decoy phone in the cupholder. Jewel slammed the door as she slumped into the front passenger seat.

"There was forty dollars' worth of pay-per-view on the bill," Kyle said.

"I was so bored. You didn't, like, want me going anywhere, remember?"

Kyle lifted his butt off the seat and removed his personal phone from the front pocket of his jeans. He texted Troy.

Jewel crossed her arms over her chest. "Are we going?"

"Now you're in a rush," Kyle replied, not looking up from his phone.

Kyle: I got a live one. What's your schedule like this week?

Kyle set his personal phone in the cupholder with the decoy phone. He started the car and turned to Jewel. "My sister won't be back for forty minutes or so. Do you wanna get something to eat?"

Jewel sat up, her sour face showing signs of life. "Can we go to Chick-Fil-A again?"

"Yeah."

They drove north on Route 1, stopping at Chick-Fil-A. They both ordered a chicken sandwich and fries. They sat in a booth across from each other. The restaurant was lively with parents and children. Their conversation was subdued as they focused on their food. Kyle's personal phone buzzed.

Troy: 10–6 MWF and all next weekend

Kyle: What about tomorrow, Sunday?

Troy: No. I have Sophie this weekend

Kyle: Thanks. So Tuesday and Thursday are open?

Troy: Yes

Kyle: I'll let you know what the douche says.

Troy: Sounds good

"Who are you texting?" Jewel asked, then popped her final fry in her mouth.

Kyle turned his phone upside down on the table and looked at Jewel. "My friend Troy. He helps me video the confrontations."

She nodded. "I watched all your videos last night. There's, like, fifteen of 'em."

"There's eleven."

She lifted one shoulder. "Same difference. How long have you been, like, doing this?"

"Almost a year."

"I think I understand what you're, like, trying to do."

"And what's that?"

"I think you wanna help kids because nobody ever helped you."

Kyle looked away for a moment, as if Jewel's gaze could see inside him. "It's not about me." He piled the remnants of their lunch on the tray. He spoke without making eye contact. "You are right though about helping kids."

"I think it's cool, you know? To, like, help kids."

Kyle looked at Jewel. "Thanks."

"Is it OK if I get dessert?"

Kyle handed her five dollars. "Yeah."

"Do you want something?" she asked, standing from the booth.

"No, … thanks."

Jewel returned with a caramel sundae and a barely contained smile.

Midway through her sundae, she said, "Thank you for helping me."

Kyle nodded. "You're welcome."

"And I'm sorry about what I said the other day. … You know, the virgin thing." She winced.

"It's fine."

After lunch, Kyle drove them north to Crosspointe. He parked in the driveway of Leigh's stone-faced colonial.

"I need you to be nice when you meet my sister," Kyle said, looking at Jewel.

She narrowed her eyes. "Why?"

"Because she hasn't agreed to let you stay yet."

Jewel frowned. "Why would you tell me that I could stay with her then?"

"Because I think she will let you stay, but it's a big request and not one you ask over the phone."

"You think she won't wanna tell me no to my face."

141

"She won't, if you're nice. This is the only option I have for you, so be nice."

"Fine. I'll be nice."

They exited the car. Kyle started for the front door.

"What about my stuff?"

"Let's not be presumptuous. It's rude."

"What does that mean?"

Kyle stopped walking, allowing Jewel to catch up to him. "It means, we're presuming that she'll say yes, which'll make her feel like she doesn't have a choice, which'll make her say no."

"OK."

Kyle rang the doorbell, opened the front door, and stepped into the foyer with Jewel on his heels. Jewel looked up at the expansive foyer, and the white-carpeted stairs leading to the second floor.

"Leigh," Kyle called out.

"I'm in the kitchen," Leigh replied.

Little feet pitter-pattered on the hardwood, coming from the kitchen. Gwen entered the foyer, her cherub face sun-kissed.

"*Unc Kye!*" she said, running, her arms flailing. "I saw big water."

Kyle picked her up and twirled her around, her giggles echoing. "You mean, the ocean?" He placed her on his hip.

"Ocean." Gwen craned her neck and pointed at Jewel standing behind Kyle. "Who *dat*?"

Kyle turned to Jewel. "This is Jewel. She's a friend of mine."

"Hi, *Jew*," Gwen said with a goofy grin. "Wanna play with me?"

Jewel smiled. "OK."

Gwen twisted in Kyle's arms, signifying that she wanted down. Kyle set her down.

Leigh walked into the foyer, her eyes on Jewel. "What's going on? Who's this?"

"This is my friend, Jewel," Kyle said.

"Hi, Jewel. I'm Leigh." Leigh extended her hand.

Jewel dipped her head and shook Leigh's hand with a weak shake.

Gwen grabbed onto Leigh's jeans. "Can *Jew* play with me?"

"If it's OK with Jewel," Leigh replied, looking at Jewel.

Jewel nodded and smiled at Gwen. "We can play."

Gwen grabbed Jewel's hand. "Let's go, my room." They went upstairs, Gwen already making the rules. "You can't be princess. I'm princess of all the land."

"Can I be queen?" Jewel asked as they disappeared upstairs.

Leigh raised her eyebrows. "*What* is going on?"

"Can we talk in the kitchen?" Kyle asked.

They sat at the round kitchen table. Leigh had a healthy tan. Her dark hair was in a ponytail.

"Well?" she said.

"Can Jewel stay with you for a few days?"

"How old is she?"

"Fourteen."

"Why are you hanging around a fourteen-year-old girl?"

"You're concerned about me hanging around young girls? You don't seem to care about Robert. How do you think I met her?"

"What the hell does that mean?"

"She's the one I saw coming and going from his house."

She shook her head, scowling. "Jesus, Kyle. We've been through this. You need help."

"He promised her a modeling contract only to take it away the moment she was supposed to go on some made-up world tour."

"He wouldn't do that."

"Ask her."

"How well do you even know her? Girls get mad all the time when they realize that they'll never make it. And most girls *don't* make it. You know that."

"I saw them kissing."

"Dad kisses girls. It's not sexual."

"This wasn't the European kiss on each cheek. It was a real kiss. And I'm nearly certain they've had sex."

"Did Jewel tell you that?"

"In so many words."

Leigh blew out a breath. *"In so many words.* I want you to leave and to take Jewel back to her parents or wherever she belongs." Leigh stood from the table.

"Her mother's boyfriend is sexually abusing her. The predators always know which ones to pick, don't they?"

She sat back down. "If that's true, you need to go to the police. Let them handle it. They can place her in a home, get her psychiatric help."

"I tried. She's not gonna do that, and she won't go back home. Her mother's on the boyfriend's side. She was gonna use Craigslist to find a place to stay. She'll run away if we push that."

"She can't stay here."

"She told me that Robert's not like the guys in my videos. She said she came on to him. She thinks she wanted it. That's what he does. He manipulates these girls and then throws them away like trash."

Leigh shook her head. "I don't believe that."

"What if it's true? You gonna risk Gwen growing up around him? You gonna leave them alone together?"

"Goddamn you, Kyle. How the hell am I supposed to believe this shit?"

"I'm not asking you to believe anything. I'm just asking you to let Jewel stay with you for a few days. I'd let her stay with me, but how would that look?"

Leigh pursed her lips. "I don't want to get involved in whatever this is."

"Forget about Robert for a minute. What about her mother's boyfriend? That guy's abusing her. I'm sure of it. She needs some time to process it all. Otherwise she'll end up as a runaway. What do you think'll happen to her on the streets? Please, Leigh. If she's any trouble, I'll come and get her right away."

"I need permission from her mother."

"She's already got that."

Leigh narrowed her eyes.

"She did. I told her that I wouldn't help her unless her mother agreed. You can have her call again, if you want."

"I want to talk to her myself."

Kyle went to the stairwell. "Hey, Jewel, could you come down here for a minute?" he called out.

Jewel and Gwen stepped down the stairs hand in hand.

"Leigh wants to talk to your mother," Kyle said, as they walked to the kitchen.

Jewel nodded, her mouth turned down.

Leigh stood from the kitchen table and offered Jewel a small smile. "Jewel, honey, you're welcome to stay. I just need to talk to your mom to make sure it's OK."

Jewel removed her phone from the back pocket of her skinny jeans. "OK." Jewel tapped on the screen and put her cell phone to her ear, while everyone watched. "Mom, ... God. I don't want anything." Jewel paused for a moment, listening to her mother complain. "I'm staying with Kyle's sister for a few days. She, like, wants to talk to you." Another pause, then Jewel whispered, "Do you want me to tell?" Jewel handed her phone to Leigh.

"What's your mother's name?" Leigh asked Jewel.

"Rhonda."

Leigh put the phone to her ear. "Hi, Rhonda, my name's Leigh Summers-Burns, and your daughter Jewel is welcome to stay with me for a short time—provided that's OK with you of course." Leigh paused, listening. "Yes. I'll text you my phone number." Leigh paused again. "Is there anything you'd like to know about me? I want you to be comfortable with this." Leigh paused again. "OK, here she is." Leigh handed the phone back to Jewel.

Jewel took the phone. "Yeah." She listened for a moment. "I *am* happy now. Happy to be away from you and Dale." She disconnected the call.

CHAPTER 26

AMBER ALERT

Bethany Beach Girl: How did U get all those muscles?

Danny Boy MMA: U did like my video?

Bethany Beach Girl: It was kinda gross

Danny Boy MMA: Don't lie made u horny

Bethany Beach Girl: Ewww

Danny Boy MMA: I know the truth

Bethany Beach Girl: Whatever

Danny Boy MMA: Got my muscles by training hard

Bethany Beach Girl: Cool

Danny Boy MMA: U want to touch me?

Bethany Beach Girl: Maybe

Danny Boy MMA: Girl says maybe she means yes ☺

Bethany Beach Girl: Maybe

Kyle yawned and glanced at the time. It was nearly midnight, and he was running on fumes. *I need to end this for tonight.*

Danny Boy MMA: I want to touch u

Bethany Beach Girl: I have to go bed

Danny Boy MMA: Too bad when u sending me that pic?

Bethany Beach Girl: Maybe never

Danny Boy MMA: Ha maybe means yes

Bethany Beach Girl: Sorry gotta go bed. Mom yelled at me

Danny Boy MMA: Talk tomorrow baby

Bethany Beach Girl: K

Kyle received a new direct-message alert from Grindr. *It must be Brandon. I should probably message him. They always get antsy when the meeting's set.* Kyle tapped "Cody's" Grindr account.

Brandon4455: Still down for Tuesday?

Cody12782: 4 right

Brandon4455: Yes 4 pm at the woodbridge five guys

Cody12782: Yeah

Brandon4455: That cool?

Cody12782: Yeah

Brandon4455: Cool can't wait

Cody12782: Me 2. My mom yelled at me to go bed

Brandon4455: Its cool. Goodnight Cody

Cody12782: Bye

Kyle plugged his decoy phone into the charger on his desk, his personal phone into the charger on his bedside table. He settled under his covers and drifted off to sleep.

* * *

His phones shrieked. Kyle blinked repeatedly, trying to focus his eyes in the dark. This wasn't a normal phone call. First, the noise was coming from both his phones. Second, it wasn't his ring tone. It sounded like an alarm, like one of those public broadcasts, where they say, "This is a test." The alarm stopped, the silence abrupt. Kyle reached for his phone on the bedside table. The screen read:

2:39 a.m.

Sunday, May 11

AMBER Alert now

Lorton, VA Amber Alert: White Chevy Pickup, Red Cap

Kyle's eyes were wide, his heart pounding. *How the hell did he get a kid at this hour?* He swiped right and clicked on the text for more details.

AMBER Alert: Lorton, VA

VEHICLE: Older White Chevy Pickup w/Red Cap

CHILD: 12 White Male 5'0" 80 pounds Brown hair Brown Eyes wearing Washington Redskins pajamas.

SUSPECT: White or Hispanic Male 6'0-6'3" 200-250 pounds wearing all black with ski mask.

Shit. He snatched this kid from his bedroom. The decoy phone buzzed, causing Kyle to flinch. He turned on his lamp, stood, and grabbed the phone from his desk.

Man with a Plan: You see my Amber Alert, Kyle?

The Big Bad Wolf got a new account.

Cody12782: Let him go. They saw you and your POS truck.

Man with a Plan: Truck's gone. Wasn't mine anyway. Do you want to save this boy?

Cody12782: Yes

Man with a Plan: Do you want to be a hero?

Cody12782: Where are you?

Man with a Plan: All good things to those who wait.

Cody12782: What do you want from me?

Man with a Plan: I told you to delete your videos. You didn't listen. I took this boy as a tribute to your disobedience.

Cody12782: I'll delete everything if you let him go.

Man with a Plan: Too late for that.

Cody12782: What do you want?

Man with a Plan: Since you want to be a hero so bad, I'm going to give you your big break. Come to the following address alone. If you call the cops, I will kill the boy and worse. Don't test me. 3570 Old Colchester Road Lorton

Cody12782: I'll be there

Man with a Plan: Tick-tock, Kyle.

Kyle's finger hovered over the keypad on his phone, his brain turning with outcomes and probabilities. He dialed 9-1-1.

"Nine, one, one, what is your emergency?" the woman asked.

"I know where the kid is," Kyle replied. "The one on the Amber Alert."

CHAPTER 27

DOUG DOESN'T BLUFF

Kyle paced in his living room, fully dressed in jeans and a fleece. He held his phone to his ear.

"Hello?" Leigh answered, her voice raspy with sleep.

"It's me," Kyle replied.

There was no response.

"Are you there?"

"It's three in the morning," Leigh said.

"He took a kid, Leigh. There was an Amber Alert."

"What are you talking about?" Her voice was high and shaky now.

"Doug, the Big Bad Wolf, whatever the hell his name is. He took a kid, then sent me a text about it."

"Gwen."

Kyle heard a *thud* followed by a rumble of quick steps. "Leigh?"

No answer.

"Leigh?" *She must've gone to check on Gwen.*

"She's sleeping," Leigh said, returning to the line.

Kyle blew out a breath of relief. "You should make sure the alarm's set and all the doors and windows are locked."

"You don't think he'd come here, do you?"

"He hasn't mentioned Gwen since the note, but I don't know."

"Damn you, Kyle. What did I tell you?"

"I know. I'm sorry. I called the police. They're supposed to be here any minute. I'll tell 'em to send someone to your house. In the meantime, check your alarm and make sure everything's locked."

"I can't believe this is happening."

The police banged on his door. *Only the police knock that rudely.*

"I gotta go. They're here." Kyle disconnected the call, hurried to the door, and opened it. Detective Sean Fitzgerald stood bleary-eyed in a rumpled suit, flanked by two uniformed officers.

"I need you to come with me and answer some questions at the station," Detective Fitzgerald said, his mouth a flat line. "And we're gonna need your phone and your computer."

"But we're running out of time," Kyle replied. "You can talk to me here. I have video of the guy and a little of his truck. It might help find him."

"We've already seen it."

"OK, … my computer's in my room, and I have two phones. I'll go get 'em."

"No, just show us where they are. We'll take them to the station."

Kyle handed his personal phone to the detective and showed the officers where he kept his laptop and his decoy phone. Kyle and Detective Fitzgerald stood in the living room while the uniformed officers placed his laptop and phones in Ziploc-style bags.

"All right. Let's go," Fitzgerald said to Kyle.

Kyle didn't move. "Can someone check on my sister? This guy threatened my niece."

"Threatened?" Fitzgerald asked. "Threatened how?"

"The guy left me a note that said, 'Gwen.' That's my niece's name."

"That's it? It just said her name?"

"Yeah."

"Have you talked to your sister?"

"Yeah, they're fine, but given what just happened …"

"What's her address? I'll call it in."

After dispatching a police officer to Leigh's, Fitzgerald and Kyle left the apartment complex. Fitzgerald drove with Kyle in the front seat of his unmarked Crown Victoria.

I'm glad he didn't put me in back like a criminal. "Have they found the boy?" Kyle asked, looking at the detective.

"I can't talk about an open investigation," Fitzgerald replied, not taking his eyes off the road.

Does that mean they haven't found him? Does that mean I'm a suspect? We're definitely not working together here. Is he gonna arrest me when we get to the station? Kyle's temples pounded from stress and lack of sleep.

The rest of the ride was uncomfortably quiet.

At the police station, Kyle gave Detective Mitchell his laptop and phone passwords, and showed her the folder that housed the digital documents pertaining to the Big Bad Wolf. Then Fitzgerald led Kyle into an interrogation room—although the detective called it an *interview* room. Kyle sat across from Detective Fitzgerald at a small square table in a small square room. At the upper corner of the room, a camera pointed down at them.

"We're recording this interview," Fitzgerald said, gesturing to the camera.

"OK," Kyle replied, glancing at the camera, his hands clasped and resting on the metal desk. "Do I need a lawyer?"

Fitzgerald narrowed his beady eyes. "Did you do something wrong?"

"No."

"Then you don't need a lawyer." Detective Fitzgerald cleared his throat. "Take me through your relationship and your face-to-face meeting with Doug aka the Big Bad Wolf and aka Man with a Plan."

"From the beginning?"

"Yeah."

"I need my phone. I can show you the messages from when we started talking."

"Detective Mitchell's looking at your phone and your computer right now. Just tell me what you remember."

"I posted a fake profile of a made-up kid named Cody on Grindr. Doug or whatever his real name is contacted me about six weeks ago. I told him right away that I was twelve and had lied about my age to get on the site."

"You're talking about Grindr, right?"

"Yes."

"How did he react to this admission of Cody being twelve years old?"

"He was fine with it. They always are. He started calling me YM, which is young man for short. He said he called me that because I was a young man, but still a man."

"What happened after his initial contact on Grindr?"

"We messaged back and forth for weeks."

"What did you talk about?"

"It's all on my phone. If you just get my phone—"

"We're already looking at it."

"I don't remember everything we talked about."

"What do you remember?"

"He sent me video of himself masturbating. He had on big sunglasses, and it was dark, so you can't see his face very well."

"Did he send you any other pictures with a better view of his face?" Fitzgerald asked.

"No, but my video got him a bit better, but he does have on a hat, and his face is shaded pretty heavy."

"Did he ever give any indication of what he does for a living in your chats?"

"No, but you should look at the messages," Kyle replied. "Maybe you'll see something I missed."

"What else do you remember about your chats?"

"He was aggressive."

"What does that mean?"

"He tried to push things sexually in an aggressive manner."

Detective Fitzgerald nodded.

"He asked me if I was setting him up. I told him no, and he said, if I was, that he'd kill me."

Fitzgerald shook his head. "And you still went to meet him?"

Kyle didn't respond.

"After I explicitly told you to stop luring guys off the internet?"

Kyle kept quiet.

"Is there anything from your chats that you can remember that might help us identify Doug?"

"No, but you have everything. It's all in that folder I showed Detective Mitchell."

"What about the meeting? Is there anything about the meeting that might help us identify Doug?"

"The truck. You guys got it mostly right in the Amber Alert, but the cap was a faded maroon, not red. And the truck was dirty. None of that may matter though. He sent me a message saying the truck wasn't his, and he got rid of it."

"When did he say that?"

"Right before I called 9-1-1. Detective Mitchell has that message string. It's the last one."

"When you met him, did you happen to get his license plate?"

"No. I snuck up to him, walking along the building, and from that angle I couldn't see the truck's plates. Then when he left, he drove too fast. It did look like Virginia plates though, like the regular blue-and-white ones. Not that that really narrows it down. Maybe one of the businesses got the plates on camera."

Fitzgerald nodded. "Anything else that might be useful from your meeting?"

"He pulled a gun on me and my friend Troy. That wasn't in the video because he stole my phone and camera."

"Then how did you get the footage that you got?"

"I was recording with my phone, and I have that continuously backed up to the cloud. It didn't get everything … obviously."

"What kind of gun was it?"

"I'm not a gun expert, but it looked kind of like the guns you guys carry."

Detective Fitzgerald removed a boxy Glock 9 mm from the shoulder holster under his suit jacket and placed it on the table in front of him, the barrel facing the wall. "Like this?"

Kyle looked at the gun. "Uh, exactly like that."

Fitzgerald put his Glock back in his holster. "Did you see any birthmarks or tattoos or anything else that might help us identify him?"

Kyle shook his head. "I didn't see any tattoos, but he was wearing pants and long sleeves. He is a big guy. Maybe six-two, 220. Stringy blond hair almost to his shoulders. A blond-and-white beard. He looked about forty or so."

"Anything else?"

"No, … sorry."

Fitzgerald nodded and stood from the table. "Wait here. We'll have more questions once we've gone through your phone and laptop."

Kyle frowned. "Are you going through *all* my stuff?"

"Just the folder you gave us." Fitzgerald glared at Kyle for a moment. "Are you hiding something I should know about?"

"No. I don't want you wasting your time. I have a lot of videos and chats. *A lot.* It would take forever to go through all that. You guys don't seem to be moving very fast on this Amber Alert. Aren't the first few hours really important?"

Fitzgerald ignored the question. "Wait here." The detective stepped outside the interview room. A uniformed police officer was posted outside.

Why is that cop standing there? Is Fitzgerald holding me here? And why is there no sense of urgency? Unless … Kyle's stomach turned.

The seconds turned to minutes. The minutes to over an hour. Without stimulation, or much sleep the night before, Kyle's eyes were heavy. He put his forearms and elbows on the desk and rested his head on his arms. He drifted off to sleep.

* * *

"Kyle, wake up," Detective Fitzgerald said.

Kyle lifted his head and blinked rapidly, his eyes adjusting to the harsh fluorescent light. Fitzgerald and his partner Detective Janet Mitchell sat across from him at the table.

Kyle rubbed his eyes and sat up straight. "What time is it?"

Fitzgerald checked his watch. "I've got 6:33."

"Did you guys find the boy?" Kyle asked.

"He's dead, Kyle," Detective Mitchell said without emotion.

Kyle looked down and swallowed.

"You OK?" Mitchell asked.

Kyle wiped his eyes discreetly with the sleeve of his fleece. "Doug said he'd kill him if I called the police." Kyle shook his head, his eyes downcast.

"Do you think this is your fault?" Detective Mitchell asked, her voice soothing.

Kyle looked up. "I don't know."

"Regardless of what he said, you did the right thing by calling us."

"You should've called us when he pulled that gun on you," Fitzgerald said. "Hell, you shouldn't have been luring men to begin with."

"Am I in trouble?" Kyle asked.

"You've been walking a fine line," Mitchell said. "We're willing to forgive and forget, but we need you to do a few things for us."

"You want me to take down my videos?"

"No," Fitzgerald said. "It's more likely that he'll contact you if you leave the videos up."

"Maybe you could feature his video somehow," Mitchell said. "Put it at the top of your page."

"I can pin it to the top on my Facebook page. It's my most recent video on YouTube, so it's already at the top." Kyle furrowed his brows. "Why do you want to antagonize him?"

Fitzgerald said, "We're gonna lure him into contacting you. We wanna tap your phone and put an undercover officer at your apartment complex in case he contacts you or comes back to your house."

Kyle shook his head. "What about my sister and my niece?"

"They're fine. We've had a cruiser parked at your sister's house since about 3:30 a.m."

"I'm not comfortable with this. He might do something to my niece. I thought he was just trying to scare me, but he's obviously not bluffing."

"What if we made sure your sister and niece are protected? We can keep an officer at your sister's house 24/7 until we catch this guy."

Kyle took a deep breath. "OK."

CHAPTER 28

PUNISHMENT

Kyle struggled to keep his eyes open as he was driven home from the police station, exhausted from lack of sleep and the three-hour interrogation. An undercover officer was supposedly assigned to Kyle's apartment complex, although he didn't see any unmarked police cars. The officer stopped his cruiser in front of Kyle's apartment building, but he didn't park. Kyle stepped from the cruiser, shut the door, and the uniformed police officer was gone without so much as a wave. Kyle trudged to the fourth floor, his black fleece over his shoulder, and his laptop held in one hand like a textbook. The police had copied everything they needed and had allowed Kyle to take his gear home. After all, he'd need it to be the bait they wanted him to be.

As soon as he crested the fourth-floor steps, he saw it. A yellow Post-it note stuck to his door. He looked around, half-expecting the Big Bad Wolf to huff and puff and blow his apartment down. He approached his door tentatively. The note read GO TO TROY's. Kyle walked next door. Another yellow Post-it note was on Troy's door. It read IT's OPEN. CHECK BEDROOM. Kyle looked around again. Nobody. He turned the knob and pushed inside.

"Troy?" Kyle called out. He shut the door behind him. Troy's boots and Sophie's little pink sneakers were by the door. It was quiet, sunlight streaming through the living room blinds, dust motes hanging in the air. "Troy?" Kyle padded past the kitchen and the living room, down the short hallway to the bedroom. There were five Post-it notes on the bedroom door, arranged in a vertical line.

You disobeyed me again by calling the police.

You still haven't deleted your videos.

You don't know who you're fucking with.

You want this to happen to Gwen?

You stop. I stop.

Kyle's heartbeat pounded; his stomach churned. He knocked on the door. "Troy?" No answer. Kyle turned the knob and pushed inside. The room was neat and appeared clean, but the air smelled putrid, like fear and feces. Two beds dominated the room—Troy's queen and Sophie's small bed. Sophie's bed was made—the pink comforter tucked in tight. Troy's bed had a lump under the comforter, the size of … Troy.

"Troy?" Kyle said, approaching his bedside.

Kyle set his laptop and fleece on the bedside table. He shook his friend, only a bit of Troy's hair uncovered. Troy was unresponsive. Kyle pulled back the comforter. "Troy?" He was facedown. A thin purple bruise circumvented Troy's neck. Kyle pushed him, turning him over. Troy's face was dark blue, his eyes open and red. Kyle put his hand to Troy's neck, searching for a pulse that he knew wasn't there. He took a step back, tears welling in his eyes. He swallowed the lump in his throat. "Sophie? Are you here? It's Kyle." He dropped to his knees, checking under the bed. Nothing. He went to the closet and opened the door. Sophie lay on her side awkwardly, her eyes red, half of her face blue, the same ligature mark around her tiny neck. Kyle dropped to his knees, tears slipping down his face.

A few minutes later, Kyle wiped his face with his sleeve and removed his personal cell phone from his pocket. For the second time in less than twenty-four hours, he dialed 9-1-1.

* * *

Kyle sat at his kitchen table with Detective Fitzgerald while crime scene investigators processed Troy's apartment. Kyle gripped the edge of the table to stop his hands from shaking. "I can't do this," Kyle said. "I'm out."

Fitzgerald exhaled heavily. "Look, Kyle. I'm sorry about your friend and his little girl. It's tragic." Fitzgerald shook his head. "I'd like for you to still help us. We can protect you and your sister and your niece."

Kyle narrowed his eyes. "You don't know that."

"I know he'll kill again, if we don't do something about it."

"He did this because I didn't do what he told me to." Kyle looked down.

"You can't reason with him. He's a psychopath."

Kyle looked up. "He said, if I stopped, he'd stop. I'm done." Kyle stood from the table. "I'm sorry, Detective."

Detective Fitzgerald stood from the table, his mouth turned down. "Let me know if you change your mind."

Kyle nodded.

Detective Fitzgerald left Kyle's apartment.

Kyle went to his desk and powered on his laptop. He deleted everything that pertained to The Predator Hunter. The Facebook page, YouTube page, Twitter account, all the videos, audio, his website, … everything.

CHAPTER 29

PUBLIC PLEA

Kyle sat in his recliner, watching his television. Rachel Franklin was on the screen in front of Kyle's apartment building. The afternoon sun faded in the background. A few police cars were parked in the lot.

Rachel wore a pencil skirt and a solemn expression. Her dark lustrous hair touched her shoulders. "Early this morning, in this Woodbridge, Virginia, apartment building"—Rachel gestured to the building behind her—"twenty-eight-year-old Troy Ferguson and his six-year-old daughter, Sophie, were murdered in their home. Troy Ferguson was the neighbor and cameraman for Kyle Summers, otherwise known as The Predator Hunter, an online sensation who poses as children with the intention of meeting, confronting, and shaming child predators in person. According to the police, the prime suspect in the double homicide is a man who Kyle Summers and Troy Ferguson confronted behind a local strip mall. Unfortunately, the police have not been able to identify the suspect from the video footage. I'll have more details as they are released from the Prince William County Police Department. Back to you, Stanley."

The news program cut to a fortysomething male anchor with plastered-in-place hair. His face was just as solemn as the reporter's. "Thank you, Rachel."

Doug aka the Big Bad Wolf's picture appeared next to the anchor. It was from Kyle's video. Doug had his trucker hat pulled low over his eyes, his ratty blond hair spilling from the sides.

Kyle ground his teeth and had a death grip on the armrests of his recliner.

"This image is of the prime suspect," the anchor said. "He's known to frequent dating sites such as Grindr under the screen names, Big Bad Wolf or Man with a Plan. His first name may be Doug, or he may use that name as an alias. He's estimated to be in his early forties. He's a large man, approximately six-two and 220 pounds." Doug's image was shown in full screen, along with a phone number and a caption that read Prince William County Police Hotline. The news anchor spoke over the picture. "If you have any knowledge of this man's identity or his whereabouts, please contact the Prince William County Police Hotline at 703-555-8621. And please, folks, under no circumstances should you approach this man. He is considered to be armed and highly dangerous."

Kyle turned off the television, his heart pounding, his shoulders tense, and his jaw stiff from grinding his teeth.

CHAPTER 30

SOMEONE TO BLAME

Danny Boy MMA: Where u at girl?

Danny Boy MMA: Jonesin 4 some Bethany

Danny Boy MMA: Where u at?

Danny Boy MMA: It's like that?

Danny Boy MMA: U R missing out

Kyle sat in his car, wearing a dark suit. He didn't respond to Danny Boy.

Brandon4455: I'm here

Brandon4455: Its 4 where are you?

Brandon4455: 4:15 are you coming?

Brandon4455: I drove a long way to see you

Brandon4455: Message me so I know your OK

Brandon4455: I'm leaving its 4:45 ☹

Brandon4455: Where were you yesterday? I waited for you

Brandon4455: I'm worried

Brandon4455: Message me please I'm worried

Kyle placed his decoy phone with his personal phone in the cupholder. The past three days had been a never-ending nightmare. When he closed his eyes, he saw Troy and Sophie, blue and lifeless. As far as he knew, the police still had no idea where Doug was or even *who* he was. Despite Kyle's lack of cooperation, Detective Fitzgerald, or more likely Fitzgerald's boss, had kept a uniformed officer at Leigh's house and Kyle's apartment complex. Kyle had no idea how long it would last or if it was even necessary. Kyle hadn't heard from Doug since Kyle had deleted everything Predator Hunter. *If you stop, I stop. Maybe he'll keep his word.*

Kyle stepped from his car, the heat radiating off the asphalt parking lot, the afternoon sun high in the sky. He walked across the parking lot to the gothic funeral home. Inside, the decor was filled with dark wood and ornate furniture. Kyle was greeted by a serious man who resembled a live skeleton.

"Welcome to Kramer Funeral Home," the man said. "Are you here for the Ferguson viewing?"

Kyle cleared his throat. "Yes."

"You can sign in here, if you like." The man gestured to the podium and the open book. "The viewing is to the left, the first room on the left."

"Thanks." Kyle moved to the podium.

An older couple entered and received the identical greeting from the skeleton man. Kyle signed the guest book and walked to the viewing room. A line snaked from the open double doors to the open caskets. One very large casket to encapsulate Troy's six-three frame and one very small casket for six-year-old Sophie. Kyle stood in the receiving line behind an elderly couple. Approximately a dozen people were in front of him, the conversations subdued.

The line inched forward, Kyle moving closer to the family of the deceased. The low conversations were now audible. Two middle-aged couples spoke to those in line. The nearest couple was tall, like Troy; the other middle-aged couple was short. *Sophie's grandparents maybe.*

"I'm so sorry for your loss," the elderly man said.

"Thank you for comin', Uncle Harry," the tall middle-aged man said, shaking hands with the elderly man.

"It's just heartbreaking." The elderly woman blotted the corners of her eyes with a handkerchief.

"Aunt Bette, thank you for comin'," the tall man said again.

The old woman hugged the tall man.

Kyle glanced at the caskets. Troy and Sophie looked like lifelike dolls, so real, yet so obviously dead. Troy was cleanshaven. Kyle had never seen him without his beard. Kyle's mind flashed back to Troy's dead red eyes and Sophie, lifeless on her side, one half of her face blue. He swallowed the lump in his throat.

"Excuse me, young man," the tall man said.

The "young man" reference jolted Kyle from his stupor.

The tall man held out his hand. "I'm Jack Ferguson. Troy's father."

Kyle shook Jack's hand. "Uh, I'm Kyle. I'm ... was ... Troy's friend." Kyle looked down, the tears welling in his eyes.

"You were Troy's neighbor."

"I'm so sorry," Kyle said, still looking down, the tears unstoppable now.

Jack put his hand on Kyle's shoulder and squeezed. "It's OK, son."

Kyle shook his head. "It's not." He looked up, his eyes red and glassy. "I'm really sorry. If he never knew me, they'd be ..."

Jack reached out and hugged Kyle, clapping him on the back. "Don't you think that. You were tryin' to do good." Jack let go.

Kyle stepped back. "Thank you." Kyle turned and headed out the way he came, his head down. He wiped his eyes with the side of his fist and bumped into someone near the double doors. Kyle stopped and raised his head. She was short, about his age, with dark hair and a little black dress. "I'm sorry," he said.

"I know who you are." She narrowed her red-rimmed eyes at Kyle. "What the hell are you doing here?"

"I ... uh—"

"Your stupid bullshit killed my little girl." Her voice trembled.

Heather. "I'm sorry. I didn't mean for—"

"You didn't mean for what? For my daughter to get murdered!"

The receiving line turned toward the pair.

Heather slapped Kyle across the face.

Kyle stood, stunned.

After a beat, she slapped him again and again. Kyle took his punishment, thinking he deserved far worse.

Jack stepped between them, facing Heather. "That's enough, Heather."

"He killed my baby. He killed my baby." She grabbed onto Jack and sobbed.

Kyle hurried for the exit.

CHAPTER 31

HELPLESS

The grass was lush—hopped up on chemical fertilizer and underground sprinklers. Kyle's pants were green from his kneecaps to his ankles. He placed the trimmer on the rack attached to the trailer. Hector put the final touches on the lawn with the last few diagonal stripes. Julio blew off the sidewalks and the driveway. Kyle hadn't spoken to anyone all day. In fact, he hadn't spoken to anyone since the day before, at the funeral. Not speaking was easy on a mowing crew with loud machines, a language barrier, and a route that everyone practically knew by heart. The noise and the repetitive, robotic work was a welcome distraction.

Back at the shop, Kyle turned in his route sheet and clocked out. Kyle's boss, Sam Irwin, approached from his office. Kyle turned and walked toward the exit.

"Hey, Kyle," Sam said, catching up.

Kyle stopped and turned to his boss.

"I'm real sorry about what happened."

Kyle nodded, his mouth a flat line.

"Detective Fitzgerald called earlier. He asked if you were workin' today. I told him that you were. He wants you to call him immediately. He said you have his number."

Kyle nodded again.

"I didn't think you'd be here today. Hector can run the crew if you need a few days."

"I need the money." Kyle turned and stepped toward the exit and the parking lot.

Kyle drove home, his windows down, breathing in exhaust from the stop-and-go traffic. Detective Fitzgerald was parked in a visitor spot in front of Kyle's apartment building. As soon as Kyle parked, Detective Fitzgerald hustled toward him. Kyle stepped from his Hyundai. Detective Fitzgerald stood, his ruddy face taut, blocking Kyle's path.

"Your phone's been off all day," Fitzgerald said.

Kyle nodded, brushing past the detective.

"We still have an officer parked at your sister's house."

Kyle stopped and turned to the detective. "I appreciate that. I really do."

"We need your help."

"You don't need me. You have video of the guy. Go find him."

"We're trying. We did a composite from your video but no hits yet."

"What about the cameras at the strip mall? Didn't they get a better angle?"

"No. The one with the best view was a dummy camera."

Kyle blew out a breath. "I said I was done." Kyle continued up the stairs.

Detective Fitzgerald followed. "Look, Kyle, you're our best lead. We need you to try to contact this guy."

Kyle stepped onto the fourth floor. He glanced at the police tape across Troy's apartment door, then to Fitzgerald. "No." Kyle continued to his apartment. He unlocked the dead bolt, stepped inside, and shut his door in Fitzgerald's face.

Kyle showered, dirt and grass washing off his body. He put on a pair of athletic shorts and a T-shirt. His phones were on his desk, dismantled, the batteries and SIM cards removed. He ate two turkey sandwiches for dinner, the long workday trumping the sick feeling in his stomach.

At the knock on the door, Kyle jumped, his stomach in his throat. He set down his half-eaten sandwich and crept to the door. Another knock came, startling him again. He peered through the peephole.

"Kyle, I know you're home. Open up," Leigh said.

Kyle opened the door.

Leigh's dark hair was disheveled. She wore a long T-shirt and running pants—no makeup. "I've been calling you," Leigh said, stepping inside, shutting the door and locking it behind her. "I was worried."

Kyle shrugged. "My phones are off."

"Jesus, Kyle, you can't do that. Not after everything that's happened."

"It doesn't matter what I do."

"It matters to me." Leigh moved closer.

"It shouldn't." Kyle returned to the kitchen table.

Leigh followed, talking to his back. "It does."

Kyle sat at the small table. Leigh sat across from him.

"Are you OK?" Leigh asked.

"I'm fine." Kyle broke eye contact for a split second.

"You sure?" Leigh pressed.

"Yeah." Kyle rubbed his eyes with his thumb and index finger.

"You don't look fine."

Kyle exhaled heavily. "What do you expect?"

"I'm just worried about you."

"I'm fine."

"You said that."

"Is there something else? I need to go to sleep soon. I have to be up at 5:30."

Leigh sighed. "I know this is terrible timing, but you've put me in an impossible position with Jewel."

Kyle rubbed the back of his neck. "What do you want me to do about it?"

"I've had her for five days now, and I don't know what to do with her. She's been great with Gwen, but she's not my child. If I send her home, she'll run away. If I give her up to the state, they'll send her home or maybe they'll arrest me. Either she stays with me or she ends up on the street. What am I supposed to do with that?"

"I don't know. I can't help her. I can't help anyone."

CHAPTER 32

ONE WAY OUT

Kyle got what he wanted. The rest of the week he worked as much as he could; he went to bed early, and he was left alone. He even worked Saturday, helping a landscape crew that was behind on a pond-and-waterfall project. He'd gone cold turkey on his cell phones and the internet. By Saturday night, he was out of distractions. He lay in bed, wide awake, staring at the ceiling. His bedroom was dimly lit by the streetlights filtering through the blinds. He thought about Troy and Sophie, and Leigh and Gwen.

Detective Fitzgerald had told Leigh that they were pulling their personal police protection on Monday, but they'd still make regular patrols by her house. *Would Doug still go after Gwen?* Kyle hadn't heard from Doug since the Post-it notes last Sunday. *But he's still out there, and the police can't find him or even identify him.* Kyle figured he had three options.

I could continue to do nothing. Or work with the police to find Doug. Or find Doug on my own. If I do nothing, that's still no guarantee of safety for Leigh and Gwen, not to mention Doug'll probably kill again. If I help the police, there's no guarantee that we'll find him, and, if Doug finds out I'm working with them, he'll kill Leigh and Gwen for sure, just like he did Troy and Sophie. If I find him on my own, what the hell can I do about it? Kyle turned on his side, restless. *There's only one thing to do. But can I do it? I don't know.*

Ultimately, he chose the option that risked the lives of the two people he *didn't* care about.

CHAPTER 33

A BIGGER NET

Rays of sun slipped between the blinds in skinny slivers. Kyle's eyes fluttered. He glanced at the alarm clock on his bedside table. He'd bought it last week when he had dismantled his phones. It was late—10:23 a.m. He had had trouble sleeping the night before. Tossing and turning with his plans, probabilities, and possibilities. Thankfully he was off today, as it was Sunday.

He stretched his arms and legs, and rose from bed. He padded to his desk, put his phones back together, and powered on his laptop and phones. While his equipment loaded, he brushed his teeth. He knew what he had to do. *I need a bigger net.* Kyle sat down at his desk and made multiple profiles of preteen boys. He used pictures fans had given him and avatars of superheroes. He made many different accounts on various dating sites for men. He received messages immediately. Nothing from the Big Bad Wolf or the Man with a Plan yet. Granted, Doug likely had new handles, but Kyle was confident that he'd know him by his messaging style and word choice. *Would Doug be stupid enough to take the bait twice? Compulsion often trumps intelligence.*

After breakfast Kyle did an internet search for gun shops nearby that were open on Sunday. He hopped in his car and drove the short distance to Griffin's Guns and Ammo. He heard muffled shots coming from the building. Kyle opened the barred door and walked inside, the bells on the door jingling. The shop was a narrow room with a long glass case filled with handguns. Rifles hung on the wall behind the case.

A burly man with a gray beard stood behind the counter. He looked up from his *Guns & Ammo* magazine. "What can I do for you?" Gray Beard asked.

"I need a gun." Kyle looked down at the case. "Like one of these."

"A handgun?"

"Yes."

The man stroked his beard. "What are you plannin' to use it for?"

"Self-defense, … like from people."

"Revolver or semiautomatic?"

Kyle shrugged. "What's easier to use?"

"A revolver. You have any experience with guns?"

"No."

Gray Beard nodded. "It's not the gun that matters. It's what you can do with it." Gray Beard picked up a flyer from the stack near the register. "Monday nights I do a class for beginners. I gotta indoor range in back. It's only fifty bucks." He handed the flyer to Kyle.

Kyle took the flyer.

"Come by tomorrow. I'll make sure you get a gun that fits you and that you know how to use it."

CHAPTER 34

GONE FISHING

Greggor the Great: Pete, like your profile pic. Hit me up.

Kyle sat in his recliner, checking his messages on his various profiles. He'd had a lot of bites over the past week, but he hadn't responded to a single message. He was waiting for the big fish.

Redman123: Lookin good, handsome. Top or bottom?

Thomas Sandberg: Hey, what's up, Peter. DM me if you want to talk.

Eatshitdie: FAGGOT I HOPE U HAVE TO WEAR A DIAPER CUZ OF ALL THE DICKS IN YOUR ASS

BIG BEARMAN: Wanna be my cub?

Connor Radley: How are you, YM?

Jackpot.

CHAPTER 35

EVERYONE HAS A PLAN UNTIL ...

Kyle parked at the CVS Pharmacy in Dumfries, VA, his Hyundai shielded by the building and other cars. He checked the time on his phone—*2:33 p.m.* He had hoped to make the trip and get into town a little earlier to get a lay of the land, but Friday traffic was always a bitch. Plus, he had been filthy from work, so he had stopped by his house, took a quick shower, and changed into a pair of jeans and a plain T-shirt. Besides, the last thing he needed was to be identified by his company uniform.

Hector and Julio had agreed to work through lunch, and they'd finished relatively early. With the heat wave, the grass growth had slowed considerably, and today's route was light. Sam always scheduled light on Fridays in case rain during the week had them playing catch up. Kyle had thought about calling in sick, but, if everything went according to plan, a sick day would look awfully suspicious. Kyle checked his messages.

Connor Radley: I'm running a little late. Might be closer to 3:15.

Peter Parker505: K no probs

Connor Radley: See you soon, YM.

Kyle studied the parking lot from his driver's seat. Nobody was looking. Kyle put on a Washington Senators baseball cap and pulled it low over his eyes. He looked around the parking lot again, his heart pumping. Nobody. He opened his glove compartment and removed the 380 revolver and ankle holster. He hiked his pant leg and attached the holstered revolver.

Kyle stepped from his car and shoved his decoy phone and his personal phone in each front pocket of his jeans. He walked around the CVS and peered out from the rear of the building to the Little Caesar's pizzeria. The pizza place looked mostly empty. Only three cars in the lot. One of them a pickup truck. It was a relatively new F-150 quad cab, nicely optioned. *That can't be Doug's truck. That's probably a $50,000 vehicle. He must be telling the truth about being late.* The cars were Japanese compacts. Also not Doug's style.

The Little Caesar's pizzeria was the meeting spot. Connor Radley or the Big Bad Wolf or Doug or whoever the hell he was thought Peter was a seventh grader at Dumfries Middle School, which was within walking distance of the pizza place. They were supposed to meet, have some pizza, then go to a movie.

Kyle hustled from the CVS parking lot, across a road, to the back of the pizzeria. Heat reverberated off the asphalt in a haze. His legs felt hot in his jeans and heavy with the gun on his ankle. He hid between the Dumpster at the back of the building and waited, his body taut and his heart pounding. Boredom and fatigue set in, and gradually he relaxed. Forty minutes later, he sat on the asphalt, leaning against the building, breathing in garbage. His stomach twisted like a knot at the sound of a diesel engine followed by squeaky brakes. It sounded close by, maybe only twenty feet away. He crept closer to the Dumpster, making sure he was concealed. His decoy phone buzzed. The diesel idled in the background.

Connor Radley: I'm here. I'm around back.

Peter Parker505: I'm in lil cesers

Connor Radley: Meet me in back.

Peter Parker505: I'm hungry lets eat

Connor Radley: I know a better place.

Peter Parker505: U said we could eat here

Connor Radley: You don't want to go someplace better?

Peter Parker505: No

Connor Radley: Order the pizza to go.

Shit. I need to get him out of his vehicle.

Peter Parker505: No money

Connor Radley: Order the pizza, tell me when it's ready, and I'll come in and pay.

Peter Parker505: K thx

Kyle waited for two minutes.

Peter Parker505: They said 20m

Connor Radley: Let me know when it's ready.

Peter Parker505: K no probs

Kyle waited for nineteen minutes, on edge, his heart pounding in his chest.

Peter Parker505: Its ready

Connor Radley: Coming now

A creaky door opened and shut with an echo. *Was that an echo or a second door? Sounded like a second door. Or maybe another car door? Shit.* Kyle removed the 380 from his ankle holster, crept to the corner of the Dumpster, and peered out. A black Dodge pickup with rust spots was parked there. The cab was empty. He moved to the driver's side wheel of the truck, the 380 in his sweaty palms. His phone buzzed.

Connor Radley: Where the hell are you? Is this some kind of joke?

Kyle shoved his phone back in his pocket, gripped the revolver with both hands, and crouched next to the tire for concealment. *It won't be long now.* His phone buzzed again. He didn't check the message. Heavy black boots rounded the corner. The boots and jeans walked in front of the truck toward the driver's side door. As soon as the person turned the corner, Kyle stood, his gun pointed at the Big Bad Wolf aka Doug's barrel chest. Doug stopped, his eyes narrowed at the business end of the revolver. He wore a black cap low over his eyes, greasy blond hair spilling from the sides.

"Turn around," Kyle said.

"I thought it might be you," Doug said, no fear in his voice.

"I said, turn around. I will *fucking* shoot you where you stand."

Doug turned slowly. "Your cameraman and his little girl. That was your fault. I told you—"

"Shut up. Walk to the passenger door of your truck." Kyle jammed the barrel of the gun into Doug's back, prodding him forward.

Doug walked around the front of the truck to the passenger door. A teen boy appeared from the corner of the building, his wide eyes focused on Kyle's gun.

"What the hell you doin'?" the teen asked.

"Go home," Kyle said. The teen stepped closer, forcing Kyle to turn his gun on the boy. "I said, go—"

Doug grabbed Kyle's wrist and twisted, the 380 dropping to the asphalt. Kyle reached for the gun, but Doug kicked it toward the teen. The teen picked up the revolver.

"I got it," the teen said, his voice high.

Doug turned Kyle and pushed him against the truck. Kyle pushed back, but Doug was too strong, too heavy. Doug wound up and smashed Kyle's jaw with a haymaker. Kyle crumpled to the asphalt. After a moment, Kyle shook his head and pushed himself to one knee, his vision blurred.

"Gimme the gun, Hank," Doug said to the teen.

Doug now pointed the 380 in Kyle's face. Hank stood next to Doug with a wicked grin. The boy had a sparse mustache and errant hairs on his oily chin. Hank bound Kyle's hands behind his back with zip ties, then patted Kyle's pockets and removed Kyle's phones, his keys, and his wallet. Kyle was forced into the truck at gunpoint. A pair of sunglasses—the lenses painted with spray paint—were placed over his eyes. They kept his hat on his head. Wherever they were going, Kyle was along for the ride.

CHAPTER 36

CAPTIVITY

Kyle sat on the bench seat, between his captors, blinded by the blacked-out sunglasses and bound by zip ties. Doug and Hank both smelled like BO, Doug mustier and Hank sour smelling. The teen had the barrel of the 380 jammed against Kyle's side. Kyle could see a little if he looked down, but just a sliver. The interior of the Dodge was cloth, weathered, and cut in places, some of the spongy guts spilling out. Kyle saw his captors' ratty jeans. A bit of their arms. The teen's skinny, Doug's beefy.

After a minute of tapping on Kyle's phones, Doug said, "Gimme some paper and a pen."

"Huh?" the teen said.

"Pay attention, Hank. Don't make me repeat myself. Open the fucking glove box and gimme some paper and a pen."

Hank opened the glove box, grabbed a yellow pad of paper and a pen, and handed it to Doug—all with one hand, his other still firmly on the revolver and trained on Kyle. Kyle couldn't see much, but he caught a glimpse of Doug's hand moving across the yellow paper. *What is he writing? Something from my phones. A phone number maybe? Whose?* Doug tore off the piece of paper, and shoved it in his pocket. He cranked the engine, the diesel motor roaring to life.

"Ain't you gonna throw those away?" Hank asked.

He must be talking about my phones.

"Not here," Doug replied.

Classic rock played on the truck radio—loud. Kyle's jaw was sore and clicked when he moved it back and forth. Hank still had the barrel of the 380 jammed into Kyle's side. Doug drove and sang along with the radio as if Kyle's abduction was perfectly normal. Doug tossed Kyle's phones out the window roughly half an hour into the trip. Kyle thought it was when they went over a bridge, but he wasn't sure.

Hank said, "They'll never find 'em now."

Kyle wondered if Hank was talking about the phones or him. *Doug must be taking me someplace secluded to kill me.* His stomach felt queasy. His underarms were wet. He had known this was a possible outcome. He had already made peace with death, but he was afraid of the pain. *I hope it's quick. Bullet to the head. They have my gun. It's not traceable to them. Why wouldn't they use it to kill me?*

It was a long ride. Kyle's shoulders and wrists ached from the zip ties and the placement of his hands behind his back. Kyle counted songs and commercials. Fifteen songs and five commercial breaks. Kyle figured they'd been driving for roughly an hour and a half, figuring four-minute songs and five-minute commercial breaks.

The smooth asphalt turned to a gravel road with potholes. The truck's old suspension was stiff and groaning over every imperfection. After two more songs—Aerosmith followed by The Eagles—the truck stopped. Hank opened his door and pulled Kyle from the cab by his arm. It was cooler here. Through the bottom of his shades, he saw the shadows from trees overhead. Leaves rustled in the breeze. Doug grabbed his other arm. They walked a few paces on gravel and stopped.

"Three steps up," Doug said.

Kyle felt for the step with his work boot, although he could see the wooden steps below the blacked-out glasses. After three steps up, three dead bolts were undone, and the front door was opened. Inside, it smelled musty, no air-conditioning. It felt warmer inside than out. Kyle was forced straight into the house, like traveling into the belly of the beast.

Doug opened another door, and Kyle was prodded down the stairs. It was cooler in the basement, but it smelled like mold. There was another smell. It wasn't overwhelming, but it was here, and it was something he'd hoped to never smell again. *Death. This is the end. This is where he's gonna do it.* Kyle's legs shook. He thought about Leigh and Gwen.

Doug removed the blacked-out sunglasses. Kyle glanced around the room, dazed, his eyes adjusting. A bare bulb hung from the ceiling. A narrow hallway led to a utility sink at the end with a garden hose and nozzle attached. Along both sides of the hallway were barred cells. *Fucking cells.* Like they were in prison or at the zoo. Eight of them. Four spanned the length of each side. A boy played a first-person shooter game in a back corner cell. He didn't seem to notice or care about Kyle and his captors. The kid's mouth hung open, his eyes vapid, as he virtually killed everything in sight.

"What the hell is this?" Kyle asked, scowling.

Doug shoved Kyle into the first cell on the right. Doug shut the barred door and locked it with a key.

Hank laughed. "It ain't so bad. You'll get used to it."

The cell was empty except for a bucket and a drain in the center.

"Turn around and put your hands between the bars," Doug said. Kyle hesitated.

"You wanna leave those ties on?"

Kyle turned around and put his hands through the bars.

"Don't move unless you want me to cut off your hands."

Hank laughed again.

Doug cut off the zip ties, Kyle's shoulders and wrists feeling immediate relief. Kyle rubbed his wrists and faced his captors. Hank wore a dirty white T-shirt, his face red with acne. Doug wasn't wearing his cap anymore. His greasy blond hair touched his shoulders. He had a receding hairline, a full beard, and bags under his eyes.

"What do you want from me?" Kyle asked.

"It used to be that children were seen and not heard," Doug said. "That's what I expect of my guests. You are to be seen and not heard. Don't speak unless spoken to. Do not try to escape. Do what you're told. If you do those three things, you might go home. If not, well, you don't wanna find out about the alternative." Doug chuckled.

Hank joined in on the laugh, as if on cue.

"You didn't answer my question," Kyle said.

Doug shook his head. "Not even five seconds later and you're already breaking the rules. I told you not to *fucking* speak unless spoken to."

"Want the Hot-Shot?" Hank asked.

"Bring it here."

Hank grabbed a long metal rod attached to a yellow-and-black handle, and handed the contraption to Doug. Doug flipped a switch and gripped the handle, the rod end crackling with electric current. Kyle thought it was a cattle prod. He'd never seen one in real life. He had a flashback to an old episode of *Cheaters*, where the philandering husband was confronted by the host and the camera crew. The husband responded by threatening them with a cattle prod.

Kyle took a step back, but Doug was quick to plunge the electrified rod between the bars and into Kyle's stomach. Kyle yelped and fell to the ground—thousands of volts coursing through his body. Doug retracted the cattle prod.

"Hurt, don't it?" Hank said.

Kyle staggered to one knee, then upright.

"Obey the rules, and I'll reward you, but, if you disobey, you will be severely punished. Do you understand the rules now?" Doug asked.

"Yes," Kyle replied.

"Good." Doug looked at Hank. "Give him one water bottle."

Hank grabbed a plastic water bottle from the utility sink and filled it from the tap. He screwed on the cap, walked toward Kyle, and tossed the bottle inside the cell. It was a small bottle, maybe sixteen ounces. Kyle immediately guzzled half of it.

Doug clapped his hands once and smiled. "Time to celebrate." He strolled to the corner cell where the boy played his game. "Turn that off."

The boy turned off the television immediately and stood at attention.

Doug opened the cell. "Let's go."

The boy followed Doug in lockstep. Kyle tried to make eye contact as the boy walked by, but he had tunnel vision. The boy was skinny and short, maybe ten or eleven. He had brown unkempt hair and buck teeth.

With his captors gone, Kyle first searched for obvious cameras. Saw none. Then Kyle searched his cell for a weakness. There wasn't much to this cage. His cell was eight by eight, like the others. Kyle shook the bars. He examined the base and the roof and the door. He could easily touch the ceiling. Everything was solid. Impenetrable. *Shit.*

Kyle studied the other cells. The one next to his had a toilet seat over a bucket and a thin mattress. The one next to that had a twin-size bed with a raggedy blanket and pillow. The next one had a working toilet to go along with the bed. The boy's cell was downright luxurious in comparison to Kyle's accommodations. He had a toilet, television, bed, and a sink, not to mention the PlayStation. That's when Kyle understood.

This is how Doug gets total obedience. He uses pain and pleasure. Hardship and comfort. Follow the rules. Do what you're told. Maybe you'll get a better cell. Kyle looked around at his barren cell. *What would I do to upgrade my circumstances?*

CHAPTER 37

PUNISHMENT

Gunshots woke Kyle from his fitful sleep. His eyes adjusted to the sparse light emanating from the boy's television. The gunshots were from his game. The single bulb was off. Kyle groaned as he sat up, his entire body sore from sleeping on concrete. He had used his boots as a makeshift pillow. Not particularly soft, but much softer than concrete. *Was it morning?* There were no windows, so no way to tell for sure.

He slipped on his boots, tied them, and stood. He turned his back to the boy and peed down the drain. His urine was yellowish-brown. His mouth was cottony dry. He had had very little to drink yesterday and nothing since that small water bottle Hank had tossed in his cell. Kyle zipped up and turned to the boy. The boy's cell was thirty to forty feet away, situated in the opposite corner from Kyle.

"Hey," Kyle said.

No response.

"Are you OK?" Kyle asked.

No response.

The boy hadn't responded last night either. Doug had brought him back to his cell a few hours after he had taken him. The boy had walked like a depressed octogenarian, his head down, his feet shuffling. He had climbed into his bed and pulled his comforter over his body like a cocoon. Now he was in a trance, zombified by his game.

"Hey, talk to me," Kyle said louder.

The boy finally turned, his finger to his lips. "*Shh.*"

"Please," Kyle said.

"We're gonna get in trouble," the boy whispered, then turned back to his game.

"What's your name?"

No answer.

"What's your name?"

Still no answer.

"What's your name?" Kyle said louder.

The boy paused his game and glared at Kyle. "It's against the rules," he hissed.

"Please," Kyle whispered. "Maybe we can help each other."

The single bulb turned on, illuminating the dank basement, followed by steps down the stairs. The boy went back to his game. Hank descended the stairs with a shit-eating grin.

"What the fuck y'all talkin' 'bout?" Hank asked.

"I was asking his name," Kyle said, gesturing to the boy, "but he won't talk."

Hank sauntered close to Kyle, wearing the same clothes from yesterday, his breath toxic, and his BO kicking. "You know the rules. No talkin'."

Kyle took a step back. "You're right, Hank. I'm sorry."

"I don't give fuck about how you're sorry. You got to be punished." Hank grabbed the cattle prod.

"I can tell you're intelligent," Kyle said.

"You tryin' to be a smart-ass?"

"No, I'm serious. You're a smart guy. You could do anything you want. I could help you. You don't have to be here."

"What the hell you talkin' 'bout?"

"What do you really wanna do with your life? You don't wanna be

187

Doug's slave forever, do you?"

Hank narrowed his eyes. "I ain't no slave."

"Doug tells you what to do, and you do it. What would happen if you told him no?"

"Shut the fuck up. You don't know nothin'." Hank flicked on the cattle prod.

Kyle thought about reaching out and strangling Hank, maybe grabbing the cattle prod, but Kyle had never seen Hank with the keys. Kyle would still be stuck in the cell. The electrical current crackled at the end of the rod. Hank lunged the rod at Kyle, but Kyle sidestepped the rod, and moved to the back of the cell, out of reach.

"What the fuck you think you're doin'?" Hank asked, glowering at Kyle.

"I just wanna talk to you. I can help you." Kyle held up his palms, as if he were trying to tame a wild animal.

"You're just tryin' to get outta here. You must think I'm stupid. You best take your whuppin', or I'm-a-tell Doug."

Kyle blew out a breath and took a few steps forward. Like a swordsman, Hank thrust the cattle prod again, this time connecting with Kyle's leg. Kyle dropped instantly, shrieking in pain.

Hank retracted the prod, cackling. "That never stops bein' funny."

Kyle staggered to his feet. He thought that this shock was less painful than the one he received last night.

Hank sauntered over to the boy's cell. "Get up, Ryan. Time to take your medicine."

"Come on, Hank. He didn't even talk to me," Kyle said.

Ryan stood, shaking like a leaf, tears streaming down his face. "Please don't. Please don't."

"Why you always cryin'? Such a fuckin' baby."

Ryan moved within striking distance, and Hank shocked him on his bare thigh, just below his shorts. Ryan dropped to the concrete, howling in pain. He rocked back and forth holding his leg. "*Ow, ow, ow, ow, owwww,*" he said in rapid succession.

Hank laughed.

Doug descended the stairs, a milk jug filled with water in hand. "What's all the fucking racket?"

Hank's smile went flat. "They was talkin', so I punished 'em."

"Ryan didn't say anything," Kyle said.

"That's a damn lie," Hank replied. "They was plottin'."

Doug rubbed his beard in contemplation.

Ryan was in the fetal position on the concrete, rocking back and forth, quietly sobbing.

Doug approached Kyle's cell. "What did I tell you about talking?"

"You told me not to," Kyle replied.

"Now you need a punishment."

Hank had a goofy grin, a film of yellow on his teeth. "I already got 'im good with the Hot-Shot."

"That's for a first offense," Doug said. "Second offenses must be more severe." A white dot of spray paint was on the floor about five feet away from Kyle's cell and every other cell as well. Doug placed the water jug on the white dot. "I might give you this water tomorrow, provided you learn how to follow the rules." Doug strolled to Ryan's cell. "Get off the fucking floor. Quit your crying."

Ryan stood, sniffling and wiping his eyes.

"Gimme your PlayStation power cord."

Ryan unplugged his game console, detached the cord, and handed it to Doug.

Doug glared at Ryan. "Disobey me again, and I'll move you back a cell ... or maybe two." Doug grinned. "You wanna go back to shitting in a bucket?"

Ryan shook his head.

"You can forget about food today too."

Doug and Hank left them alone.

Kyle rubbed his temples. *They haven't killed me yet for a reason. What do they want? To torture me?* Kyle shuddered. He looked at Ryan, and the boy turned his back and crawled into his bed. Kyle lay on the concrete and reached through the bars for the water jug. It was out of reach. He took off one of his boots and tried to reach it with his boot. When he really stretched, he barely touched the jug with his boot, but he couldn't pull it toward his cell. He felt faint from the exertion. *Just out of reach. I guess that's the point.*

Kyle caught his breath, put on his boot, and stood. He moved to the corner of his cell, facing Ryan, who was in bed facing away from Kyle. He spoke in a whisper. "Hey, I'm sorry, Ryan. I'm assuming that's your name, because that's what they were calling you. Don't worry. You don't have to talk to me. I'll do all the talking. That way, if they hear, it'll just be me who gets in trouble. My name's Kyle, by the way. Do you know where we are?" Kyle paused. "Can you give me a thumbs-up for yes or a thumbs-down for no?"

Ryan sat up in bed and turned toward Kyle, the comforter wrapped around him. He gave a thumbs-down.

"Are you hurt?" Kyle whispered.

Thumbs-up.

"Bad? Do you think you need to go to the doctor?"

Thumbs-down.

"I'm really sorry they hurt you. Are you scared?"

Thumbs-up.

"Me too, but don't worry. I'll figure out a way to get us out of here."

Thumbs-up.

"Do you know how long you've been here?"

Thumbs-down.

"How old are you? Eleven?"

Thumbs-down.

"Ten?"

Thumbs-up.

"I'm twenty-seven." Kyle paused for a moment. "Do you have any brothers or sisters?"

Thumbs-down.

"Do you like sports?"

Thumbs-up.

"You look tough. Are you a football player?"

Thumbs-down.

"Soccer?"

Thumbs-down.

"Baseball?"

Thumbs-up.

"Cool. I love baseball. What position do you play? Shortstop?"

Thumbs-down.

"Catcher?"

Thumbs-down.

"Pitcher?"

Thumbs-up.

"Awesome. You must be really good. Coaches always put the best players at pitcher."

Thumbs-up and a small smile.

"I think you're really brave, Ryan. Maybe we can work together, like Batman and Robin. Maybe we can help each other to get out of here. What do you think?"

Ryan paused, his little face serious as cancer. He turned his thumb up.

CHAPTER 38

DISOWNED

"*Whew-wee*, smells like shit in here," Hank said as he sauntered up to Kyle's cell.

Kyle had used the bucket yesterday. He lay on the concrete, exhausted, only awake because of his massive headache. His mouth felt like desert sand. He was too thirsty to notice his hunger.

"Water," Kyle said, his voice raspy.

Hank glanced at the shit bucket. A few flies buzzed about. "That's fuckin' nasty. You're like a fuckin' animal."

"Water."

Hank stepped back, standing next to the water jug. "You want this?"

Ryan watched the scene from his bed.

Kyle crawled closer to the bars. Closer to the plastic jug. "Water."

Hank moved the jug a few inches closer with his boot. Kyle reached through the bars, his fingertips touching the jug, but the handle was on the other side, so he couldn't grab it.

Hank chuckled. "You are one sorry sack of shit. That's what my daddy used to say to me. But now I'm *your* daddy." Hank picked up the jug and spilled a bit on the floor, the water running to a drain in the middle of the hallway between the cells. Hank laughed again.

"I'm just fuckin' with you." He placed the jug next to Kyle's cell.

Kyle grabbed the jug, but it wouldn't fit through the bars without losing some of the precious liquid. Kyle unscrewed the top on the jug and put his upturned face between two bars. He tilted the jug to his mouth and guzzled. Once it was mostly empty, he crumpled the plastic jug to fit between the bars and pulled it into his cell.

"Tastes good, huh?" Hank said, with a smirk. "I bet you would've sucked my dick for that water."

"That what you do to Doug?" Kyle's voice was still raspy.

Hank grabbed the cattle prod. "You're gonna pay for that."

A door slammed upstairs. Heavy footsteps were overhead.

"Sounds like *your* daddy's home," Kyle said, one side of his mouth raised in contempt.

Doug stomped down the stairs and approached Kyle's cell. He glowered at Kyle, his jaw set tight. Kyle was eight feet away, against the wall.

"You wanna know why you're here?" Doug asked.

Kyle nodded.

"I did a background check on you after you tried to fuck with me. I found out about Leigh and Gwen, and your daddy and his company. I figured he had a few extra dollars laying around. I called *Robert.* Your daddy thinks he's King Shit, High and Mighty. You ask me, he's too big for his britches. You know what he said?" Doug paused, placing his hand on the knife attached to his belt.

Kyle didn't respond.

"He said he doesn't have a son. I pressed the piece of shit, told him that I knew Kyle Summers was his son and that I had him locked up and that I'd kill him if I didn't get what I wanted. Then he said some shit that surprised me. I don't get surprised often, but I tell you, Kyle, your daddy surprised me. He told me that he disowned you ten years ago and that he won't be blackmailed. He said he was reporting my number to the police." Doug paced to the utility sink and back. "What am I supposed to do with you now?"

Kyle didn't respond.

"What the fuck did you do to make your daddy disown you?" Doug asked, shaking his head.

Kyle still didn't respond.

"It could be that he's bluffing. Maybe he thinks I'll let you go if I think you're not worth a shit."

"He *ain't* worth a shit," Hank said.

Doug turned to Hank. "Did I ask for your fucking opinion?"

Hank dipped his head. "No."

Doug turned back to Kyle. "Maybe your daddy's hard of hearing. Maybe he doesn't think I'm serious. Maybe he needs an ear to hear me better." Doug removed handcuffs from his back pocket. He glanced at Hank. "Take him down with the Hot-Shot."

Hank turned on the cattle prod, the current pulsing. Doug opened the cell. Hank entered with the cattle prod out front like a spear, but Kyle shot from the cell like a rocket, avoiding the electrical current and smashing Hank in the face with a straight right. Hank dropped like a sack of potatoes.

Just as quickly, Doug had his meaty arms cinched around Kyle's neck. Kyle, weak from lack of food and water, struggled against the big man, but he was no match. Kyle collapsed, Doug on top of him. Kyle was dazed and oxygen-deprived as his hands were wrenched behind his back and cuffed together. Doug ground his knee into Kyle's back, keeping him firmly pressed against the concrete, just outside his cell.

There was a pause for a moment. Kyle didn't feel the pain at first. Blood poured down his cheek and neck. Then the pain hit. Red-hot searing pain. His ear fell to the floor, mere inches from his eyes. He passed out.

CHAPTER 39

NO HOPE

Kyle woke with a start. It was dark except for the blue screen of Ryan's television. Kyle's head pounded; his ear throbbed. Hearing from his left ear was muffled. He touched his ear softly, with just his fingertip. It was bandaged. Soft gauze and medical tape covered whatever was left of his ear. His T-shirt was stained with dried blood. His mouth was dry. Kyle glanced around his cell, searching for the water jug. It was gone. Thankfully the shit bucket had been emptied. He had worried about the flies.

"Ryan," Kyle said, his voice hoarse. "Ryan?"

No answer. The boy was still sleeping. Kyle struggled to his feet, using the bars for help. He peed into the drain. Afterward, he sat on the concrete, his back against the wall. He couldn't sleep—not with the throbbing pain in his head and ear. *I was so fucking stupid. I should've shot him in that parking lot. I'm gonna die in this shithole. And nobody will give a shit. And they shouldn't.*

"Kyle," Ryan whispered, sitting up in bed, a dark form across the room.

"I'm here," Kyle replied, also whispering.

"Are you … OK?"

"I think so."

"I'm scared." Ryan's voice was barely audible.

"Me too."

"I thought we were gonna be Batman and Robin."

"We are. I'm still working on a plan to get us out of here."

"We're never getting out of here, are we?"

A lump formed in Kyle's throat. There was a long moment of silence, Ryan's truth-bomb detonating and destroying their bubble of hope.

"I need a really good plan, and really good plans take time to figure out. We're getting out of here. Trust me." Kyle knew it was a lie, but he needed to believe the lie just as much as Ryan.

"OK."

They heard steps above them.

"*Shh*," Kyle said.

Ryan gave him a thumbs-up.

The single bulb clicked on, and heavy footsteps followed by lighter ones descended the stairs. Doug carried a tripod and a camera. Hank carried a jug of water. He had a bandage on his nose and two black eyes. Kyle smiled to himself.

"Good morning," Doug said, setting up the tripod and pointing the camera at Kyle.

Kyle stood, his legs a bit wobbly. He faced Doug, his arms crossed over his chest. Doug wore baggy jorts and construction boots. Hank stood just behind Doug, glaring at Kyle. Ryan watched from his bed, silent.

"Do you know how long a human being can live without water?" Doug asked.

"Three days," Kyle replied.

"No. Three to five days, depending on the conditions. Maybe even a week in some extreme cases. It's been a day since you had anything to drink, so I'll guess you got about four days left. It's not hot down here, and you're not exerting yourself, but who the hell knows for sure? You could drop dead two days from now." Doug grinned at

Kyle, his teeth yellow. "Here's how things are gonna go from now on. You help me get my money, I'll give you water. You don't, and I'll let you die from dehydration. Do you understand?"

Kyle nodded.

"Speak up."

"I understand."

Doug clapped his hands together. "Good. I'm glad we're on the same page. You're gonna record a video this morning. You need to beg your daddy to send me my money. Tell him, if he goes to the police again, I'll kill you. Tell him how I'm gonna let you die of dehydration. Tell him how you only got a few days. Tell him how I cut off your ear. Show him the bandage. I mailed your ear to Robert, but I don't know if he got it yet. By the way, you're welcome for my expert medical attention. I used to be a medic. Did you know that?"

"No."

"If you do a good job, Hank's got a nice jug of water for you. You ready to do this?"

"Do I have a choice?"

Doug pressed a button on the camcorder. "Three, two, one, … action." Doug pointed at Kyle with a grin.

"Robert, if you don't send this man money, he's going to kill me. I know you don't wanna help me, but I'm asking you to. He cut off my ear." Kyle turned his head, showing the bandage to the camera. "I only have a few days. He's not giving me any water. You need to get him the money as soon as possible and no police. He said if you go to the police again, he'll kill me."

Doug pressed a button on the camcorder. "Cut, cut, cut. That was half-ass, Kyle. Not enough emotion. And why the fuck are you calling your daddy *Robert*? That's disrespectful. Do it over. This time with feeling. Beg your daddy. If you don't care about your life, how's anyone else supposed to care?" Doug restarted the camcorder. "Three, two, one, … action." Doug pointed at Kyle again.

Kyle looked at the jug of water at Hank's feet. He thought about what his dad did to Kate. He stared into the camera, his eyes glassy. "Dad, please, I need your help. I've been electrocuted, beaten, and my ear was cut off." Kyle turned his head, showing the camera the bandage. "I'll be dead soon if you don't send this man the money he wants. Please, Dad. He's not bluffing. I am 100 percent sure he will kill me if you don't send money. Do not talk to the police again. He will kill me immediately if you do. Please." A tear slipped down his cheek.

Doug pressed a button on the camcorder. "Cut! Damn, that was good, Kyle. The tear at the end. I got a close-up of your face. I should've been a director." Doug picked up the water jug and stepped to the center of the room. He unscrewed the cap and stared at Kyle as he dumped the water down the drain.

Kyle watched in horror as his lifeline disappeared.

Doug tossed the empty plastic jug into the utility sink like a three-point shot. "*Swish*," he said as the jug rattled around the sink. "Didn't see that coming, did you?"

Hank cackled.

Kyle was silent, his jaw set tight.

"Did you know that I like to read?" Doug asked Kyle.

Kyle didn't respond.

"That surprise you?"

Kyle was still silent.

"I read this book about marketing, and it said that it was important to put a time limit on sales. Makes people more likely to buy right away. If I give you water, it gives your people more time to pay and less incentive to pay. I know it might seem cruel to you, but I'm doing you a favor. I'm making it more likely that your daddy will pay and that you'll get outta here. People respond to incentives." Doug smiled at Kyle.

Hank raised one side of his mouth in contempt. "I'd kill this motherfucker either way."

Kyle glared at Hank.

Doug grabbed Hank around the neck with the speed of a viper. "You get your ass kicked, and now you're gonna act tough?"

Hank's face was red, his hands trying to pry Doug's off his neck.

"You're a worthless piece of shit. I should put you back in a cell." Doug tossed him aside, Hank falling to the concrete and gasping for air. Doug stood over him, his finger in his face. "You ever disrespect me again, I will make you *beg* for death."

* * *

That night, after the single bulb turned off, and the footsteps overhead ceased, Kyle crawled from the back of his cell to the corner, facing Ryan's cell. Kyle's cell was only eight by eight, so it was a short crawl, and crawling expended less energy than standing and walking.

"Hey, Ryan," Kyle whispered. "You awake?"

Ryan was in his bed, the only light from the blue of his television screen. Ryan rolled toward Kyle. He sat up and moved from his bed to the front corner of his cell, facing Kyle. Ryan waved as he sat cross-legged on the concrete floor.

"How are you doing?" Kyle whispered.

Ryan shrugged. "OK."

"I'm still working on a plan."

"I know." Ryan whispered this without conviction.

"How did you get here?"

"My mom was supposed to pick me up from baseball practice. Doug asked me if I needed a ride." He hung his head. "I didn't know that he was gonna ..."

"It's not your fault, Ryan. He took me too."

Ryan nodded.

"Where's your house? Like where your parents live."

"It's just my mom." Ryan sniffled. "I want my mom."

"I'm sorry, buddy. I'm gonna get you home, OK?"

Ryan wiped his eyes with his T-shirt sleeve. "OK."

"Do you remember where your house is?"

"In Virginia … Dale City."

"I live in Woodbridge. Not too far from you. Maybe we can play catch when we get outta here?"

Ryan gave a thumbs-up.

CHAPTER 40

I'M LOVIN' IT

Kyle lay in the fetal position on the concrete. His stomach felt hollow; he had a pounding headache. Last night, Kyle had promised Ryan that he'd get him out of here. It was a promise he knew he couldn't keep. Kyle wondered if his empty promises were to comfort Ryan or himself. He had also said that he was working on a plan. He wasn't exactly working on a plan. More like working on coming up with a plan.

It had been four days since he'd eaten and two days since he'd had any measurable amount of water. Whenever he stood, he felt woozy, almost drunk. *I've never gone even a day without food or water before this.* He smelled sausage and eggs and hash browns. It reminded him of the Big Breakfast at McDonald's. *Am I hallucinating?* The single bulb clicked on. Doug descended the stairs, holding a paper McDonald's bag, and a tray with two large orange juices. Kyle's mouth watered.

Doug passed Kyle, walking directly to Ryan's cell. "Wake up, Ryan. Time for breakfast. I got your favorite. McDonald's."

Ryan rose from bed, wiping his eyes. He grinned at the food. "Thank you, thank you, thank you, Doug. I love McDonald's."

Doug opened the cell with a key. "Of course, you've been good." Doug removed a Styrofoam container from the McDonald's bag and handed it to Ryan along with an orange juice. "You got it?" Doug asked as he placed the juice in Ryan's hand.

"Got it," Ryan replied with a plastered smile.

"Enjoy your breakfast," Doug said, shutting the cell door. "I almost forgot." Doug removed a power cord from his pocket and tossed it between the bars. "No playing after lights out."

"Thank you, Doug!" Ryan sat on the floor in front of his bed and placed his juice carefully to the side.

"Don't spill it," Doug said.

"I'll be careful," Ryan replied.

"I know you will." Doug turned and walked over to Kyle's cell. "I bet you're thirsty and hungry."

Kyle stared at the orange juice, imagining the sugary liquid coating the back of his throat.

Doug set the bag and the juice on the floor precisely on the white dot.

Kyle wondered if that was really his breakfast or just another taunt. *Maybe he got his money?*

Doug entered an empty cell and grabbed a skinny mattress. He leaned it against the cell next to Kyle's. He removed a pair of handcuffs from his back pocket. "Put your hands through the bars."

Kyle narrowed his eyes, but didn't move.

"You want breakfast and a bed?" Doug motioned him over. "Face me. Put your hands through the bars."

Kyle did as he was told, and Doug handcuffed him there. Kyle was now effectively stuck to the bars.

"I gotta response to your video," Doug said, meandering to the wall and the cattle prod. "Wanna know what your dad said?"

"Not really."

Doug grabbed the cattle prod and returned to Kyle. "Not a fucking thing." Doug flicked on the electrified rod, the end crackling.

Kyle jerked back from the cattle prod, the handcuffs smacking against the steel bars and holding Kyle in place.

"I spoke to a *fucking* negotiator. Your father broke the rules. Unfortunately for you, he's not here to pay for it."

Kyle pulled at the handcuffs, his wide eyes trained on the cattle prod.

Doug plunged the prod into Kyle's stomach and held it there under constant current. Kyle screamed in agony, his body jerking. His threadbare T-shirt did little to lessen the jolt. He smelled burning flesh. Doug retracted the prod, and Kyle slumped against the bars.

"That'll wake you up!" Doug said.

A hole was burnt through Kyle's T-shirt. A patch of skin on Kyle's stomach sizzled with searing pain. Doug put the cattle prod back against the wall and returned to Kyle. He removed the knife attached to his belt, reached through the bars and placed the tip of the blade to Kyle's neck. A bit of blood dripped down.

"You got three seconds to tell me why I should keep you alive," Doug said. "Three, two—"

"My sister," Kyle said, breathless.

Doug retracted the blade. "What about her?"

"Send my video to her." Kyle paused for a breath. "She'll sent it to my mother." He paused again. "Or she'll put pressure on my father to pay. Either way, you'll get your money."

Doug chuckled. "I hope for your sake you're right. You won't get another drop of water until I get my money. According to my calculations, you might survive two and a half more days without water. *Tick-tock.* We know Daddy doesn't give a shit about you. Let's see if Mommy does."

Kyle glanced toward Ryan. He was in the back corner of his cell, turned away from the carnage, his breakfast half-eaten on the floor.

Doug picked up the untouched breakfast from the white dot on the floor, walked to Ryan's cell, and opened the door. "Let's go, Ryan. I need a stress reliever, and you need a bath."

CHAPTER 41

DAVID AND GOLIATH

His hands were over his head, still bound to the bars, the patch of skin on his stomach burning. While sitting on the concrete, in his discomfort, Kyle had an epiphany. He remembered a quote he'd seen on Facebook. *Appear weak when you are strong and strong when you are weak. By Sun somebody or other.* Kyle thought he had a plan, but he needed three things for it to work. He needed food and water for strength. He needed to figure out how to defeat the cattle prod, and he needed a weapon.

A few hours later, Doug returned with Ryan in tow. Ryan was despondent, averting his eyes as he walked past Kyle. Ryan walked into his cell, and Doug locked the door.

"Make sure you finish that food," Doug said, pointing at the remnants of Ryan's breakfast.

"Yes, Doug," Ryan replied in monotone.

Doug turned and sauntered to Kyle.

"You look like shit," Doug said.

"I need water," Kyle said.

"That's up to your sister and your mother." Doug chuckled and looked at Kyle's stomach. "Damn, I got you good. Burned right through your shirt." Doug removed a handful of keys from his pocket. "I'll do something nice for you because I'm in a good mood." He unclasped the handcuffs.

Kyle's body collapsed to the floor.

Doug climbed the stairs and shut the door.

Kyle waited until he no longer heard footsteps upstairs to whisper to Ryan. "Are you all right?"

Ryan was in bed, his covers over his head. He didn't respond.

"Ryan?"

Still no response.

Ryan eventually got up, plugged in his PlayStation, and killed the enemy, the volume cranked. Kyle tried to get his attention, but Ryan wasn't biting. No hand signals either or even eye contact. The rest of the day Ryan was silent, engrossed in his game. Kyle focused on his first problem. Food and water. He glanced at the uneaten food in Ryan's cell. He had an idea, but Ryan would have to take a serious risk.

That evening, Hank brought Ryan's dinner—pizza and soda. Hank glared at the uneaten food in Ryan's cell. "You better eat all that shit before mornin', or I ain't bringin' breakfast."

Ryan nodded.

"Speak up, faggot," Hank said.

"I said, yes," Ryan replied, mildly exasperated.

"You gettin' smart with me?"

"No. I'm sorry."

"That's what I thought."

Hank looked in on Kyle. "You want some water?"

"Please," Kyle said from the floor.

"Suck my dick, and I'll get you some water."

Kyle turned away.

Hank cackled and left the basement.

* * *

After lights out, Kyle listened intently for Hank's and Doug's overhead footsteps. Once he was satisfied it was safe, Kyle whispered, "Ryan, you awake?" Kyle paused. "Ryan."

Ryan lay in a heap under his covers, unresponsive to Kyle.

"Ryan?"

Still nothing.

Kyle lay on his hip, thinking about the second problem with his plan—how to defeat the cattle prod. *It won't work. There's no way I won't react to being electrocuted.* After an hour of fruitless thought, Kyle thought about the third problem. A weapon. Again, he needed Ryan.

"No, no, … stop," Ryan said.

Kyle rolled off his aching hip, the patch of skin on his stomach still burning and now blistering.

Ryan rustled in his bed, bathed in the blue light from his television screen. "Stop, … please."

"Ryan," Kyle said, his voice raspy. "Wake up. You're having a nightmare."

"Kyle?"

"I'm here," Kyle whispered. "Are you all right?"

Ryan sniffled. "I wanna go home. I miss my mom."

"I know." Kyle took a deep breath. "We're gonna get out of here. I have a plan, and I think it'll work, but I need your help. Do you wanna be Batman or Robin?"

There was a pregnant pause. "Batman."

"All right, Batman. If I'm going to be Robin, I need food and water, so I can be strong. Do you think you could throw me some of your food? Maybe fill up your water bottle and toss it over here?"

"It's kinda far," Ryan whispered.

"You're a pitcher, right?"

Thumbs-up.

"Then you know how to throw accurately, right?"

Another thumbs-up. Ryan looked at his half-eaten breakfast and pizza crusts. He held up an English muffin.

"That's perfect."

Ryan held up pizza crusts.

"I'll eat those too." Kyle stuck his hands through the bars, dead center of the cell. "Aim for my hands, just like I'm your catcher."

"If Doug finds out …" Ryan whispered.

"I know. And I know you can do this. Maybe throw it underhand. Try the English muffin first."

Ryan grabbed the English muffin. He put his right arm through the bars and turned his body diagonally toward Kyle's cell. He tossed the English muffin underhand. Kyle winced; it was short. The muffin skidded on the concrete, a few feet away. Kyle hurried to the corner of his cell and reached through the bars. He had just enough reach to grab the muffin with his fingertips.

"Got it," Kyle whispered.

Ryan did a better job with the pizza crusts. Kyle caught two of the three in midair, and the third skidded right next to his cell for easy retrieval. Ryan filled up the plastic water bottle in his sink.

"Make sure the cap's on tight," Kyle whispered.

Ryan tightened the cap and gave Kyle a thumbs-up.

"This one's a lot heavier than the bread. Why don't you practice tossing it on your bed first?"

Ryan tossed the small water bottle on his bed a few times and returned to the bars, giving Kyle another thumbs-up.

Ryan put the water bottle right on the money, and Kyle caught it in midair. Kyle guzzled the water immediately.

"Great job, Batman," Kyle whispered. "Now I need to get this bottle back to you. I'm not sure the best way to do that. It's too light now."

Ryan held out his hands as if to say, *I don't know.*

Kyle removed the cap and scrunched the bottle, removing much of the air. Then he replaced the cap, the bottle still scrunched. The bottle was now much more compact and was less likely to roll.

"You ready?" Kyle asked.

Ryan put his hands through the bars and turned up both his thumbs.

Kyle tossed the plastic bottle just short of Ryan's cell. It skidded across the concrete and stopped against the bars. Ryan grabbed the bottle. He held it up with a wide grin, his buck teeth gleaming in the darkness.

"Awesome job," Kyle whispered, matching his smile.

Ryan gave another thumbs-up.

"Think you can send the water back one more time? I'm still pretty thirsty."

They did it one more time without incident. Kyle ate the English muffin and the pizza crusts with the second bottle of water. Kyle was still thirsty, but he didn't want to push his luck.

"There's one more thing I need for you to do," Kyle whispered.

Thumbs-up.

"Do you know the story of David and Goliath?"

Thumbs-down.

"Goliath was this big bully that beat up kids and stole their lunch money. Everyone hated Goliath, but he was so big that the kids were afraid to stand up to him. Then one day Goliath went up to David and said, 'Gimme your lunch money.' David was the smallest kid in the whole school. What do you think David said?"

Ryan shrugged.

"He said, 'You can't have my lunch money, and I'm not afraid of you.' Goliath was seriously pissed off. He said, 'After school I'm gonna kick your butt.' Everybody thought David was gonna get beat up ... bad. The bell rang, and everyone went behind the school so the teachers wouldn't see. Goliath stood over David, ready to beat him to a pulp. But David pulled a slingshot from his pocket and shot a rock that hit Goliath in the face. Goliath started to cry, and he ran home. He never hurt any kids ever again." Kyle paused for a moment.

"You want me to shoot Doug with a slingshot?" Ryan whispered.

Kyle smiled to himself. "No, it's a metaphor."

"Is that something that means something else?"

"Yes, exactly. Do you have pockets in your shorts?"

Thumbs-up.

"When you go upstairs, are there any scissors or knives or any small weapons that you could take without Doug seeing?"

Thumbs-down.

"How about tools lying around, like a box cutter or a screwdriver?"

"I can't fight Doug," Ryan whispered.

"I don't want you to. I just need you to bring me something that I can use as a weapon. I can fight Doug, but I need a weapon."

Thumbs-down. "I could get in big trouble."

"I know."

CHAPTER 42

SCREAM FOR THE CAMERA

The next day, Hank and Doug waltzed into the basement. Doug wore black pants and a black hoodie. Hank held onto a Halloween mask. Kyle lay on the concrete in the fetal position. Doug set up the tripod and camera in front of Kyle.

"They always want more time," Doug said, shaking his head. "You awake, Kyle?"

Kyle raised his head. "Water."

"That's good. I oughtta get that on video." Doug pointed the camera at Kyle and pressed Record. "What do you need, Kyle?"

"Water ... please," Kyle said, his voice raspy.

Doug stopped the recording. "That was good." He approached the cell, kneeling in front of Kyle. "Your mother needs more time to get the money, but you don't have much time, do you, Kyle?"

"Water."

"Shit, you may not make it five days without water. Here's what we're gonna do." Doug removed handcuffs from his back pocket. "You're gonna stick your hands through those bars again, like yesterday, and we're gonna make a little film for your mother. If you holler extra loud, maybe it'll speed up payment, and then I'll get you some water."

Kyle crawled to the back of the cell.

"Don't make me come in there," Doug said. "You're only making it worse." He paused for a moment. "You got five seconds to put your hands through these bars. Five, four, three, two, one and a half, … one."

Kyle stayed in the corner, curled up, his head under his arms. The cattle prod buzzed. The door clicked and opened. Kyle peeked at Doug with the cattle prod. His face was covered by a grotesque mask, the skin leathery and the mouth sewn with metal wire. He grabbed Kyle by the elbow and dragged him to the middle of the cell. Doug faced the camera as he electrocuted Kyle.

The shocks came fast and furious, Kyle howling for the camera. Doug didn't hold the prod in place like yesterday. The pain was intense, but it was more for show than punishment or permanent damage. After thirty seconds of intermittent shocks, Doug relented.

Kyle learned a valuable lesson. The cattle prod hurt a lot more against his skin than it did against his jeans.

CHAPTER 43

RUNNING OUT OF TIME

Last night, Kyle and Ryan had played "toss the food and water" to perfection. They had gone over the plan. Ryan had to do his part, or Kyle would never be able to do his. Kyle had slept most of today. Ryan had catnapped after his meals. They didn't communicate when the overhead light was on during the day. Hank had come down to bring Ryan breakfast and lunch. Each time he had yelled at Kyle to see if he was still alive. And each time Kyle had awoken disoriented, begging for water and a blanket. Hank had had a good chuckle at Kyle's expense.

Late in the afternoon, Kyle awoke to a grumbling in his stomach. He worried that he might have to move his bowels. *How would I explain that?* Doug hadn't given Kyle anything to eat since he'd gotten there. *How many days have I been here? Five, ... six? It was that damn apple.* Kyle had eaten the entire thing last night, even the core. He had fit the stem between the slats of the drain.

Doug sauntered down the stairs and stopped in front of Kyle. "You still alive? Hank said you were still ticking."

Kyle lay huddled, shivering in the back corner, like a dog waiting to die. Kyle turned his head toward Doug.

"You cold?"

"Water, … blanket," Kyle croaked.

"You're cold because you're gonna die. Your body's trying to protect your major organs. Blood is only circulating to the necessary organs, making your body cold." Doug blew out a breath of resignation. "I'm surprised you made it through the night. This is day four and a half, give or take, without water and food. How much longer can you hang on, Kyle? I doubt you'll make it through another night. I tell you what, Kyle. Your parents surprised me. I thought they'd come through, but they don't give two shits about you." Doug shook his head.

"Water, … blanket," Kyle croaked again.

"What the fuck did you do to your parents?" Doug shrugged. "I've been watching my Bitcoin account. Still waiting on the cash, not that I'm expecting it at this point, and, even if I do get the cash, you won't survive this. It's too late." Doug turned and walked to Ryan's cell.

Ryan stood, his hands on the bars. "He can have my blanket."

Doug chuckled and opened Ryan's cell.

"He's cold," Ryan said, grabbing the comforter from his bed.

Doug glared. "Let's go, Ryan. Leave your fucking blanket."

"Please, Doug. Just this once. I'll do anything."

"You think you can bargain with me?"

Ryan looked down. Doug smacked Ryan on the side of the head, knocking him off his feet.

Kyle winced at the violence.

"Get the fuck up," Doug said.

Ryan stood, crying and sniffling.

"You wanna give him your blanket so bad?" Doug snatched the comforter from the twin bed. He marched to Kyle's cell, Ryan following like a beaten puppy. Doug tossed the blanket on the floor next to Kyle's cell, then turned to Ryan. "You're not getting another one. Let's go."

Ryan followed Doug upstairs.

CHAPTER 44

PITCH AND CATCH

The overhead light turned off. Ryan lay in bed, wrapped in a thin sheet like a burrito, his blue television screen providing the only light. He hadn't moved since Doug had brought him back. Kyle lay on Ryan's thick blanket, feeling grateful for the small luxury and yet guilty for what Ryan had to do. Kyle listened and waited for the steps overhead to cease.

Kyle stood, his hands on the bars. The sensation of having to move his bowels increased. "Ryan? You OK? You did great with the blanket."

Ryan shifted in bed. He unwrapped himself and sat up. Ryan stood and raised his arm to the ceiling. In his hand was a screwdriver.

Kyle smiled wide and made a concerted effort to whisper. "You did it, Batman."

Ryan held the screwdriver in one hand and gave a thumbs-up with the other.

"Practice tossing the screwdriver on your bed. Take your time. When you're ready, let me know."

Ryan tossed the tool on his bed, getting a feel for the weight of the screwdriver. After a few minutes of practice, Ryan gave Kyle a thumbs-up.

Kyle put his hands through the bars. "I'm ready when you are."

Ryan tossed the screwdriver underhanded. It was off the mark. Kyle tried to retract his hands and place them where the screwdriver was headed, but he was too slow. The screwdriver clanged against the bars, dropped to the ground, bouncing away from Kyle's cell. *Shit.* The screwdriver stopped a few inches in front of the white dot.

"Doug's gonna kill me," Ryan said, probably louder than he intended.

"*Shh*," Kyle said, his finger to his lips. Kyle waited, concerned that the *clang* of the screwdriver against the bars might stir Doug or Hank. His bowels churned. He clenched his sphincter. After a few minutes of silence, Kyle said, "It's fine. I think I can reach it with my boot." Kyle took off his boot and reached through the bars, the toe just long enough to pull the screwdriver toward him. Kyle grabbed the screwdriver and pulled it into his cell. "We're good."

Ryan smiled. "You want water now?"

"Please."

Ryan filled up the water bottle at his sink and returned to the bars. Kyle gave him a thumbs-up, and Ryan tossed the water bottle on the money. Kyle caught it in midair.

"Nice throw," Kyle said.

"Good catch."

Kyle guzzled the water. A moment later, the urge to defecate became overwhelming. Kyle looked around his cell, desperately searching for an answer, his sphincter clenched. He looked at the bucket. *If I go in the bucket, they'll know I was eating.* His eyes flicked to the drain. He grabbed the screwdriver and got on his hands and knees. The drain cover was held in place with two screws. Thank God, they were Phillips-head screws.

"What are you doing?" Ryan asked.

"I have to go," Kyle said, unscrewing the cover on the drain.

"Like, ... poo?"

"Yeah." The screwdriver was a bit small. He stripped the screws, but he was still able to remove the cover.

Kyle squatted over the hole. The feces dropped into the pipe, giving Kyle immediate relief. Thankfully it was relatively dry, so the lack of toilet paper wasn't disastrous. The smell was dreadful though. Kyle pulled up his pants and peered into the hole. The white PVC pipe appeared to turn after a short drop. *The shit is sitting in the elbow, stinking up the place. Shit, … literally.*

"It stinks," Ryan whispered, his shirt over his nose.

Doug will know I was eating. He'll take it out on Ryan. "Sorry, Ryan. That was probably in me for a long time." Kyle put the grate back on and covered it with the bucket. "Hopefully the bucket'll make it better." *They're still gonna smell shit in the morning.*

"It's a little better now."

Kyle thought about how this impacted their plan. His mind flashed to an episode of *South Park* that showed what happened to people when they died. He smiled to himself.

Despite his proximity to shit, Kyle was hungry. Ryan threw some food to Kyle and another bottle of water. Kyle ate two rolls, a package of Pop-Tarts, and he drank the water. He shoved the Pop-Tart wrapper into the water bottle, leaving a bit of the wrapper hanging out of the top of the bottle, so Ryan could easily remove it. Kyle condensed the water bottle, put the cap on, and tossed the bottle with the wrapper back to Ryan. The bottle dropped right next to Ryan's cell for easy retrieval.

"Good throw," Ryan whispered. "Do you want more water?"

"Yeah, one more." *I'm gonna need all my strength for tomorrow.*

Ryan removed the Pop-Tart wrapper and filled the water bottle again. His return toss was a little low. The water bottle bounced off the bottom of the bars and rolled away from Kyle. He bent down and reached through the bars for the plastic water bottle, but it was out of reach. Kyle adjusted himself, pushing against the bars, extending a little farther, but it was still out of reach. He tried his boot, but again, it was still out of his reach. *Shit. We're in trouble.*

"Doug's gonna kill me," Ryan hissed.

CHAPTER 45

TURNING THE TABLES

The light clicked on, followed by soft footsteps. Kyle lay in the corner, against the wall, Ryan's thick comforter wrapped around him. The footsteps stopped at the bottom of the stairs.

"What the fuck?" Hank said. "Why's a water bottle on the floor? Hey, faggot, wake up." Hank paused. "What's that smell. Is that shit? Hey, wake up."

Kyle faced the wall, his breathing as shallow as possible.

"Wake up. Don't make me get Doug."

Kyle was unresponsive.

"I think he's dead," Ryan said.

"Did I ask you?" Hank replied.

"No."

"This is your water bottle."

Ryan didn't reply.

"How'd it get over here?"

Ryan was quiet.

"You threw it over here, didn't you?" Hank paused, waiting for Ryan to explain. "Doug's gonna fuck you up. You'll be in the dead dude's cell. No more TV. No more PlayStation. You won't even have a bed. You'll be back to shittin' in a bucket. Dumbass."

Hank climbed the basement steps. A few minutes later, heavy boots led Hank back down to the basement.

"See? That's Ryan's water bottle," Hank said. "I think Ryan tried to give him water. He might be dead though. He ain't moved a muscle, and it don't look like he's breathin'."

The heavy boots stepped toward Ryan's cell. "That true, Ryan?" Doug asked.

"He was begging for water," Ryan replied, barely above a whisper.

"You think that water you have is yours to give?"

"No."

"If you wanted to give him water, don't you think you should've asked me first?"

"Yes. I'm sorry."

"You're not sorry yet, but you will be."

Doug's heavy boots moved closer to Kyle's cell.

"I think he *is* dead," Hank said. "I smelled shit. Why do they always shit themselves?"

"Only if they have food in their colon," Doug replied stepping back toward Ryan's cell. "Did you give him food?"

"No, ... I didn't," Ryan replied.

"He hasn't had food in a week, but somehow he shit himself? I'm not buying it." The jingle of keys followed the creak of Ryan's cell door. "Don't you fucking lie to me, Ryan."

"I, I, I'm not lying."

A dull *thud*, then a yelp from Ryan. A few slaps, skin on skin, followed by breathless sobs. Kyle winced, feeling responsible for each blow.

"Get up," Doug said.

Ryan sniffled, still crying, but catching his breath.

"I tried to be nice to you. Got you a fucking TV and a PlayStation, and this is the gratitude I get?"

"I'll take the PlayStation," Hank said.

"Shut up," Doug replied, walking with Ryan to the cell next to Kyle. "Go on. Get in."

218

Ryan walked into the Spartan cell. The door shut behind him.

"Kyle, still no money from your people." Doug paused. "You still alive? If you are, gimme a sign. Raise your hand. Something. If you do, I'll give you some water. Last chance." Doug paused again. "You know what's gonna happen if I come in there." Another pause. "Hand me the Hot-Shot."

The cattle prod crackled with electricity. Keys jingled. The cell door opened. Kyle kept his body limp, like a lifeless lump of flesh and bone. The prod jammed into his back, but he didn't feel a jolt, the thick comforter providing just enough protection. The prod jammed into his back again. Nothing.

"Hold this," Doug said, presumably to Hank.

Thick hands grasped Kyle's shoulder and pulled, rolling Kyle's body face up. As his body rolled, Kyle jabbed the screwdriver into Doug's neck. The metal skewer plunged deep—all the way to the black-and yellow handle. Doug stood up straight, his eyes wide, his hands vaguely touching the screwdriver handle. Dark blood seeped from the puncture wound and pooled at the collar of his T-shirt. Doug looked at the blood, his face frozen with fear.

"What the fuck?" Hank said, moving to Doug's side to get a look.

Kyle stood, grabbed the handle of the screwdriver, and yanked it from Doug's neck. When the blood sprayed Kyle in the face, he dropped the screwdriver. Now a deluge of blood poured from the hole, and Doug fell to his knees.

Ryan looked on in horror from the adjoining cell. Hank was in a daze, his mouth wide open, his eyes unblinking.

Kyle snatched the cattle prod from Hank's weak grasp. This action woke Hank from his stupor. Hank turned and ran from the cell. Kyle found the trigger and thrust the prod at Hank, narrowly missing him. Hank ran up the basement steps.

CHAPTER 46

LET'S GO

Doug choked on his own blood. Kyle dropped the cattle prod and felt the pockets of Doug's jeans. He pushed Doug on his side and grabbed the keys from his pocket. Kyle exited his open cell, leaving Doug gasping and bleeding.

The keys were numbered. He tried the number one key. It didn't work. He tried the number eight key. That one worked. Kyle locked Doug inside the Spartan shit-infested cell.

"You did it," Ryan said, standing by his cell door.

"*We* did it," Kyle replied, as he shoved the number seven key into Ryan's cell door. "Let's get outta here." Kyle opened the door.

Ryan hesitated at the threshold, glancing at Doug bleeding out in the cell next to him. Doug's body seized, his hands grasping the air. He went limp. Kyle watched Doug's chest for the rise and fall of breath, or any movement whatsoever, but Doug was perfectly still.

"It's over." Kyle motioned for Ryan to exit the cell.

Ryan rushed to Kyle and hugged him, his bony body against Kyle's, his head to Kyle's chest. Kyle patted Ryan's back and his head. The boy shook and cried.

"It's over," Kyle said. "We're going home. It's over."

The boy pulled back, sniffling. "Are we really going home?"

"Yes."

Ryan knitted his brows. "What about Hank?"

"I can deal with him. We do need to be careful though. Stay close to me, OK?"

Ryan smiled wide. "OK."

They climbed the wooden steps leading from the basement, Kyle in front. The door at the top of the steps was open. Kyle looked right and left down the hallway. Sunlight pierced the windows, the house quiet except for the songbirds outside. They went right, creeping down the hall toward the metal door with three dead bolts. Along the way, they passed the living room. A big-screen television hung from the wall. There was black leather furniture and a wooden bar with neon beer signs. At the front door, Kyle started from the top lock and worked his way down, unlocking dead bolt after dead bolt.

"Where do you think you're going?" Hank said, approaching from the hall, one side of his mouth raised in contempt, and Kyle's 380 pointed in their direction.

Kyle moved in front of Ryan, shielding the boy. His eyes were on the 380; his heart pounded. "It's over, Hank. Doug's dead."

"It ain't over till I say it's over."

"You're not gonna get in trouble. You're a victim. You need help, Hank. You can come with—"

Hank fired the revolver, the sound deafening.

Kyle felt a hot bite to his shoulder, adrenaline masking the pain. He turned and opened the front door, the sunlight blinding them. Another shot fired. Another bite, this one to his upper back.

"Run," Kyle said to Ryan.

Out front, Doug's truck was parked, but Kyle knew the key ring in his pocket was only keys to the cells. The small front yard was grass and weeds and clay and rocks. Beyond that, forest all around them. Kyle and Ryan ran down the gravel road, the trees tight to the roadside. Kyle was out of breath after a few hundred yards, his energy spent. Blood streaked down his right arm. He touched his shoulder, his hand wet with blood. As he did so, his upper back barked in pain.

The *click-clack* of the diesel pickup roared to life. The truck gained ground. Kyle led Ryan into the forest. They ran, avoiding deadwood and tree roots. The truck stopped on the road behind them. A door opened and shut.

"You ain't gettin' away," Hank called out, crashing through the brambles at the forest edge.

Ryan streaked ahead, high on adrenaline. Kyle struggled to keep up, his legs heavy. After a few minutes, Ryan turned and motioned for Kyle to hurry, but Kyle leaned against a tree.

Ryan jogged back to Kyle. He stared at the blood on Kyle's arm. "You're bleeding."

Kyle sat on the ground, gingerly resting his back to the tree. "I need you to run and get help."

"I can't. I don't know where to go." Ryan's eyes were glassy.

"Just pick a direction and stay straight. You'll eventually find someone. If you find a creek or water, just follow the flow of the water downhill. You can do it."

"I hear you," Hank called out in a singsong voice, leaves rustling under his feet.

"Go," Kyle hissed at Ryan.

Ryan turned and ran. Hank gave chase, passing the tree Kyle sat against.

Hank's gonna catch him. "Hey, faggot!" Kyle called out.

Hank stopped and turned toward Kyle's taunt.

"You heard me," Kyle said. "I'm right here."

Hank followed Kyle's words until he found him slumped against a large oak. "Damn, I got you good." Hank's lips were curled into a snarl, the 380 pointed at Kyle's chest.

"Did you like it?" Kyle asked.

"Like what?"

"Did you like what Doug did to you?"

"Shut the fuck up."

"You must've liked it."

"I said, 'shut the fuck up.'"

"Then why are you still doing his dirty work?"

"You don't know what you're talking about."

"Can't you think for yourself? He's dead, and he's still telling you what to do. Put the gun down."

Hank aimed, gripping the gun with one hand, the barrel unsteady. He fired twice and stared at Kyle, admiring his handiwork.

Kyle stared back, his eyes glassy. He felt faint. He slumped to his side, blood and life leaking from his body. *Run, Ryan. Run.* Kyle pictured Ryan finding a house, a couple taking him inside and protecting him.

Hank ran after Ryan once more.

Kyle turned his head, just enough to see the forest canopy overhead. Slender sunbeams streaked through narrow openings in the canopy. He drifted out of consciousness.

CHAPTER 47

GOING HOME

Kyle drifted in and out of consciousness, listening to squirrels scurrying on leaves, the life draining from his body. He heard Ryan's chirpy voice, deeper voices, and heavy boots, then shouting.

"He's over here!"

Kyle was hoisted on a magic carpet. He floated along the forest floor. Then the bright sun direct overhead and the *whomp-whomp* of God coming for him. *It's so windy, like a storm. That can't be right. It's so sunny. So beautiful. A great day to work.*

He was heaved upward. Everything went fuzzy again. Then black. He was gone, but he felt it. His body was lifted higher, lifted to the heavens.

CHAPTER 48

VISITING HOURS

Cool oxygen entered Kyle's nostrils from the attached hose. The room was dim, flowers and cards crammed along the wall. Kyle didn't know the well-wishers. A *tick, tick* came from the IV drips—one in each arm. A pulsometer was clamped to his finger. A fresh bandage was on his ear. Both shoulders were bandaged and one side of his chest and upper back. Two through-and-throughs and two bullets lodged in his body—one in his shoulder and one in his chest. He had had multiple transfusions and surgery to remove the bullets. The doctor had said that Kyle was incredibly lucky. Hank was a poor shot, his unsteady hands moving the shots off-target just enough to miss Kyle's vital organs.

Kyle had been in the hospital for two days. The first day was a drug-induced semiconscious haze. His first recollection was a nurse, followed by a doctor, followed by Leigh. She had looked rough. Red-rimmed eyes and disheveled hair.

He tried not to push the button for the pain meds, but his upper torso hurt terribly, especially when he moved. He gingerly grabbed the remote from the overbed table. The sharp pain bit despite the narcotics. He turned on the flat screen and flipped through the channels, stopping on Doug's face.

Kyle was transfixed, reliving his captivity, only hearing bits and pieces of the newscast. Nothing he hadn't already heard. Doug Chambers. Former Spotsylvania County Police Officer. Fired for multiple complaints of inappropriate touching of minors. But never prosecuted criminally.

Kyle's face appeared onscreen, along with footage from the confrontation with the weatherman, Aaron Wells. News stations loved to use the clip of Kyle riding on the hood of the weatherman's BMW.

A light knock, then a nurse entered the private room. "Your sister's here. Are you OK to have visitors?"

"It's fine," Kyle replied, turning off the television.

The nurse brightened the lights a bit. "Is the light OK?"

"It's fine."

The nurse left, and Leigh entered the room, holding hands with Gwen, Jewel behind them.

"*Unc Kye!*" Gwen said, running for the bed.

Leigh hurried after Gwen, scooping her up, stopping her from jumping on the bed. "Kyle's hurt, honey. You can't jump on him."

"But I wanna hug." Gwen crossed her arms over her chest.

Kyle laughed and pointed to his cheek. "It doesn't hurt here."

"Kiss," Gwen said, grinning.

Leigh leaned Gwen over the bed. Kyle groaned and leaned toward his niece. She planted two kisses on his cheek.

Leigh set Gwen on the floor. "You're getting too heavy." Leigh smiled at Kyle. "Gwen and Jewel wanted to see you."

"Hey, Jewel," Kyle said.

Jewel approached the bed, offering a shy wave. "Hey, Kyle."

"You gonna die?" Gwen asked.

"Gwen," Leigh said with furrowed brows.

Kyle laughed. "I'm gonna be fine, sweet pea."

"How are you feeling?" Leigh asked.

"Like I was shot four times."

Jewel smiled.

Leigh was unamused. "Well, you look better than yesterday. Do you need anything? Are you thirsty?"

Kyle nodded to the water on the overbed table. "I'm good."

"Something to eat?"

"I think I'm supposed to have dinner in a few hours."

"*Sumpin* to eat. *Sumpin* to eat," Gwen said, tugging on her mother's sundress.

"Honey, you just ate," Leigh said.

"How are you guys doing?" Kyle asked, his gaze flicking from Leigh to Jewel and back again.

"Better," Leigh replied.

Jewel smiled again, this one reaching her eyes. Kyle had never seen her smile like that.

"*Sumpin* to eat. I'm hungry," Gwen said.

Leigh riffled through her purse and extracted a few bills and some change. She turned to Jewel. "Can you take her to the vending machines? Feel free to get yourself something too."

"OK," Jewel replied, taking the money. "Come on, peanut."

Jewel and Gwen walked hand in hand from the hospital room.

Leigh watched them leave, then turned back to Kyle. She took a deep breath. "Mom asked me to ask you if she could visit. She's only in town for a few more days."

Kyle frowned. "You can't be serious. I thought you hated Mom."

"She's trying, so I'm trying." Leigh pursed her lips. "Look, Kyle. I know you're really mad about the ransom. I would be too, but Mom and Dad did what the police told them to."

"How do you know?"

Leigh paused. "That's what they told me."

"They're both full of shit. They left me to die. I'd expect nothing less from them."

"Kyle, please."

"You know what? Fuck it. If she wants to see me, fine."

"If you're going to be an asshole, I'll tell her not to come."

"Do whatever you want."

Leigh sighed. "I thought, after everything, you might have some … perspective."

"I have plenty of perspective."

"If you say so."

Kyle glared at his sister. "Nearly dying tends to put things in perspective."

"I really don't want to fight with you."

"Neither do I."

There was an awkward silence.

"How long is Jewel gonna stay with you?" Kyle asked, changing the subject.

Leigh took a deep breath. "She's leaving on Tuesday for Paris. Dad signed her to a contract."

Kyle clenched his jaw. "Why? You and I both know she's not gonna make it. Something's up. It doesn't make sense."

"Because he's a good guy, Kyle. Jewel went to see him. Apparently, she made him reconsider. I think she told him about her mother's boyfriend. He's gonna give her a job in the office if she doesn't book enough work." Leigh put her hand on top of Kyle's. "Maybe this whole thing with Dad's a huge misunderstanding."

Kyle removed his hand from hers. "I know what happened."

"Memories are unreliable."

"I *know* what happened."

Jewel and Gwen stepped into the room, Jewel sipping a soda, Gwen eating from a bag of Famous Amos chocolate chip cookies.

"What did you get?" Leigh asked, turning to Gwen.

"Cookies," Gwen said, holding up the bag.

"Can I have one?" Kyle asked.

Gwen shook her head with a mischievous grin.

"Come on, little cookie monster."

Gwen giggled. "OK. But only one." She handed Kyle a solitary cookie, placing it directly in his hand, so he didn't have to reach.

"Thanks, sweet pea." Kyle ate the cookie.

They talked for ten minutes about nothing of substance. The weather. Gwen's day-to-day. Movies Jewel had seen recently. It was hard to avoid the elephants in the room.

Gwen tugged on her mom's hand. "I wanna go home."

"In a minute, honey," Leigh replied.

Gwen twisted her little body back and forth, tugging Leigh's hand in the direction of the door. "I'm bored."

"Why don't you take her home?" Kyle said.

"I'll drop her off with Jewel and come back," Leigh replied.

Kyle shook his head. "Go home. I'm fine."

"I'm coming back." Leigh stared at Kyle for a moment, as if sealing a promise. She looked at Gwen, then Jewel. "I need to run to the bathroom. Can you watch her for a minute?"

"Wanna go now," Gwen said, her voice whiney.

"In a minute," Leigh said. "I'll be right back."

"Wanna go with you."

Leigh sighed. "Come on, honey." She glanced at Jewel. "I'll be right back." They left the room.

Jewel sat in the chair next to Kyle, trying to contain a smile.

"Leigh said you're going to Paris," Kyle said.

She smiled wide. "Yeah, … on Tuesday."

"What made him change his mind?"

Jewel looked away for a moment and lifted one shoulder. "I guess my look is back in."

"So quickly?"

"I guess so."

"Fashion changes quick, but not that quick."

Jewel chewed on her lower lip.

"Why did he really change his mind?"

"Maybe he realized he, like, made a mistake."

"According to Robert, he never makes mistakes."

She was quiet.

"Leigh thinks you told him about your mom's boyfriend. Is that what happened?"

Her cheeks flashed pink. "No. That's, like, … nobody's business."

"Robert's using you."

She stood from the chair, her head held high. "Maybe I'm using him."

Leigh and Gwen returned.

"You ready?" Leigh asked.

Jewel was already out the door.

CHAPTER 49

BATMAN

An overhead view of Doug's house appeared on the screen. Originally, it had been his parents' house. They'd died many years ago—his dad of a heart attack, his mother lung cancer. The old farmhouse was crawling with FBI crime scene investigators and black SUVs. The caption read Chamber of Horrors. The press used Doug's last name—Chambers—for their catchy titles. Doug had the cells installed and began snatching kids after his parents died. Ryan had been in the Chamber of Horrors for four months and five days. Hank had been his first victim and one of the very few who made it out alive, Ryan and Kyle being the only others.

A woman spoke over the images. "Multiple bodies have been found buried around the property—"

Kyle turned off the television and closed his eyes. He lay in bed, sunlight from the window bleeding through his eyelids, creating a reddish haze with various moving shadows. The shadows turned into figures, people, small people, big people. A big person grabbed a small person around the neck. Sophie's half-blue face appeared. Kyle opened his eyes.

Leigh waltzed into the hospital room, carrying a clear plastic container filled with greens and a plastic bag.

"How was lunch?" Kyle asked.

"It was OK. I had a chicken salad." She placed the container and the bag on Kyle's overbed table. "I brought you a turkey sub and a salad."

"Thanks." Kyle removed the sub, plastic utensils, and bottled water from the bag.

He was still sore, still moving carefully, but less so than yesterday. Kyle ate in silence, his bed adjusted to a nearly seated position. Leigh checked her email on her phone.

After lunch, a nurse knocked on the open door. "You have visitors. Carla and Ryan Evans."

Kyle smiled wide. "Send 'em in."

Ryan walked in first. His brown hair was cut and clean, parted on the side. He wore a polo and khakis. He grinned as he approached the bed, his big front teeth bright and white. A chubby woman followed him, her dishwater-blond hair cut to chin-length. She wore mom jeans, a billowy blouse, and a silver cross around her neck.

"Ryan," Kyle said.

Leigh stood from the seat next to the bed.

"I wanted to come see you," Ryan said, sidling up to the bed.

"Hi, I'm Leigh, Kyle's sister," Leigh said to the woman.

"I'm Carla, Ryan's mom," she replied.

They shook hands.

"We tried to visit before, but they said only family," Carla said.

"This is perfect timing," Kyle said.

"I've heard so much about you," Leigh said to Ryan. "I'm Leigh, by the way. I wanted to thank you for being so brave. You saved my brother."

Ryan blushed.

"May I hug you?"

Ryan nodded.

Leigh glanced at Carla. She nodded.

Leigh hugged Ryan briefly, whispering, "Thank you so much," in his ear. Afterward Leigh said, "I have some work to do. It was very nice to meet you both." Leigh left the room with her computer bag on her shoulder.

"So, how're you doing?" Kyle asked Ryan.

Ryan shrugged. "It's been kinda weird. You know? Being able to go all around my house. And the news is always calling. I've seen *you* on TV, like, a hundred times. But it's been OK. People have been nice."

"That's good." Kyle nodded. "My sister's right. You saved my life. Thank you. In my book, you're braver than Batman."

"You saved me too." Ryan glanced at his mom, then back to Kyle. Ryan leaned over the bed and hugged Kyle.

Kyle wrapped his arms around the bony boy, his shoulders aching. After a moment, they disengaged. Kyle swallowed the lump in his throat. He looked at Carla. "He's a great kid. You must be thrilled to have him home."

She dabbed the corners of her eyes with a tissue, a bit of black mascara coming off. "I never thought I'd see him again. He's my whole world."

"Mom," Ryan said, frowning.

She sniffled. "I know. I'm not supposed to cry so much. But these are good tears." Carla stepped forward and put her hand on Kyle's. "I know it was awful for you both, but I'm so happy God brought you two together. I never gave up hope. I prayed every day. I think God sent you as an answer to my prayers." There was an awkward silence. Carla removed her hand.

"I'm very lucky to know your son," Kyle said to Carla.

She smiled.

Kyle turned to Ryan. "You must've run pretty fast through the woods. I heard you found a house."

"I ran *really* fast," Ryan replied. "I couldn't hardly feel my legs. I ran until the woods stopped, and I was on a road. I didn't know which way to go, so I picked one way and ran on the road, and I found a house. This old man was in front. His name's Mr. Tanner. He had a knife, so I was a little scared at first, but he was using it on a piece of wood. He was making a bird."

"That's cool. He was whittling."

"I told him that you were in the woods, and he called the police. Then I told him about Hank, and he got out his shotgun, told me to wait inside. We never saw Hank, but the police said they caught him, but they didn't put him on the news. He's in a hospital, but not a hospital like this."

"A psychiatric hospital," Carla said.

"Yeah, that," Ryan said. "Then the police came and I took them to you. I had a little trouble remembering, but you weren't too far from Mr. Tanner's house."

"I'm glad you remembered. You must have a good memory. I would've gotten lost."

"Mr. Tanner sent me the bird. It's all painted and everything. It came in the mail yesterday."

"That's cool. What kind of bird is it?"

"A cardinal. Mr. Tanner said it's the state bird."

"I'd love to see it sometime."

"You can come over anytime." Ryan glanced back at his mother. "Right, Mom?"

"Of course," Carla said, her gaze locked on Kyle's. "You're welcome anytime."

CHAPTER 50

OLIVIA AND FRANCOIS

Thirteen years ago. That was the last time he'd seen his mother, Olivia, and the first and last time he'd seen Francois. They took Kyle to the country club. Back then Olivia was thirty-seven, but looked ten years younger. She had dark voluminous hair, an athletic physique, and impeccable style. People often said she looked like Catherine Zeta-Jones—a comparison she definitely didn't discourage.

Francois was twenty-one then—only seven years older than Kyle. Francois was at the country club, a personal guest of Olivia. At the time Francois was the picture of health, sporting his washboard abs, tan skin, and banana hammock as they lounged around the pool.

Kyle had been appalled and embarrassed. Leigh had driven Kyle home early. They had masked their pain by making jokes about Francois's swimwear.

The star-crossed lovers had left in the middle of the night. Gone to France, never to be seen again. There had been letters and cards but never any visits or invitations to visit. Kyle had read the first few letters. Olivia went on and on about being in love with Francois and how Kyle would understand when he was older. He had stopped reading his mother's letters, depositing them directly in the trash when they arrived.

Now these two were in his hospital room. Olivia stood like she didn't want to touch anything. Her heavy makeup and multiple plastic surgeries masked her age, but her veiny hands told the truth. She was still thin, but a little top heavy from her implants.

Francois looked around the room, inspecting the medical equipment as if he were an expert. He had a perpetual five-o'clock shadow, and his washboard abs had been replaced with a paunch. He wore glasses and slacks and a designer button-down. No doubt to look distinguished and smart since he was no longer young and hot. Their marriage—once steamy and exciting and illicit—was now pathetic and weird and sad.

"Do you have any idea how much money he wanted?" Olivia asked.

"Does it matter?" Kyle replied, sitting upright in the hospital bed.

"Even if we paid, he probably wouldn't have let you go."

"This is true," Francois chimed in, with his French accent. "The police said so."

Kyle pinched the bridge of his nose. "You know what? It doesn't matter. It doesn't change a thing. You two can go now."

"I dropped everything to be here for you," Olivia said.

"And what have you done for me?"

Olivia was speechless.

"We've already established that you care more about money than me."

"That's not fair," Olivia said.

"I've been in the hospital for six days. This is the first I've seen you."

"The first few days you were too sick."

"Leigh said we should wait," Francois said. "We were trying to be respectful."

Kyle raised one side of his mouth in contempt. "Respectful, huh?"

"Yes, respectful."

"You two wanna be respectful?"

Olivia and Francois glanced at each other.

"You can take your asses back to France and stay there," Kyle said. "*That* would be respectful."

"I do not understand you," Francois said. "My mother died when I was a child. I'd give anything to see her again."

Kyle glared at Francois. "Get out."

Francois put up his hands in surrender. "Fine. I am going."

"Kyle, please," Olivia said.

Francois left the room.

"I don't understand you either," Olivia said.

"Of course you don't," Kyle said. "I haven't seen you in thirteen years."

"All this business with pedophiles. Why, Kyle? I don't understand why you'd get involved in this." She spoke softly, barely above a whisper. "Is it because of what happened?"

Kyle clenched his jaw and pointed to the open door. "Get out."

"Please, Kyle. You were young. I know you didn't mean it. That's why she didn't press charges—"

"Get the fuck out!"

CHAPTER 51

THE UGLY TRUTH

"You met Doug Chambers with a 380 that you recently purchased. It wouldn't be hard to prove intent to kill," Detective Mitchell said, her hands on her hips, standing over Kyle.

"You're lucky the DA's not gonna prosecute," Detective Fitzgerald said.

Kyle sat in a chair next to the hospital bed, wearing jeans and a T-shirt. "It would be a PR nightmare for you guys if you tried to prosecute me."

Fitzgerald shook his head. "The DA has prosecuted unpopular cases in the past. She's tough. Like I said, you're lucky, Kyle."

"Very lucky," Mitchell said.

"I think your nine lives have been used up," Fitzgerald said.

"I did find and kill a serial murderer," Kyle said, scowling. "Who was a pedophile. And a cop. *Jesus.* You guys really screwed up by not arresting him when you had the chance."

Fitzgerald crossed his arms over his chest. "Wasn't our county."

"Look, Kyle, we're not here to harass you," Mitchell said. "We're just here to let you know that you're in the clear."

Fitzgerald glared at Kyle. "And to give you a final warning about taking the law into your own hands."

"*And* to let you know that we're happy you're alive, and we're grateful for what you did." Detective Mitchell smiled.

"You don't listen for shit, but you got guts. I'll give you that." Fitzgerald shook his head, but he was smiling. It was brief and barely visible, but it was there.

* * *

An orderly pushed Kyle from the hospital entrance in a wheelchair. Leigh walked alongside, carrying a duffel bag with Kyle's accumulated belongings. Kyle stood with a groan and glanced up, letting the sun wash over him. He hadn't been outside in a week, not since he and Ryan ran from the farmhouse.

"Are you OK to walk to your car?" the orderly asked.

"Yeah, I'm good. Thanks," Kyle replied.

Leigh and Kyle walked to her SUV. The sun reflected off the cars and reverberated off the asphalt. Kyle sweated as they trudged across the parking lot. He settled into the front passenger seat, and Leigh cranked the AC. She drove from the hospital toward home.

"I made up the guest room for you," Leigh said.

"Thanks." Kyle cleared his throat. "I appreciate you helping me. Dr. Van said I should be OK to be on my own in a couple weeks."

Leigh smiled at Kyle, then looked back to the road. "We probably shouldn't put a time limit on your recovery. You're welcome to stay as long as you like. Gwen'll be in her glory. She was sad about Jewel leaving. She liked having a playmate."

"She left the day before yesterday, right?"

"The day before that."

Kyle nodded. "Have you heard from her? How's she doing?"

"She sent me a few texts. It seems like she's having a blast. Who knows? Maybe she'll make it. She is a pretty girl."

They drove in silence for a few minutes.

"I need my car for my physical therapy appointment tomorrow," Kyle said.

"You don't want me to take you?" Leigh asked.

"I can drive, especially if I keep my arms low on the wheel. It only hurts when I lift them."

She frowned at Kyle, then looked back to the road. "I can take you. It's no problem."

"I'm fine to drive."

"Then you can take my car. I'm not going anywhere tomorrow."

"All right."

They pulled into Leigh's garage. Leigh showed Kyle to his room, not that he didn't know where the guest room was.

"I put fresh towels in the bathroom, and fresh sheets are on the bed."

Kyle glanced around the room at the country decor, queen-size bed, fake flowers, and the nearly sheer curtains that made sleeping late impossible. There was a subtle hint of cheap perfume. Remnants of Jewel.

"Thanks, Leigh." Kyle turned to his sister. "I need to go home at some point and get some more clothes."

She smiled wide and opened the closet. The closet was filled with men's clothes. "I bought you some clothes. You needed it." Leigh ran her hand across the hanging shirts. "I left the tags, so, if you don't like something, you can leave it here. When you go home, I can return it." She moved to the dresser and opened a drawer revealing sport and dress socks. "I also got you socks and underwear and T-shirts."

"I don't know what to say."

"You're welcome."

"You're a good person, Leigh."

She smiled again.

The house was quiet. No beeps or buzzing or ticks from medical equipment.

"Where's Gwen?" Kyle regretted asking the question as soon as it left his mouth. He hated to hear about what a great babysitter Robert was. They were probably doing something cool and educational. Grandfather of the fucking year.

240

"She's with Mom and Francois. They went to the Smithsonian."

Kyle clenched his jaw.

Leigh checked her watch. "They'll be by to drop her off soon. I'd like to invite them to stay for dinner."

Kyle frowned.

"They're going back to France tomorrow," Leigh said. "Gwen loves being around her. Calls Mom her fairy grandmother."

"I should go by my apartment to pick up a few things and check on the place. Can I borrow your car?"

Leigh tilted her head. "She's trying. Maybe you could try too."

"I can't."

"I was mad at her too. I still am to a certain extent, but it's not healthy to hold on to that hate forever. And it's not all about me anymore. I have Gwen to think about, and she wants a grandmother."

The doorbell rang, followed by the front door opening.

"Mom!" Gwen called out.

"Leigh, honey, we're here," Olivia called out.

Speak of the devil. "Can I have your car keys?" Kyle asked, blank-faced.

Leigh sighed. "They're in the kitchen." She left the room, headed downstairs.

Their voices carried from the foyer.

"Hi, sweetheart," Leigh said. "Did you have fun?"

"Yes! I saw dinosaurs and *spacesips* and tigers with big teeth," Gwen said. "My fairy gramma bought me space ice cream."

"Like the astronauts eat," Olivia said.

"Tastes terrible," Francois said.

"I'm grilling burgers tonight," Leigh said. "Would you guys like to stay for dinner?"

"We don't want to put you out," Olivia said.

"Nonsense, Mom."

"Stay for dinner. Stay for dinner," Gwen chanted.

"We'd love to stay for dinner," Francois said.

"Great."

"Where's *Unc Kye*?" Gwen asked. "He's 'posed to be here."

"He's upstairs resting, honey," Leigh said.

"*Unc Kye*," Gwen called out, her little feet climbing the stairwell.

"Kyle's tired. Let's leave him alone."

Kyle stepped from the guest room to the top of the stairs.

"*Unc Kye!*" Gwen said.

Kyle met her halfway down the stairs.

She hugged his legs, then held up her arms. "Up."

"I can't, sweet pea. My shoulders are still hurt."

Kyle held Gwen's hand as they walked down the stairs to the awaiting audience.

"Hi, honey. How are you feeling?" Olivia asked as Kyle approached.

"Fine." Kyle walked past Francois and Olivia, not making eye contact.

"Kyle," Leigh said to his back.

Kyle grabbed Leigh's keys from the kitchen counter.

Francois's voice carried from the foyer. "He has too much guilt."

"Leave it alone," Olivia said.

"He needs to stop punishing *you* for *his* actions."

"Francois." There was a pleading in Olivia's voice.

Kyle overheard, clenching his fists around Leigh's keys, the jagged edges poking his skin.

"What are you talking about?" Leigh whispered, her words still carrying to Kyle in the kitchen.

"It's nothing, honey," Olivia replied.

"Would you two like something to drink?" Leigh asked.

"Something to *dink*," Gwen said.

The fractured family moved toward the kitchen, toward Kyle. Rage and adrenaline coursed through his veins. He glanced at the garage door, thinking about a speedy retreat, but he was tired. So tired ... of everything.

Kyle glowered at Francois and his sweat rings and fanny pack.

"How is it that I'm punishing Olivia for *my actions*?" Kyle's hands were shaky, his heart pounding.

"Francois spoke out of turn," Olivia said, giving her husband a look.

"I did no such thing," Francois said. "Too many things go unsaid in this family."

"Then say it," Kyle said through gritted teeth.

"You made a mistake. You were young. I understand, but it is not right to punish your mother all these years."

"Stop it, Francois," Olivia said. "This is neither the time nor the place."

"What mistake?" Leigh asked.

"It was a long time ago," Olivia replied. "It's not important anymore."

"This is the problem," Francois said.

"Well, whatever it is, it's still a problem," Leigh said, glancing at Kyle.

"Tell her then," Kyle said to Francois.

"It is not for me to tell," Francois replied.

Kyle shook his head. "You're a real piece of shit, you know that?"

"Kyle!" Leigh said.

"Piece of *sit*, piece of *sit*," Gwen said.

Leigh scowled at Kyle, then bent down next to Gwen. "Go in the other room and watch cartoons."

Gwen pouted.

"Go."

Gwen went to the living room.

"You remember Mom's friend, Rebecca?" Kyle asked Leigh.

"We don't need to dredge up the past," Olivia said.

"You remember those parties at our house? Mom and Dad and their stupid friends, getting drunk and high?"

"It was a long time ago," Leigh said. "I don't blame Mom and Dad anymore. They were young once too."

"One night, Rebecca was wasted and came in my room." Kyle's body trembled with rage. His eyes were glassy. "I was thirteen years old, but Francois and Olivia think I raped her."

The television flipped on and blared in the background, goofy voices and sound effects of a cartoon.

"It was a big mistake," Olivia said, her eyes watery. "She was out of it. She didn't know Kyle was in there. She took off her clothes to go to sleep. Kyle didn't know any better. He was just a boy."

"It was a bad circumstance," Francois said.

"Shut the fuck up," Kyle said, pointing at Francois, then turning to Leigh. "That's not what happened. She came into my room. She came on to me. I didn't know what I was doing. *She* made it happen." Tears slipped down his face. He wiped them away with his T-shirt sleeve.

"My God," Leigh said, turning to Olivia. "Did you go to the police?"

"I was protecting Kyle," Olivia said. "He could've gone to prison or juvenile detention."

"You were protecting your friend and your reputation!" Kyle said, pointing at his mother.

"I've known Rebecca my whole life. She wouldn't—"

"She did."

They were speechless.

"You know what? Fuck this. Enjoy your dinner." Kyle opened the door to the garage and slammed it behind him.

CHAPTER 52

BLAME AND RESPONSIBILITY

Kyle drove home in Leigh's SUV, his hands still shaky. His phone chimed. It was Leigh. He swiped left, ignoring the call. She followed up with a text.

Leigh: Come back and talk to us. Nobody blames you.

Kyle gripped the steering wheel, his knuckles white. *It's us now? Nobody blames me? What that really means is nobody believes me.*

He didn't return the text. He parked in front of his building and trekked to his fourth-floor apartment. Troy's apartment no longer had police tape covering the entry. Inside his own apartment, Kyle checked the food in his fridge. He dumped and washed the yogurt-like milk down the sink. He sat in his recliner and flipped on the television, looking for something mindless. His phone chimed again. He ignored Leigh's fourth call. He watched *Coming to America* on TNT.

* * *

A knock on his door startled him upright in his recliner. He glanced at the time on his phone—*9:11 p.m.*

"Kyle," Leigh called out from the other side of the door.

Kyle opened the door and stepped aside without a word. Leigh stepped inside, carrying Kyle's duffel bag.

"I wasn't sure if you were coming home," she said, holding out the duffel bag.

Kyle took the bag and dropped it at his feet. "I am home."

Leigh frowned. "I need my car."

Kyle fished her car keys from his pocket and handed them over. "How'd you get here?"

"Francois dropped me off." She paused. "He means well."

"He's an idiot."

Leigh pursed her lips. "Mom told me everything."

Kyle crossed his arms over his chest. "What did she say?"

"We don't have to rehash it. I just want to help you."

"What did she say?" Kyle asked a bit firmer.

"She feels awful. She wishes they'd never had those parties."

"*What did she say*?" Kyle said louder.

Leigh swallowed. "She said that Rebecca was in bad shape. Drunk and high. Mom sent her upstairs to sleep it off in the guest bedroom. She was mixed up and went in your room. She was hot, so she took off her clothes and passed out. When she woke up she had … semen on her inner thighs and her vagina. You were thirteen, Kyle. A naked woman just shows up in your bed. That's every teenage boy's dream. I know you didn't know what you were doing. Nobody blames you."

Kyle dropped his arms and closed his eyes for a moment as if he could will himself to be teleported someplace else—anyplace else. "Is that what you believe?"

"It does make sense." Leigh winced. "I mean it helps me to understand why you are the way you are. You need help. My therapist could really help you. If I made an appointment, would you go? I'll pay for everything."

"What's wrong with the way I am?"

"You're self-destructive. You're not kind to yourself. You've never

246

even had a serious girlfriend. You're a good-looking guy. It's not normal. I think all these problems you've had started then. You need to forgive yourself."

He had a lump in his throat. His voice quivered. "That was the first and last time I had sex."

"It doesn't have to be like that." Leigh reached out and touched Kyle's hand.

Kyle pulled away. "What happened, … I don't have to forgive myself because *I* didn't do anything wrong. I do have to live with it."

"Nobody's saying you did anything wrong—"

"Bullshit. She got into my bed in the middle of the night and made it happen. I didn't know what I was doing." Kyle blinked, a tear slid down his cheek. "She told me not to tell, and I wasn't gonna tell. Then, when Mom and Dad found out, she lied to save her ass, and nobody gave a shit because boys can't be raped by girls, especially not by attractive ones. It was easier for everyone to believe I did it."

"Kyle—"

"You know how Mom found out?" Kyle paused, his hands trembling now. "When I got sick, and she took me to the doctor. Rebecca gave me herpes."

Leigh gasped and put her hand to her mouth.

"Mom didn't tell you about that, did she? You always wanna know why I don't have a girlfriend? This is why. They hear *incurable STD*, and they're out the door." Kyle shook his head. He wiped his eyes with his thumb and index finger.

Leigh was speechless, her eyes wide and eyebrows arched. "I, um, I didn't know."

"You didn't wanna know."

"That's not fair."

"It's not? I've been telling you about Dad for years. You don't wanna believe it, so you don't. Why would this be any different?"

"You could've talked to me about it."

"There's nothing left to say. I'm done talking. Take your car and go back to Mom and Dad, since they're such awesome grandparents now."

"Don't be like that."

Kyle marched to his door and opened it. "Go."

"Fine." Leigh left the apartment.

CHAPTER 53

BAGGAGE CLAIM

Kyle placed the exercise band in the jamb and shut his bedroom door. He grabbed the band, held his arm straight, and stretched it across his chest for ten repetitions. His shoulder burned, but it was a good burn. Then he turned around and did his other arm. He was on the lightest band, but he was definitely getting better.

He had only been out of the hospital for eleven days, but he could now lift his arms over his head without pain. He had been sleeping and eating, watching mindless television, and doing his rehab. He had gone cold turkey on the internet. His phone buzzed.

Sam Irwin had texted to see how Kyle was doing, and had been to the hospital for a brief visit. He had told Kyle to let him know when he was ready to work, that he'd hold his job for him. Kyle wasn't in good-enough shape to do manual labor yet, but he had no choice. His bank account was nearly empty.

Sam: Great to hear from you. Glad you're getting better. When did you want to come back?

Kyle: I was hoping next week. I can run the zero turn. Probably can't line trim all day though. Too much strain on my shoulders.

Sam: The grass is slowing down now. You know how summer is. Guys are striping up the dirt. Hector has the crew under control. I don't think it makes sense to put you back on the crew.

Kyle: You don't have a job for me?

Sam: Not on a crew. Mike quit. I need an estimator. You interested?

Kyle: Yes, but I'm not qualified.

Sam: It's estimating not rocket science. I'll train you. Besides you're a celebrity now. Something tells me you'll be a damn good salesperson.

Kyle: Thanks Sam. See you Monday.

Sam: Yep

Kyle went back to his exercises. Toward the end of his workout, his phone chimed. He grabbed his phone and stared at the name. He had been avoiding her, but his anger and resolve had diminished. He swiped right. "Hi, Leigh."

"I'm surprised you picked up," Leigh replied. "You still mad at me?"

"Do you believe me?"

"I never said I didn't."

"You seemed skeptical."

"I know. I'm sorry. It's a lot to digest. I do believe you though."

"OK." Kyle took a deep breath. "I'd rather not talk about it anymore."

"That's fine. How are you feeling? You been going to physical therapy?"

"I can't afford it. It costs me forty bucks every time I go. My health insurance sucks, but I'm lucky Sam paid my premium to keep me on the plan."

"Kyle, you know I can help you."

"Don't worry. I'm doing therapy here. I bought some bands. I can do most of the exercises at home."

"Are you getting better?"

"Yeah, I am."

"That's good. I was calling because I'm supposed to pick up Jewel at the airport later on. Do you want to go with me?"

"Sure."

* * *

Kyle and Leigh and Gwen watched the line of weary travelers exit customs on their way to baggage claim. They searched the faces for Jewel. The wave of passengers dwindled to a trickle, but no Jewel. They went to baggage claim for Air France flight 4678. Jewel wasn't there. Kyle went to the Air France customer service counter. Leigh and Gwen waited at baggage claim in case Jewel showed up.

Kyle stepped to the counter and the young woman behind a computer screen.

"Hello, may I help you?" she asked.

"I was here to pick up Jewel Holloway. She was supposed to be on flight 4678."

She tapped on her keyboard. "That flight landed on time fifty minutes ago."

"I know. I was waiting for her, but she never got off with the other passengers. Can you tell me if she was on the flight?"

"I'm sorry, sir. I can't give out that information."

"But she's a minor."

"I still can't give out that information."

"What if I had her mother call?"

"I can only give out that information to law enforcement."

Kyle pushed off the counter. "It might come to that." He went back to baggage claim.

Leigh was on her phone. "OK, call me back." Leigh disconnected the call. "What did they say?"

"They won't tell me if she was on the flight," Kyle replied.

"What about family?"

"I asked about that. Only law enforcement."

"I called Dad. He's checking with the Paris office to see if she made it to the airport." Leigh tapped on her phone. "I should call Rhonda. Maybe Jewel changed her flight and told her mom but forgot to tell me." Leigh put her phone to her ear. "Hi, Rhonda. It's Leigh." She listened for a moment. "By any chance did Jewel change her flight? I was supposed to pick her up tonight, but she wasn't on the flight." Leigh listened again. "I already talked to Robert. He's checking with the Paris people to see if she made it to the airport." She listened again. "Of course. I'll let you know as soon as I do." Leigh disconnected the call and looked at Kyle. "Her mother hasn't spoken to her in weeks."

"We should call the police," Kyle said.

"I'm sure there's a logical explanation. She probably just missed her flight. She is a teenager. Dad should call me back in a minute." Leigh's phone chimed. "There he is." She swiped right and put her phone to her ear. Leigh listened for a moment. "Well, she's not here." She listened again. "Then she's missing, and we need to call the police." She paused. "Call me back if you hear anything more." Leigh shoved her phone in her purse, a scowl on her face. "Dad said that his Paris handler dropped her at the airport on time."

"Did he take her inside? At least get her checked in? Show her where the gate is?"

Leigh shook her head. "Sounds like the idiot just dropped her off. She's probably still in Paris. Dad's calling the police in Paris."

"I still think we should call the police here. They can at least check the flight information."

"I'm calling now." Leigh tapped 9-1-1.

CHAPTER 54

BLACKMAIL

After the airport, Kyle agreed to stay with Leigh as they waited for word. Hope dwindled a little with each passing hour. After two days, Kyle braced himself for the worst. A storm raged outside, raindrops pelting the roof and the high winds blowing against the windows. Leigh rinsed the breakfast dishes, and Kyle loaded the dishwasher. Gwen was in the other room, watching cartoons. Leigh's cell phone chimed on the kitchen table. She looked at Kyle, dried her hands, and hurried to the phone. She glanced at the caller ID, swiped right, and put her phone to her ear.

"Did they find her?" Leigh asked.

It must be Robert. Kyle watched her expression for any clues.

Leigh listened. Her mouth turned down; her eyes were glassy. "What happened?" She listened again, tears overflowing and slipping down her cheeks. "I have to go, Dad." She disconnected the call and dropped her phone on the table. She braced herself against the table, crying softly, her head bowed.

Kyle approached, a lump in his throat. "She's gone, isn't she?"

Leigh sniffled and looked up. Her eyes were red, her voice shaky. "They found her in a park outside of Paris. She was stabbed to death."

Kyle hung his head and rubbed the back of his neck. He closed his eyes for a moment, picturing Jewel, the tall skinny girl who thought she had it all figured out. He wiped his eyes with the side of his index finger. Kyle remembered the last thing she had said to him. *Maybe I'm using him.* He thought about Kate. He thought about his dad's penchant for young girls. His stomach churned. He looked up at Leigh, his jaw set tight.

"Robert did this," Kyle said through gritted teeth.

"What?" Leigh asked.

"I think Jewel was blackmailing Robert."

"I can't entertain your, your ... *bullshit.* Not now. Dad hasn't been to Paris in months."

"You really think he'd get his own hands dirty?"

"Just stop—"

"Jewel told me that she was using him. I think she blackmailed him about their relationship to get the contract, and Robert had her killed."

"Are you completely insane?"

"You don't know what he's capable of."

Leigh glared at Kyle. "Yes, I do." She walked away.

Kyle removed his cell phone from his pocket and called Detective Fitzgerald.

CHAPTER 55

EVIDENCE

"Kyle," Detective Fitzgerald said, striding to the police station waiting area.

Kyle stood and shook the detective's hand. "Thank you for meeting me."

Fitzgerald nodded. "I wish it were under better circumstances."

They took the elevator to the third floor. Detective Fitzgerald ushered Kyle to his office. They sat across from each other at the desk.

"Looks like you're healing up. How are you feeling?" Fitzgerald asked.

"Pretty good. Thanks," Kyle replied.

"Like I said on the phone yesterday, this is way out of my jurisdiction. I do have some contacts, and I found out a few things about your friend. Paris PD followed up with your father's modeling agency. Everything appears to be on the up-and-up. Paris PD seems to think she was picked up by human traffickers. They have video footage of her being dropped off at the airport, then being picked up by another car with stolen plates. No image of the guy. She probably met someone, fell in with the wrong guy. These guys charm these young girls, isolate them, then turn them out. She probably wasn't cooperative, or maybe she tried to escape. At this point Paris PD doesn't have any leads. I'm sorry, Kyle."

"I think my dad's involved."

"You said that on the phone, but there's no evidence of that."

"The last thing Jewel said to me was, 'Maybe I'm using him.' I told her that my dad was using her, and that was her response. I think he had a sexual relationship with her, and she was blackmailing him for a modeling contract."

Detective Fitzgerald leaned forward, his elbows on the desk. "Do you have any evidence?"

Kyle looked down for a moment. "No."

CHAPTER 56

MAN TO MAN

Kyle drove home from the police station. He was agitated, pacing his bedroom. He sat at his desk and grabbed a piece of paper and a pen. He wrote exactly what he wanted to say. It took four drafts to get it right. He opened the voice changer app on his phone. He had never actually used it because you couldn't have conversations in real time. He read from his written message as he recorded his voice with the app. The app had many options for voice disguise. He could even sound like Darth Vader if he wanted. He selected female and sped it up a bit. He grabbed both of his phones and a screwdriver—not the famous Phillip's head; that one was in an evidence locker some-where—but a regular old flathead. Kyle left his apartment.

It was a beautiful day—cottony white clouds, low-eighties, gentle breeze. He drove to the shopping center across from Roseland Estates. His windows were down, the warm breeze whipping through his Hyundai. He parked in the back of the grocery store lot and hiked across Ox Road to Roseland Estates. Kyle kept tight to the woods so he wouldn't be easily noticed. He cut through the forest and peeked at his dad's red brick mansion. The Lincoln was gone. The house looked vacant. Kyle stayed in the woods as he hiked to the rear of the property. He sprinted across the lawn to the back door. The back door was actually a bank of several glass doors used to take advantage of the sunlight for the walkout basement. He peered inside. No signs of life.

The alarm system had contacts on the doors and windows and motion alarms. At least it did ten years ago. Kyle took the screwdriver from the back pocket of his jeans. He jabbed a small pane of glass next to the door handle. The pane broke, a bit of glass falling on the floor just inside the door. The house was silent, no beeping from the alarm. He figured it wouldn't trigger the motion alarm, because, when he'd lived at the house, he had to walk inside several feet before the alarm sounded. He didn't put his hand through the hole to unlock the door. Instead, he moved along the side of the house and hid at the front corner, behind a large holly hedge.

He waited for hours, the heat of the day retreating. An engine rumbled closer. Kyle stood and peered around the corner. It was the Lincoln. He hustled to the back door and waited, listening intently. Doors opened and shut, the dull *thud* of a well-made car. A quieter opening and shutting of a door. *Must be the house.* The alarm beeped, giving the owner thirty seconds or so to type in the code before the siren blared and the police were notified. Kyle reached through the hole he'd made in the glass, unlocked the door, and entered the basement. He shut the door softly.

The basement was a mother-in-law suite with a full kitchen, living area, two bedrooms, and a home theater. Kyle stepped on the white carpet, past the living room and kitchen. He turned left down the hall, then right into a square room. The walls were painted black and soundproofed. A sectional couch faced a massive built-in plasma television. Kyle shut the door behind him, removed his phones from his pockets, and sat on the couch. His heart pounded. He readied the voice recording on one phone and dialed Robert's cell phone with the other. He dialed *67 to disguise his phone number. It would show up as Restricted or Unavailable.

The cell phone rang. One ring, two. Then Robert's voice mail. *He screened my call.* "You've reached Robert Summers. Please leave a name and number, and I will return your message as soon as possible. Thank you."

Kyle waited for the beep and pressed Play on his recording. He held the two phones so they faced each other. The "female" voice spoke fast. "I know what you did to that girl. You may have fooled the Paris police but not me. I have proof. I know she was blackmailing you for that bullshit contract. I know you arranged for the human traffickers to take her. I have proof.

"If you don't wanna be arrested, you need to purchase eight hundred ounces of gold bullion split evenly among one-ounce coins and ten-ounce bars. Place the gold in a sturdy rolling suitcase. Tomorrow at noon, I will call with instructions on when and where to drop the gold. Don't fuck with me. I'm just as likely to call the police as I am to kill Leigh and Gwen and you." Kyle disconnected the call.

Kyle called the home phone and repeated the process after he was sent to voice mail on the fifth ring. After leaving the messages, Kyle crept from the theater, up the basement steps, one phone in hand. He stopped at the top of the steps and put his ear to the closed door. Robert paced in the kitchen, but, other than that, it was quiet. *Maybe he was listening to one of the messages. He had to be curious after getting back-to-back messages like that.*

"There's a problem," Robert said.

Heavier steps came from the front door, past the dining room, and into the kitchen.

"What's wrong, Mr. Summers?" the driver said.

They came in loud and clear through the thin interior door. Kyle started the audio recorder on his phone. He put the mike near the space between the door and the floor.

"I just got a disturbing message. Listen," Robert said.

The men were quiet for a minute, the driver probably listening to the message.

"You wanna call the cops?" the driver asked.

"It's a serious threat. I have to. I'm not worried about myself, but I'd never forgive myself if anything happened to Leigh or Gwen. I *would* like to know more about the caller before calling the police. It might be Kyle. I really don't want to send my son to prison. I know he's pissed about the ransom. And he's been obsessed with Jewel. Maybe he's losing it because of her murder. I worry about him, Joe. He needs help."

"I hope it ain't him. It sounded like a woman. Could be a disgruntled model. Lots of them floatin' around."

"Something's off about that message. Even though the voice was high, and the person spoke fast, it still sounded a bit like my son. I wonder if he used a voice-disguiser."

Shit.

"Did a phone number come up?" Joe asked.

"It said Unavailable," Robert replied.

"Probably used *67. I could call my guy at the FBI. They can get that info."

"Yeah, do it, and go check on Leigh and Gwen. Don't tell them about the threat. If it turns out to be Kyle, Leigh will never forgive him."

"I don't feel comfortable leavin' you here alone. I'm sure Leigh and Gwen would love a visit."

"I'll be fine here. I need to call Paul. He knows the Paris girls better than me. Maybe one of them does have a grudge or a boyfriend with a criminal—"

Kyle's phone chimed. The one in his pocket. He ran down the stairs and down the hall. He heard heavy footsteps behind him. Kyle opened the back door and sprinted outside. He ran through the manicured lawn to the front, headed for the woods, and ultimately the shopping center. He knew he was too fast for two middle-aged guys. He glanced back to see if he was still being chased. Nobody there.

Kyle turned back around and was blindsided, tackled. The impact knocked him off his feet and took his breath away. He lay on the ground, writhing and hyperventilating.

Joe, the driver, stood over him like Ronnie Lott. The driver must've come from the front door, the shortcut beating Kyle to the woods. Robert joined them, jogging from the rear. Robert stood, his hands on his hips, wearing khakis and a polo. His white hair was perfectly in place and parted on the side, despite the run. He always had a handsome face, with symmetrical features and mostly wrinkle-free skin. His lack of exercise showed in his thin pasty arms and paunch.

Kyle's wheezing subsided.

"Take his phone," Robert said, standing over his son.

Joe patted Kyle's pockets and removed his phones. "He has two." Joe handed the phones to Robert.

"Did you send that threat?" Robert asked.

Kyle rose to one knee and looked up at his dad. "Fuck you, *Robert.*"

"Get him up," Robert said to Joe, ignoring Kyle. "Let's go inside."

Joe grabbed Kyle and yanked him to his feet. Joe walked behind Kyle, pushing him inside. They sat Kyle in the sunroom on a wicker chair. Joe stood over him, his meaty forearms crossed over his chest. Robert stood next to Joe, tapping on one of Kyle's phones.

"Did you send that threat?" Robert asked again.

Kyle glared, saying nothing.

Robert switched phones, checking the call log. "Well, that was easy. Here are the two phone calls. One to my cell followed by one to the house."

"Extortion, death threats, breakin' and enterin'," Joe said. "You're lookin' at some real time, Kyle."

"Your sister will be heartbroken." Robert shook his head. "I can't believe you'd threaten Gwen and Leigh. You need help, Kyle. I don't know if that'll be in a hospital or a prison, but I know you need help. I've given up hope that we can have a relationship, but I can't continue to ignore your belligerent behavior. What were you planning to do with all that gold?"

"It wasn't about the gold, and I wasn't threatening Leigh and Gwen."

"The police will disagree with you on that." Robert sighed. "You leave me little choice."

"I wanted to get you talking. I thought you might talk about how you ordered a hit on Jewel."

Robert exhaled heavily. "I wouldn't even know how to do such a thing. It saddens me to see you this way. Jewel's passing nearly broke my heart. I had high hopes for the young lady. She had had an awful childhood."

Kyle glowered at Joe. "How can you work for a fucking pedophile?"

Joe glowered right back at Kyle. "I've never seen your dad do anything unprofessional with the girls."

"You're either lying or not paying attention. My money's on the former."

Joe looked at Robert. "You want me to call the cops?"

"I'd like to have a private conversation with my son first," Robert replied. "I need to say some things that are long overdue, and I imagine he'd like to say some things to me."

Joe knitted his brows. "With all due respect, Mr. Summers, he threatened your life. I don't think it's a good idea."

"I appreciate your concern, but I'll be fine," Robert said. "We'll talk on the deck. You can watch from here. Let's step outside, Kyle. It's a beautiful day."

Kyle didn't move.

"Get up," Joe said, his eyes narrowed.

Robert exited the sunroom onto the deck, Kyle following behind. Kyle glanced back at the door. Joe shut it and kept watch from inside the sunroom. The massive wooden deck had a three-foot railing and built-in benches. Robert walked to the railing, turned around, and leaned back. Kyle approached, standing five feet away from Robert, his arms folded over his chest.

"You're in big trouble, Kyle," Robert said.

"I don't care. I know the truth. That's what matters."

Robert laughed. "Still so naive."

Kyle clenched his jaw. *This piece of shit thinks he's untouchable.*

"What's the truth, Kyle? That I'm some sort of monster? Why is that you're the only one who thinks that? I've never been arrested. Never been charged. Did you ever think that you're mistaken?"

"People don't wanna believe in evil. They think it's for stories. They think, in real life, people are flawed but mostly good. But that's not true, is it? There is evil. I've seen it up close, over and over again. I've seen it in you. I know what you're capable of."

"Mark Twain once said, 'It's not what you don't know that kills you. It's what you know for sure that ain't true.' Do you understand what I'm trying to tell you, son?"

"The thing is, I never wanted to believe it, but I know what you did to Kate. She told me everything. I saw her come out your office. She was crying, her shirt undone."

"She's a liar and a whore."

"Shut up."

"She threw herself at me. Took off her clothes. Grabbed my crotch. Told me how bad she wanted it."

"Shut up." Kyle dropped his arms and clenched his fists.

"What's wrong, Kyle? Can't handle the truth? I know you loved her, but she was trash. She wanted to fuck her way to the top. A girl like that's not capable of love."

"I said, 'Shut up.'" Kyle's eyes were glassy.

"Kyle, you're sick. You need help. You've been projecting all this time. It started with Rebecca. You were only thirteen. It was a terrible situation. Your mother and I never blamed you, but I think it flipped a switch inside you. Made you incapable of a healthy adult relationship. That's why you're so focused on these young girls. Jesus, Kyle, you even pretend to *be* a young girl. I've seen those disgusting chats you have with those perverts. You enjoy it, don't you?"

"Fuck you."

"You wanted to be with Kate, but she didn't want you. It was easier to blame me than to look at the demons in you. You wanted Jewel too, didn't you?"

"Shut the fuck up." Kyle shook with rage.

"It's the truth, isn't it, Kyle? You wanted to take her in every way possible."

Kyle rushed forward and smashed into Robert, full speed, leading with his elbows. The force of Kyle's blow upended Robert, sending him over the railing, and free falling twenty feet to the depths below. Kyle peered over the railing, Robert hitting the ground headfirst and landing awkwardly, his legs splayed apart. Joe rushed onto the deck and peered over the railing at Robert's awkward pose and lifeless body.

CHAPTER 57

ARRAIGNMENT AND BAIL

The courtroom was packed, the lighting bright white. The audience sat on rows of wooden pews. They were separated from the judge and the lawyers by a short wooden divider. While the judge could not bar the media from attending the trial, no audio recordings or cameras were allowed. Cell phones were even banned by the sitting judge. The judge was up high behind his elevated desk, the lawyers lower and at opposing tables, facing the judge.

Kyle was ushered into the courtroom by two court officers. He shuffled, his legs and hands bound, wearing a forest-green jail uniform. Kyle had been arrested on Friday, so he was forced to spend the weekend in jail. He was exhausted after a mostly sleepless weekend. He stood front and center, the judge looking down on him.

Kyle's court-appointed attorney, Brock Winston, rose from his seat, and joined his client in front of the judge. Kyle had met him briefly in the court's holding cell. Brock was small in stature, stressed, and baby-faced. He looked like he had just graduated from high school, not law school. They'd barely had five minutes to discuss the case, which wasn't uncommon for arraignment of a defendant represented by a public defender. Brock had advised Kyle on how to plead.

The clerk said, "Case number zero-seven-dash-five-seven-three-two, the *State versus Kyle Summers*, one count capital murder."

The elderly man glared down from the bench. "In the matter of the *State versus Kyle Summers*, how do you plead?"

Brock nodded to Kyle.

"Not guilty," Kyle replied.

The judge looked at the prosecuting attorney. "I'll hear from the state regarding bail."

A compact woman with blond hair and heavy makeup rose from behind the prosecutor's table. "We have evidence of extortion and death threats by Mr. Summers—one of which was against a three-year-old child. We have a firsthand witness to the murder and a confession from Mr. Summers affirming his guilt."

The judge flipped through the file, his face twisted with disgust. He looked back to the prosecuting attorney. "Ms. Emerson, does the state have a recommended bail amount?"

"We're recommending bail be set at two million dollars."

There was an audible gasp from the audience.

Ms. Emerson continued, "Given the severity of the charges, the likelihood of conviction, and the fact that the defendant's mother lives in France with sizeable resources, we believe the defendant to be a serious flight risk."

The judge looked at Brock. "Mr. Winston?"

"Mr. Summers is not a flight risk. He does not have a criminal record, and, while his mother may have sizable resources, my client does not. If he did, I imagine he wouldn't have a state-appointed attorney. Two million dollars is excessive in this case."

The judge frowned. "Bail is set at two million dollars."

CHAPTER 58

VISITING DAY

Leigh sat across from Kyle at the round table. He was permitted one personal visit per week for twenty minutes on Saturdays or Sundays. Not that anyone was interested in visiting. The room was beige and bland, the table and chairs cheap metal with faux wood laminate and barely enough padding to sit comfortably for twenty minutes. Other inmates sat at their own tables, talking with their parents and friends and wives and children.

Kyle hadn't expected Leigh to come. He hadn't asked her to. But there she was, no makeup, dark circles under her eyes, her hair in a ponytail, and a few wrinkles he hadn't noticed before.

"Why?" Leigh asked. "I have to know why."

Kyle leaned forward, his elbows on the table. "Because he was a child predator, and nobody was ever gonna stop him."

"Where's your proof?"

"Kate. I know what she told me, and I know what I saw."

"She could've lied. The truth is, you don't have any credible evidence. Gwen keeps asking where her grandfather is. What the *hell* am I supposed to tell her?"

A guard glared at her for being too loud.

Kyle showed his palms. "We're OK."

The guard scowled but turned away.

Kyle looked back at Leigh. "I didn't mean to hurt her, but I couldn't allow him to continue doing what he was doing."

She shook her head. "I'm not buying your bullshit anymore, Kyle. If you were so altruistic, why'd you try to extort money from him and why did you threaten Gwen?"

"I was in his house. I wanted to get him talking about Jewel so I could record him. I thought, if I threatened you and Gwen, he wouldn't think it was me. Obviously, I'd never do anything to hurt you guys."

"That's for sure, because you're never getting out of here."

Kyle leaned forward, his gaze locked on hers. "Leigh, please. You said you believed me before. You have to believe me now."

"I'm done believing you, Kyle. You killed our father." She sniffled, her eyes red. "I loved him. Gwen loved him. And you took that from us."

"I'm sorry."

"No. You can't say you're sorry for this. It's too big. I'm done, Kyle. I won't be visiting you in prison. Gwen certainly won't. I wanted to tell you that to your face, so there's no misunderstanding." She stood from the table and pointed at Kyle. "We're done. Do you understand me?"

Kyle nodded, a lump lodged in his throat.

She turned on her sneakers and marched for the exit.

CHAPTER 59

GOING TO TRIAL?

The Fairfax County Detention Center was a transient place: inmates going to trial or released on bail; or transferred, being sent to prison; or, on rare occasions, being found not guilty. Kyle was almost an old-timer with three weeks at the jail. He had already been through two cellmates. His last one got out on bail two days ago. The guy was all right. Busted for fleeing the scene of an accident. Kyle was treated OK by his fellow inmates. Most knew of his exploits as the Predator Hunter. That seemed to go over well here, as pedophiles were the lowest form of scum in lockup.

Kyle lay on the thin pad that passed for a mattress, his arm shielding his eyes from the fluorescent light.

"Kyle, your lawyer's here," the guard said, peeking his head into his cell.

Kyle stood and followed the guard to the private meeting area. Inmates were only allowed one short personal visit per week, but there were no limits on meetings with lawyers and police officers. Kyle was ushered down a hallway with a bank of small rooms on either side. The rooms had large thick windows, so the guards could ensure the safety of visitors without hearing the privileged conversations.

Brock Winston stood as Kyle approached. The guard shut the door behind them. The room was stark white with a card table and three plastic chairs. Surprisingly, the Spartan rooms had Wi-Fi. The two men shook hands and sat across from each other.

"You doing all right?" Brock asked, as he unbuttoned his suit jacket.

"I'm fine," Kyle replied, expressionless.

Brock nodded, not particularly interested in Kyle's response. "I'm gonna level with you, Kyle. I know I've told you this before, but your case does not look good, and the prosecution knows it. DA Emerson is prosecuting, and she's a freaking ball-buster. There's the witness, your confession, the extortion, and death threats. Emerson said she'd accept life in prison without parole for a guilty plea. You'd avoid the needle, but she won't budge on life without parole."

Kyle took a deep breath. "So I plead guilty and get life in some hellhole, or I go to trial and get the needle?"

"That's the long and short of it."

"I'd like to go to trial."

"Think about this before you make your decision. You're being charged with a capital murder, so the death penalty is on the table, and Virginia is quite efficient at killing people. The second most of any state since 1976. And they do it quickly. If they convict you, they'd likely kill you in eight years."

Not soon enough. Kyle nodded, nonplussed.

Brock continued, "With capital murder, the best sentence you can hope for is life without parole. Emerson's gonna push for the death penalty. She's a political animal. She's licking her chops on this one."

"I don't care. I'd like to go to trial."

Brock sighed. "I had a feeling you'd say that. Then we have a lot of work ahead of us. I think you should change your plea of not guilty to not guilty by reason of insanity."

"I'm not insane."

"Look, Kyle. I can't argue that you're innocent. I mean, I can, but we'll lose. At least with an insanity defense, we have a chance. I can argue that your father was a child predator, and you flew into an uncontrollable rage because of it."

"How does that work? They find me guilty and send me to some mental institution?"

"Not exactly. If you're found guilty of the crime, you'll have a second trial to determine your mental competence. You could end up in a mental institution, or you might still end up in prison or on death row."

"OK. Let's do the insanity plea."

Brock nodded. "All right."

"What happens next?"

"I'll reject the plea bargain, enter the new plea."

"When would the trial start?"

"Depends. In Virginia, you have a right to a speedy trial, unless you waive that right. Felony cases are tried within five months of arrest. DA Emerson's chomping at the bit though. She thinks they have an open and shut case. It wouldn't surprise me if we ended up on the docket in a couple of months. I can ask for a continuance, to try to stretch things out. The longer we can delay, the better chance we have."

"No. I wanna get this over with."

"That's not a good strategy."

Kyle glared at his lawyer. "Don't drag this out. Do you understand me?"

Brock looked away for a moment. "Yes."

"Where do we go from here?"

"We'll have jury selection first. Jury selection can make or break a case. Emerson will want a bunch of rich white guys on the jury. Guys who identify with Robert."

"Who do we want on the jury?"

"Young women with children. Empathetic women. Teachers maybe. It helps that you're a good-looking guy." Brock tilted his head, looking at Kyle's ear.

Instinctively Kyle touched his ear canal, the pinna mostly gone. "What?"

"Just seeing what side it's on. Luckily it's on the left."

"What difference does it make?"

"The jury box is on your left. I want them to see your ear and think about what you've been through."

CHAPTER 60

OPENING STATEMENTS

The judge addressed the jury from his desk on high. "Opening statements are not evidence but only what each side believes the evidence will show." Judge Charles Cooley had a full head of brown-and-gray hair swept to the side, a large pointy nose, and a reputation for being tough on criminals. "Ms. Emerson," he said.

DA Emerson stood from the prosecuting table and strutted in front of the jury, her heels masking her diminutive stature. Despite the heavy makeup, she couldn't hide the loss of elasticity in her face. No longer the beautiful woman who turned heads, she was now the powerful woman who bent wills.

"Ladies and gentlemen of the jury," she said with a curt smile.

The twelve jurors stared back, expressionless. Six men and six women. Nearly all white, except for two women. The African-American teacher and the Hispanic homemaker. The men were well-dressed, middle-aged to elderly. Handpicked by Emerson to identify with the victim.

"I've prosecuted many murder cases, but never have I prosecuted a case with such solid unshakeable evidence. You'll hear the death threats that the defendant sent to Robert, his daughter, Leigh, and his three-year-old granddaughter, Gwen." Emerson shook her head, her mouth turned down. "Three years old." She paused to let that sink in. "You'll hear from Joe Romero, Robert's driver, bodyguard, friend of nine years, and eyewitness to the crime. Joe was only twenty feet away when the defendant pushed his own father over the deck railing. Joe didn't want Robert to speak to the defendant alone on that deck, but Robert still loved his son—the defendant." Emerson turned and gestured toward Kyle.

Kyle sat next to Brock at the defense table, his hands folded on the table, his tie too tight and his feet swelling in his shoes. It was the only suit he had, so he'd have to wear it every day. Brock had said that appearance was important, but it was good that he wasn't wearing an expensive suit. Brock had told him to try to look innocent. *How the hell do I look innocent? How am I supposed to look? Scared? Confident?* He went with how he felt. Empty.

Emerson turned back to the jury. "The defendant had just sent death threats and an extortion demand for over a million dollars in gold bullion. Robert had planned to call the police about the threats, not because he wanted to hurt the defendant, but because he feared for the life of his daughter and granddaughter. The defendant, out of options, pushed Robert over that ledge—a ledge that was over twenty feet high." Emerson touched the jury box, another ledge. "Sadly, Robert broke his neck and died from the impact of the fall.

"You'll hear from the arresting officer, Lance Dunne. The defendant confessed his guilt to Officer Dunne minutes after the murder." Emerson held up one finger to the jury. "We have the defendant's threat of murder recorded, showing intent beyond a shadow of a doubt." She added a second finger. "We have an eyewitness whose sole job was to watch the victim. An eyewitness who was expecting trouble and watching with the utmost of care and worry." She added a third finger. "We have a confession from the defendant minutes after the murder." She gestured to the defense table. "Three strikes, they're out."

Diane Emerson turned back to the jurors. She took a deep breath, her face showing concern. "To take a life is the most heinous act that can be committed by a human being. The evidence in this case is irrefutable. *Irrefutable*. I am confident that you will wholeheartedly agree. Thank you." Emerson marched back to her table, the court-room silent.

Kyle glanced back at the audience, packed into the wooden pews, like church on Christmas Eve. A few women offered small, sympa-thetic smiles. He scanned the faces for Leigh. She wasn't here. He didn't recognize anyone.

Brock Winston stood from the defense table and buttoned his suit jacket, bringing Kyle's attention forward again. Brock stepped to the jury box. "Good morning," he said.

A few jurors nodded, but there were no audible responses.

"DA Emerson's right. The evidence is strong and irrefutable. Murder *is* the most heinous crime a human can commit. Lemme ask you a serious question. Is there any circumstance where you might kill another human being? What if you were defending an innocent person? Police officers do this every day. Soldiers do this every day. What if you knew a man was raping children?"

"Objection, speculation," Emerson said.

"Sustained," Judge Cooley said.

Brock pursed his lips. "What if your first and only love told you that your father raped her? Would you want to kill him?" Brock gestured to Kyle. "Kyle's never committed a crime in his whole life. In fact, he's dedicated his life to finding and exposing child predators. He risked his life to stop Doug Chambers, the most heinous serial murderer and child rapist in Virginia's history. The death of Robert Summers is not as simple as Ms. Emerson makes it sound. You have to ask yourself, what would you do to stop a pedophile?"

After a brief recess, Diane Emerson called Officer Lance Dunne to the stand. Officer Dunne wore his uniform and sat behind the desk, lower, but next to Judge Cooley, and near the jurors. Dunne was clean-cut and fit. Emerson asked a series of questions about

Dunne's impeccable background and experience. She then asked questions about the call he'd received to Robert Summers's house on June 29.

"When you arrived at the victim's home, what did you find?" DA Emerson asked.

"I found the victim lying on the ground below the deck," Officer Dunne replied. "I checked for a pulse, but there was none. I called for backup. The victim's bodyguard yelled down at me from the deck. He told me that he had the killer under control."

"Objection, prejudicial," Brock said.

"Sustained," Judge Cooley said.

Diane Emerson glared at Brock, then turned back to Officer Dunne. "Do you remember what Joe Romero said when he yelled down to you from the deck?"

"He said something like, 'I got the killer right here. He's under control.'"

"What happened next?"

"I drew my weapon and went up the steps to the deck to secure the assailant."

"Objection, prejudicial," Brock said.

"Sustained," Judge Cooley said.

"Who did you see on the deck?"

"The bodyguard, Mr. Romero, and the presumed assailant."

"What were they doing?"

"Mr. Romero had his gun drawn, and he was standing over the presumed assailant."

"Is the *presumed* assailant in the courtroom today?"

"Yes," Dunne replied.

"Can you point him out?" Emerson asked.

Dunne pointed to Kyle.

"Let the record show that Officer Dunne pointed to the defendant, Kyle Summers."

"So noted," Judge Cooley said.

"What was the defendant doing when you first saw him?" Emerson asked.

"He was sitting on a bench, his head down," Dunne said. "He looked depressed."

"What happened next?"

"I handcuffed Kyle Summers and read him his rights. Then I asked him if he pushed the victim off the deck."

"What did the defendant say?"

"He said, 'I had to do it. I had to do it.'"

"Are you certain that's what he said?"

"Absolutely certain. He said it twice and was very clear."

"Thank you, Officer Dunne."

DA Diane Emerson wore a small smirk as she sat down. Brock stood and approached Officer Dunne for the cross-examination.

"Did you see Kyle Summers push the victim from the deck?" Brock asked.

"No," Dunne replied.

"Did you see or hear the argument preceding the alleged incident?"

"No."

"Do you know what Kyle Summers and the victim spoke about before the alleged incident?"

"No."

"Was Kyle Summers belligerent at any time?"

"Not while I was there."

"No more questions at this time, Your Honor," Brock said.

The state called Joe Romero to the stand. He was sworn in, and DA Emerson asked him a series of questions regarding his employment by Robert Summers. Joe described Robert in numerous superlatives: honest, great guy, standup guy, professional, caring, and a great father and grandfather.

Kyle felt like vomiting.

Emerson then asked a series of questions to set up the punch line.

DA Emerson played the message with Kyle's extortion attempt and death threats. Afterward, she approached Joe. "Was that the message that Robert shared with you?"

"Yes."

"Did Robert think that the defendant might've been behind the message?"

"Yes."

"But the message sounds like a woman?"

"Robert thought that Kyle might've used a voice-disguiser."

DA Emerson approached the center podium and tapped on the keyboard. The LCD screens around the courtroom went from black to an image of one of Kyle's phones. The jurors leaned toward the screen in front of the jury box.

Kyle listened and watched, blank-faced, like a good poker player.

"This is one of the defendant's phones," Emerson said. She clicked the mouse, showing a closeup of the phone, with the apps appearing on the screen. A red circle was drawn on the screen around the app, Voice Disguiser. "This is the Voice Disguiser app used by the defendant to disguise his voice in order to send the death threat and extortion demand." She clicked the mouse again. The recording file was shown. "This is the file of the message you just heard, which was found on the defendant's phone."

Emerson approached Joe Romero. She asked questions about Robert's and Joe's discovery of Kyle in the house and his subsequent capture. She asked questions about Joe's reticence to allow Robert to talk to Kyle alone.

"How far away were you from Robert and the defendant?" Emerson asked Mr. Romero.

"About twenty feet away," Joe replied.

"During their conversation, did you ever take your eyes off them?"

"No, not for a second. I had a bad feelin'."

"Did you hear their conversation?"

"No. I was in the sunroom, watchin' through the window."

"Did you notice anything about their body language?"

"Robert was relaxed. Kyle got angrier and angrier."

"How could you tell that the defendant was angry?"

"His fists were clenched. He widened his legs in an aggressive stance."

"Why didn't you go out to the deck and intervene?" Emerson asked.

"I did. As soon as I stepped on the deck, Kyle pushed him over the railin'. I was too late." Joe shook his head. "It's the biggest regret of my life."

CHAPTER 61

SKELETONS RISING

The Fairfax County Detention Center was a noisy place. Incessant chatter, boots on the ground, televisions. Kyle lay facedown in his bunk, his pillow over his head. The first day hadn't gone well. Brock was right; the evidence *was* stacked against him. And Diane Emerson *was* a ball-buster. Kyle wished for lights out, but they still had a few hours.

"Yo, Kyle," a guy called from his open cell door.

Kyle turned and looked at the large man in a forest-green prison uniform. Jerome. Armed robbery.

"You gotta see this," Jerome said.

"Maybe later," Kyle said, careful not to offend.

"Naw, you gotta come now. It's about your case."

Kyle followed Jerome to the common area. Hexagonal steel tables were spaced throughout with attached metal discs for seats and a handful of soft chairs, usually occupied by the biggest and baddest inmates. At this time, everyone huddled below the wall-mounted television. Jerome and Kyle approached the crowd.

"Move, motherfucker," Jerome said, claiming a space.

Kyle watched from the back, his eyes like saucers. Ava Noel was on the screen. The biggest supermodel that his dad's agency had under contract. At the bottom of the screen, read the headline, Supermodel Claims Rape by Deceased CEO, Robert Summers.

"I was only thirteen, but he promised that he'd make me a star," Ava said on television.

Jerome turned back to Kyle with a gap-toothed grin. "That fine woman ain't the only one neither. There's, like, eight more."

CHAPTER 62

LEIGH'S TESTIMONY

"The motion was denied," Brock said to Kyle.

They sat at the defense table, whispering, the courtroom mostly empty. It was the third day of the trial, half an hour before the scheduled start time.

Kyle held out his hands, exasperated, the denial extinguishing his hope like a bucket of water on a lit match. "But it shows that I'm telling the truth."

"It's too late," Brock replied. "We can't submit new evidence and witnesses after the trial has begun without a damn good reason."

"We do have a good reason. This just came out."

"The judge thinks otherwise."

"Then I'm screwed."

"This is still great for us."

"What difference does it make, if the jury can't hear about it?"

"What does the judge say to the jury at the end of every day?"

"Not to talk about the case or watch television or read the news or listen to the radio."

"Exactly." Brock smiled wide. "If you were on the jury, would you listen to the judge?"

* * *

Brock Winston called Leigh Summers-Burns to the stand. Leigh looked professional in her skirt suit, heels, and updo. She avoided Kyle's gaze as she took the stand. Kyle didn't want to include her on the defense witness list, but Brock was smart. He'd said, "You never know what might happen between now and the trial. Ultimately, if we don't wanna call her, we won't." With the models coming forward with allegations, Kyle thought Leigh might be on his side now, even though they still weren't talking. Brock agreed and thought it was worth the risk.

Brock sidled up to Leigh. "How long have you known Kyle Summers?"

She still didn't look at Kyle. "Almost my whole life. He's my younger brother. I'm two years older."

Brock smiled at Leigh. "Do you get along with Kyle?"

"We got along when we were younger, but not so much anymore."

"And why is that?"

She gestured to the courtroom. "All this hasn't helped."

"Anything else?"

"He didn't get along with our father, but I did."

"I see." Brock nodded. "To your knowledge, has Kyle ever hurt anyone apart from your father and Doug Chambers, the serial murderer?"

"No."

"Never even bullied a kid in school?"

"No."

"Has Kyle ever done anything to hurt your daughter, Gwen?"

"No."

"Has he ever yelled at her?"

"No. He's always been kind to her."

"Do you think he loves his niece?"

"Yes."

"Do you think, if given the chance, Kyle might've hurt you or Gwen, as was suggested in the alleged death threat?"

"No."

"Do you think he wanted money?"

"No."

"Why not?"

"My brother doesn't care about money. He could've taken a job working for our dad. He would've been CEO eventually, but he walked away from everything."

"Why did he do that?"

"Because he thought our dad was having sex with underaged girls."

"Objection. Hearsay," Emerson said.

"Sustained," Judge Cooley said.

Brock paused for a moment, considering his options. "Do you think your dad was having sex with underaged girls?"

"*Objection*. Prejudicial," Emerson said.

Judge Cooley thought for a moment. "Overruled. You may answer the question, Ms. Burns."

Leigh's dark eyes filled with tears. She looked at Kyle as she said, "Yes."

Kyle blinked, his eyes glassy.

"No further questions. Thank you, Ms. Burns." Brock unbuttoned his suit jacket and sat next to Kyle at the defense table.

DA Diane Emerson sauntered toward Leigh.

Leigh wiped the corners of her eyes with a tissue.

"Ms. Burns, are you able to continue?" Emerson asked, dripping with artificial sweetener.

Leigh nodded. "Yes. I'm fine."

"Do you love your brother?"

"Yes."

"Of course you do. It's normal and natural to love our siblings. But sometimes that love can make us blind."

"Objection," Brock said. "The prosecution is spinning a story."

"Ask a question or move on, Ms. Emerson," Judge Cooley said.

Emerson paused for a beat. "You testified that the defendant never yelled at your daughter and was only ever violent with your father and Doug Chambers. Is that accurate?"

"Yes," Leigh replied.

Emerson stepped to the prosecution table and grabbed a single piece of paper from a small stack. She read from the page. "Yet, the defendant said, and I quote, 'Don't fuck with me. I'm just as likely to call the police as I am to kill Leigh and Gwen and you.' Emerson set the paper back on her table and strutted toward Leigh. "What was your reaction when you found out that the defendant made that threat?"

"I was angry," Leigh replied.

"Of course. The defendant threatened you and your three-year-old girl. Were you afraid that he might hurt you or your daughter?"

"No."

"Why not? You were angry about the threat."

"He was in jail when I heard about it."

"What if he wasn't? Would you have allowed the defendant to babysit your daughter?"

"No."

"Why not?"

Leigh pursed her lips. "Kyle wouldn't hurt her or any child."

Emerson spoke sternly. "Answer the question, Ms. Burns. Why wouldn't you have wanted the defendant to babysit your daughter?"

Leigh looked away for a moment. "I was afraid that he would hurt her, but I'm not now."

"You said the defendant wouldn't hurt your daughter or any child. Is that correct?"

"Yes."

"Would it surprise you to know that Kyle hurt a fifteen-year-old child? Broke the boy's nose."

"That's not true," Leigh said.

Emerson nodded, walked to the prosecution table, and picked up another piece of paper from the small stack. She returned to the witness stand. "According to police reports, Kyle punched Henry Duncannon in the face, causing a broken nose and black eyes." Emerson showed Leigh the circled passage from the police report.

Leigh glared at Emerson. "You're talking about—"

"I did *not* ask a question," Emerson said, cutting off Leigh.

"Please do not provide additional commentary, Ms. Burns," Judge Cooley said.

"Yes, Your Honor," Leigh replied.

Kyle scribbled on a yellow notepad and pushed the note across the table to Brock. The note read *Do something. She's talking about Hank.*

Brock turned to Kyle and mouthed, *I got it.*

Emerson showed the circled passage from the police report to the jury. She sat down at the prosecution table and said, "No further questions."

"Redirect, Your Honor?" Brock asked.

"I'll allow it," Judge Cooley replied.

Brock stayed seated as he questioned Leigh. "Do you know who Henry Duncannon is? He actually goes by Hank."

"Yes," Leigh replied.

"Can you think of *any* reason why Kyle might've punched this young man in the face?"

"Hank was one of my brother's captors, and the man who shot my brother four times."

CHAPTER 63

CUDDLY KATE

Kyle was mesmerized as Kate Sloan took the stand. They were gonna be Kyle and Kate forever. But that was eleven years ago, and too much had happened. She was still beautiful—tall and thin and athletic. Pale skin and straight blond hair to her shoulders. She was like a Swedish volleyball player, with a face that men wanted to protect or violate. Button nose, tiny chin, full lips, and bright blue eyes. Kyle hadn't seen her in over a decade, but the old feelings flooded back. The friendship and love. The love that got too close. The double betrayal. The anger and despair.

"Ms. Sloan, how do you know Kyle Summers?" Brock asked.

"I met him when I worked as a model for his father's agency," Kate said. "Kyle was working in the office."

"Do you remember when this was?"

"I was fifteen, so it was eleven years ago."

"What was the nature of your relationship?"

"We were really good friends."

"Just friends?"

"I guess we were boyfriend and girlfriend, but we were so young."

"Did you love Kyle?"

"I was too young to know what I was doing."

Brock nodded. "Now that you're an adult, looking back, would you say that you two were in love?"

She pursed her lips. "Yes."

Kyle's stomach floated on her affirmation.

"Why did the relationship end?" Brock asked.

She averted her eyes. "My family moved to California."

"Did you have a sexual relationship with Kyle Summers?"

"No."

"Did you have a sexual relationship with Robert Summers?"

She flushed red, her pale skin like a mood ring. She spoke barely above a whisper, her head bowed. "I didn't want to."

Kyle gripped the armrests, suppressing the urge to go to her, to shield her from the ugliness.

Brock moved closer to Kate. "I'm sorry, Ms. Sloan. I didn't hear your response. Could you please repeat that?"

She looked up, her face beet red. "I didn't want to."

"Did Robert Summers force you to have sex with him?"

She nodded. "Yes."

CHAPTER 64

CLOSING ARGUMENTS

DA Diane Emerson approached the jury. She looked across the jurors and back again, making eye contact with each one. "The facts of this case are still firmly intact. The defendant threatened the victim and carried out that threat. We have an eyewitness who watched the event from a short distance away. The defendant confessed to the arresting officer. These facts are undeniable and irrefutable.

"The defense has called into question the character of the victim. They want you to believe that Robert Summers deserved to die. Robert Summers has never been arrested or even charged with a crime. He was a pillar of the community, a devoted father and grandfather. But we are not here to judge the victim. We are not here to *blame* the victim. We are here to judge the defendant."

Emerson gestured to Kyle, then looked back to the jury. "The defendant threatened and murdered his father in cold blood. The law is clear on what constitutes murder, and this was clearly capital murder, the most heinous crime in the state of Virginia." Emerson paused, her eyes sweeping across the jurors. "It is up to each of you to examine the facts of this case and to follow the law. Do the right thing." Emerson turned on her heels and returned to the prosecutor's table.

Brock Winston stood and buttoned his coat. He stepped to the jury box, the courtroom dead silent. "The prosecution loves to talk about facts, but they outright lie about key points and leave out facts that are inconvenient to their case. This was not cold-blooded murder as DA Emerson asserted in her closing argument." Brock gestured to Emerson and the prosecution table. "Kyle went to his father's house with the intention of gathering evidence to prove that his father, Robert Summers, was a child rapist and a murderer. Kyle had every intention of going to the police, but he was accosted by Robert Summers and Joe Romero and held against his will. Kyle did push Robert Summers off that railing, but it wasn't cold-blooded murder. It was justified rage and temporary insanity.

"Ms. Emerson said that Robert Summers was a devoted father and grandfather. However, you heard testimony from his own daughter that she believed Robert raped children. *Children.* You heard testimony from Ms. Sloan that Robert Summers raped her when she was fifteen. Ms. Sloan was Kyle's girlfriend, the love of his life, and his father raped her. If that doesn't turn your stomach and get your blood boiling, there's something wrong with you." Brock shook his head. "Put yourself in Kyle's shoes. What would you do if someone you loved was raped? What if that person was never brought to justice? What if they kept doing it? What if they were raping *children*? What if the man was standing in front of you, taunting you? What would you do? Would you push him off that deck? I hope I would have the courage to do what needed to be done. Kyle had that courage, and now his fate rests in your hands." Brock paused. "I hope you have the courage to free this young man. Thank you."

CHAPTER 65

DELIBERATIONS

Brock and Kyle ate dinner in a holding cell at the courthouse. The deputies provided a card table and two chairs. It was takeout from a local Italian place. Kyle had barely touched his homemade ravioli. His stomach was in knots.

"Do you think I have a chance?" Kyle asked.

"There's always a chance," Brock replied. "I like our chances much better now than when we started. Ultimately, it's up to the twelve people in that room."

Kyle checked the clock on the wall, outside of the cell. "It's been almost five hours. What's taking them so long?"

"It probably means they don't agree, or it could mean that they're in agreement but want to be thorough. It's more likely that they're arguing. It's probably a gender war in there. The women wanting to save you, and the men wanting to …"

Kyle pushed away his plate. "Put me to death?"

"Yeah." Brock winced, then smiled. "This is a good thing. I think it's possible we'll have a mistrial."

"Then we have to do this thing over again."

"Maybe. Sometimes cases are dismissed after a mistrial. And if it's not, the next time we can bring all those victims in front of the jury."

PHIL M. WILLIAMS

"I just want this to be over."

Brock wiped his mouth with his napkin. "Well, best-case scenario, we get not guilty. Then it'll be over right here, right now. Second choice would be a mistrial."

"Whatever happens, I want you to know that I appreciate everything you've done for me."

Brock smiled again. "It's my job."

"Something tells me that you've put in a few extra hours on this one."

"Just a few."

"What do you think the chance is of a guilty verdict?"

Brock sighed. "The sixty-four-million-dollar question that every client asks at some point."

"Well?"

"I think the women coming out really hurt the prosecution …"

"But?"

"But the evidence is clear and without rebuttal. I think we're fifty-fifty for a guilty verdict." Brock spoke plainly, as if he were talking about fifty percent chance of rain.

Kyle nodded, buoyed by hope. "So a 50 percent chance for a not guilty verdict."

"No, I think a 49 percent chance of a mistrial."

Kyle hung his head and blew out a breath.

"Remember though, even if we get a guilty verdict, we still have the second trial to prove competency." Brock's phone buzzed. He checked the text. "They're back from deliberation."

Brock and Kyle were escorted to the courtroom by deputies. Emerson and Judge Cooley were already in place. The crowd filed into the pews. Finally, the jurors took their seats in the jury box, somber expressions on their faces.

They're gonna kill me. Kyle looked at his lawyer. *Brock saw it too. He looks concerned.*

The jury foreman gave a piece of paper to the bailiff who handed it to Judge Cooley. The jury foreman was one of the white men. A burly guy, successful, supposedly owned a construction company.

Judge Cooley read the form and glared at the jury. "Am I to understand that you cannot come to a unanimous verdict?"

The foreman, still standing said, "I'm sorry, Your Honor. We cannot come to a unanimous verdict."

"Will you be able to come to a verdict if you deliberate for another day?"

"I'm not sure, Your Honor."

Judge Cooley frowned. "I would like for each and every one of you to go home, get a good night's sleep, and report back here for deliberations at 8:00 a.m. tomorrow. If you cannot come to a unanimous verdict, I will be forced to declare a mistrial, and the case will have to be tried again with a new jury, but I don't think that's necessary. I think the twelve men and women of *this* jury can and *will* come to a consensus. As always, I expect that you will not talk about this trial to anyone, and you will avoid any and all media in regard to this trial."

CHAPTER 66

THE VERDICT

Kyle spent most of the next day alone in a holding cell at the court-house. He hoped the jury hadn't listened to the judge's warning about ignoring the media. Another dozen models had come forward last night. The count was up to twenty-two. Kyle thought it was really in the hundreds. Most victims of rape don't report it. And for good reason. The conviction rates were atrocious. Brock had brought him a few books to read, but Kyle couldn't concentrate enough to read. Late in the afternoon, the jury was back in the courtroom.

As Kyle was ushered into the courtroom by deputies, he surveyed the audience. The place was jam-packed. Kyle looked for a friendly face. He thought he saw Ryan's mother, but he couldn't be sure; she was toward the back and shielded by the crowd. Many of the faces had been to the trial every day, but he had no idea who they were or why they were there.

Once everyone was seated and accounted for, the jury foreman handed a piece of paper to the judge. Kyle sat next to Brock, his foot tapping nervously. Judge Cooley read the form, nodded, and handed it back to the bailiff. The bailiff handed the form back to the foreman.

"Kyle Summers, please stand for the reading of the verdict," Judge Cooley said.

Brock stood, then Kyle stood, his legs like rubber.

The jury foreman read from the form. "For the charge of capital murder, we find the defendant … not guilty."

The audience erupted, standing, clapping, shouting, some jumping up and down, arms in the air. Kyle and Brock embraced. Over Brock's shoulder, Kyle saw DA Diane Emerson. If her look could kill, they'd both be dead.

"I can't believe it," Kyle said to Brock.

"Me either," Brock replied, nearly shouting over the crowd noise.

Judge Cooley banged his gavel. "Quiet. Quiet!"

The crowd quieted a bit, voices still chattering.

The judge addressed the jury. "Ladies and gentlemen of the jury, thank you for your service." He turned toward Kyle. "Mr. Summers, you are free to go."

The audience erupted again. Brock hugged Kyle again, and they shook hands. People from the audience clustered around him, a makeshift line forming.

A middle-aged woman with big hair approached. "I wanted to thank you," she said, tears in her eyes. "That piece-of-shit weatherman, Aaron Wells, raped my daughter. They didn't do nothin' neither. Some horseshit about not enough evidence for trial." She shook her head. "It made me and my girl feel so good when you got him fired. Finally someone did somethin'." The short woman reached out and hugged Kyle tight around the waist.

Kyle smiled. "You're welcome."

She faded into the crowd, replaced by a burly man, who's daughter had been molested by a soccer coach. They shook hands. The man thanked Kyle and rapped him on the back. Kyle periodically searched the audience for Leigh and Ryan, but only unfamiliar faces surrounded him. People from the audience shook his hand, hugged him tight, and told him how he had helped them in some way. Many were survivors of sexual abuse. Many had loved ones who were survivors. Some were survivors of the men he'd exposed. Kyle couldn't help the tears of joy.

He caught a glimpse of Ryan and his big teeth exposed in his big smile. Kyle moved through the crowd toward the boy, people patting him on the back as he did so. Kyle hugged the boy; Ryan reciprocated. Kyle let go of Ryan and looked up to see his mother. She stepped aside, and Leigh stepped forward, her face blank. They stood face-to-face, only a few feet away.

"I'm sorry," Leigh said.

Kyle hugged his sister and said, "Me too."

CHAPTER 67

SWEET PEA

After the trial, Kyle exited the courthouse with Leigh and Brock. Ryan and his mother had broken off from them, not wanting to navigate the media hordes. Ryan had invited Kyle to his baseball game, which Kyle had accepted enthusiastically.

Kyle stopped on the courthouse steps, the media jockeying for positions around him. He gazed at the cloudless sky. It was a beautiful fall day—upper-sixties, light breeze. He looked at the reporters and exhaled.

"You don't have to talk to them," Brock said.

"It's fine," Kyle said.

"Mr. Summers, how does it feel to be free?" a young reporter asked, shoving her microphone in Kyle's face.

"I'm still processing," Kyle replied.

"Mr. Summers, how does it feel to get away with murder?" another reporter asked.

"Don't answer that," Brock said, glaring at the guy.

"What will you do now?" a male reporter asked.

"I don't know. I haven't thought about it. To be honest, I thought I'd be on death row."

"Were you surprised by the verdict?" the young reporter asked.

"Yes, I was. I'm very grateful to the jury."

"Will you go back to exposing child predators?" a male reporter asked.

"I don't know."

"Did you coordinate with your father's victims to help your case?"

"I'll take that question," Brock said to Kyle. "No, we didn't know any of these women were victims. We are thankful for their courage in coming forward and hopeful that they can heal from the awful traumas that they have suffered."

After the media barrage, Leigh and Kyle finally made it to the courthouse parking garage. Kyle sat in the passenger seat of Leigh's SUV.

"I was thinking you could stay at my house for a few days." Leigh said. "Gwen misses you. She's had it rough … with everything. I told her that you might not come home. I didn't want to lie to her. She cried herself to sleep last night."

"I'm sorry, Leigh."

"It's not your fault."

Kyle's eyes were downcast.

Leigh put her hand on top of his. "Really."

"Thanks." Kyle looked up. "Can we stop by my apartment, so I can get a few things?"

They drove to Kyle's apartment building. Kyle and Leigh walked to the fourth floor. A notice hung on Kyle's door. The big bold headline read Delinquency Notice. Kyle snatched it off the door, folded it, and shoved it in his pocket.

"What's that?" Leigh asked as they entered his apartment.

"I'm behind on my rent," Kyle said, not looking at Leigh as he headed for his bedroom.

Leigh followed. "Do you even have any money? You haven't been working for months."

Kyle grabbed his duffel bag from the closet. "I'll figure it out."

"Why don't you come live with Gwen and me for a while? There's plenty of room."

Kyle tossed the duffel on his bed. "I appreciate it. I really do, but I need to get my life together. Sponging off you isn't getting my life together. I feel like I've been given a second chance, and I don't wanna waste it."

"It's not sponging. I could actually use your help. Gwen needs family around, especially with me working so much. I had to hire a nanny, since ... I was willed the agency. Of course, there might not be an agency with the lawsuits coming."

"I was wondering how that was going."

She sighed. "It's a terrible thing to have dumped on your lap. I'll settle with every one of those girls, even if it bankrupts the agency. I can't fix what he did then, but I can do what's right now."

"What'll you do if the agency goes bankrupt?" Kyle opened his dresser and grabbed some T-shirts.

"I still have my trust and I have some savings. I thought about selling the house, downsizing, maybe starting my own company. I have the contacts. I know the business backwards and forwards."

Kyle shoved clothes in his duffel bag and looked at his sister. "I think you'd do great."

"If there's anything left of the agency after litigation, I'd like to split it with you."

Kyle shook his head. "Thank you, but I don't want it."

"If you change your mind, let me know."

Kyle nodded.

"A big part of me hopes the agency goes under," Leigh said. "I'm actually looking forward to a fresh start."

Kyle zipped up his duffel bag. "Me too."

"So, what do you think about living with Gwen and me?"

"I'd like to spend more time with Gwen, and I can stay with you for a few weeks if you need my help, but I can't live with you long term. I need to find my own way."

"I understand."

They left Kyle's apartment, his full duffel bag slung over his shoulder. Leigh drove them across town to her home. She parked the SUV in her garage. They stepped into the house, into the kitchen. In the living room, a young woman watched cartoons with Gwen.

"Look who's here," Leigh said, standing in the kitchen with Kyle.

Gwen broke from her television trance, turning her head. "*Unc Kye!*" She ran from the living room to Kyle.

Kyle scooped her up and hugged her. She had her little arms around his neck, her chubby cheek against his face.

"I missed you, sweet pea," he said.

CHAPTER 68

WHAT NOW?

The next day Kyle stood on Leigh's patio, the cordless phone to his ear, watching Gwen prepare a make-believe lunch in her playhouse.

"Hey, Sam, it's Kyle."

"Kyle! Congratulations on the acquittal," Sam said. "My wife and I've been followin' your trial. I gotta say, I was seriously worried."

"I wanted to apologize for never showing up for the estimator job."

Sam chuckled. "I've heard a lot of excuses for not comin' to work but never *I was arrested for murder.*"

Kyle went silent for a beat. The phone beeped. Call waiting. He ignored the other call.

"Sorry, that was rude," Sam said.

"No, it's fine. I was calling because I wanted to see if that job was still available."

Sam sucked air through his teeth. "Sorry, Kyle. I filled the position."

"OK, … no problem."

"I do need a mowin' helper. I could pay you eleven dollars an hour. I know that's a huge step-down for you, but I don't have any crew leader positions available. You'd be first in line if and when one opens up."

"Can I think about it for a few days?"

"Take all the time you need. I always need helpers."

"Thanks, Sam. You've always been good to me."

"Can I be straight with you, Kyle?"

"Yeah." The phone beeped again. Another call waiting that Kyle ignored.

"You're welcome to come back to work here anytime, but I hope I never see you again. Don't get me wrong. You're a hard worker, an honest guy. You got guts and integrity. Two things that are in short supply these days. I think you can do better than workin' for me. You let me know if you need anything."

"Thanks, Sam. I will."

"Take care of yourself, Kyle."

Kyle disconnected the call, the phone immediately ringing. "Hello?"

"This is Glen Gray from *The Washington Post*. I'm looking for Kyle Summers."

Kyle disconnected the call and approached the playhouse.

"Lunch is ready," Gwen said, handing Kyle an empty plate through the open window.

"Looks great," Kyle replied. "What are we having?"

"*Sssghetti*," she said, as if it were obvious.

* * *

After a real dinner and ice cream, Leigh and Gwen and Kyle sat on the couch. Gwen was asleep in Kyle's lap. Kyle flipped through the channels.

"Stop," Leigh said. "Go back."

Kyle had seen it too, but he had hoped Leigh hadn't. Kyle flipped the channel back to the big burly guy talking to a female reporter. Underneath the man, a caption read Jury Foreman Matthew Riggs.

"The evidence showed that he did murder his father," Riggs said.

"Then why didn't the jury find Kyle Summers guilty?" the reporter asked.

"A few of the jurors did wanna vote guilty. That's why we were in deliberation for two days."

"What changed their mind?"

"It was probably a combination of things. One juror said that we didn't have to follow the law, that we could vote our conscience. He called it jury nullification. We looked it up, and he was right. The other thing was, we could all see ourselves killin' that son of a *bleep*."

The ten o' clock news went to a commercial break, and the phone rang in the kitchen.

Leigh scowled. "It's after ten." She stood from the couch.

"I forgot to unplug the phone," Kyle said.

"I got it." Leigh was already walking to the kitchen. She picked up the phone, silencing the ring. "On what planet do you think it's OK to call at this hour?" Then she listened for a minute, her lips pursed. "Hold on." She went back to the living room, carrying the cordless phone. "A producer from TNT wants to talk to you."

CHAPTER 69

BASES LOADED

It was the bottom of the fourth inning, the score two to zero in favor of the visiting team. There were two outs, the bases loaded. Ryan was on the mound, trying to preserve his shutout and the lead. Kyle stood by himself, leaning against the right field fence. Ryan knew he was here. Kyle had told him where he'd be. He didn't want to sit in the stands and be a distraction. The media attention had been relentless over the past few days since the verdict. Twice Ryan had waved in his direction after a strikeout. Kyle had waved back with a huge smile.

Their big hitter was up. The kid was huge. He had hit a double off Ryan in the second inning. The first pitch was a ball. Kyle winced as the big slugger tattooed the second. It looked like a home run, but it pulled a bit too far left. Foul ball. Two more balls brought the count to three and one. Ryan was avoiding him, trying to paint the corners, but with three balls and the bases loaded, he'd have to come after him.

Ryan did exactly that. He threw a fastball right down the middle, the batter taking a big swing and a miss. The count was full. Ryan looked focused but relaxed. Ryan checked the runners, like he was in the big leagues, and threw a changeup. The slugger was way out in front. Strike three. Ryan waved at Kyle and walked off the mound like a boss.

"Hey," a woman with a soft voice said, sidling up to Kyle.

Kyle turned as Kate rested her hands on top of the short fence. She stood next to him, her sundress and blond hair billowing in the breeze.

"Kate," he said, his eyes wide.

She smiled. "Your sister told me you'd be here."

"You were looking for me?"

"I'm headed back to California tomorrow. I wanted to see you before I left."

"Really? I thought you hated me."

She pursed her full lips. "I didn't like dredging all this up."

"I'm sorry."

"That's why I'm here actually. I wanted to tell you that I'm sorry about what I did to you. It was cruel and selfish—"

"You weren't—"

"Please, Kyle, let me finish."

Kyle nodded.

"When you rejected me, I was humiliated—"

"I shouldn't have."

"No, you were right. We were too young, but I didn't understand it. Even at fifteen, I was so used to guys coming on to me. Then, when you rejected me, it hurt."

"I didn't wanna reject—"

"Please, let me finish."

Kyle showed his palms in surrender. "OK, I'm shutting up."

Ryan's team was at bat, already with a runner on first.

"I was mad at you, and your dad had been coming on to me, so I thought I'd show you. I kissed him." She blinked, her eyes watery. "I didn't want it to go any further, but I started it to get back at you. I felt so much guilt, like it was all my fault. Your dad told me to lie to the police. He said that they'd never believe me and that I'd lose my career and that my family would be devastated. He was right. My family would've been devastated. I'm not even sure my mother would've believed me. He had her charmed. So I lied, and we moved to California, and I just wanted to forget the whole thing." Kate took a deep breath. "I wish I could take it all back. I'm really sorry."

"So am I. I only rejected you because I was ashamed of what had happened to me, and I didn't think you'd want to be with someone who was ruined." Kyle went on to tell Kate the whole story about Rebecca showing up in his bedroom that night and the lasting effects.

Kate listened intently, her face showing empathy instead of the pity or even the disgust that he expected. "I'm sorry, Kyle. I didn't know."

"If I could change anything, it would be that. I would've pushed her away. I never would've rejected you. Robert never would've ..." Kyle swallowed the lump in his throat. "I wish I could do it all over."

She inched closer, her arm touching his. "What if we could?"

Kyle forced a smile. "I wish." He took a deep breath. "All this time, I never stopped thinking about you."

"Me too," Kate replied.

They were quiet for a moment, watching the game.

Kyle turned to Kate. "Ryan and his mom and I are going out for pizza after this. You wanna come?"

"I don't want to intrude. Ryan will probably want your undivided attention."

"Maybe next time?" Kyle asked.

She nodded, her eyes downcast.

"We won't be out late. You wanna get together after?"

She smiled, blushing. "I'd like that."

CHAPTER 70

THE PREDATOR HUNTER

It was dark in the living room except for the Christmas tree lights. The house was a nicely decorated suburban colonial. Kyle hid behind the wall separating the living room from the kitchen. An open entryway to the kitchen was only a few steps away. The doorbell chimed; his heartbeat increased. The front door opened.

"Danny?" the girl asked, her voice squeaky.

"Bethany?" the man replied.

The girl giggled. "Who else would it be?"

"You know how it is, girl. A guy's gotta be careful."

"Come on in."

Light footsteps moved down the hall to the kitchen. The front door shut, and heavy boots lumbered behind.

"Where you goin', girl?" the man asked.

"The kitchen," the girl replied over her shoulder. "You want something to drink?" The girl walked past the kitchen, the laundry room, and into the garage.

"Can I get a hug?" the man asked, now in the kitchen. "Where you at?"

Kyle stepped from the living room to the kitchen. "What's up, Danny?"

Danny's eyes were like saucers. He was a massive man. Stubbly beard, big puffy black coat, knit cap, thick neck, and tree-trunk legs.

"Who the hell are you?" Danny said, his hands already balled into fists.

"Why don't you have a seat," Kyle said, ushering the man to the kitchen table.

Danny sat, looking around as he did so. "Who are you?"

Kyle sat across from the man at the small round table, wondering if Danny had spotted one of the hidden cameras or microphones. "I'm Kyle Summers, the Predator Hunter."

Danny raised one side of his mouth. "The who?"

"Why did you come here?"

He took off his knit cap, his shaved head gleaming in the fluorescent light. "Bethany and I were gonna have some dinner. What's it to you? Where did she go?" Danny craned his neck, looking around for "Bethany." "Bethany" was actually Cassie, a very-young-looking eighteen-year-old theater student.

"That's it? You're just here to have dinner?"

"Yeah, so what?"

"So, she's thirteen. It's not appropriate for a twenty-eight-year-old man to meet a thirteen-year-old girl for dinner."

Danny furrowed his brows. "How'd you know how old I am?"

"That's not important. What is important is, why you're here." Kyle removed his phone from the pocket of his fleece. "You're Danny Boy MMA, right?"

"How the *fuck* do you know that?"

"When 'Bethany' asked what you wanted to do tonight, you texted, and I quote, 'I wanna give it to you all night long.' What exactly did you mean by that?"

Danny Boy's face was red, every muscle in his body tense. It looked like he was about to explode. "What the fuck, man?"

"Why did you send a picture of your genitals to a thirteen-year-old girl?"

Danny Boy stood. "Are you some kinda cop?"

"I'd sit down if I were you."

"I'll do whatever the fuck I want."

Kyle stood from the table and went back to his phone. "Why did you text and I quote, 'I'm gonna make you come so hard.' What did you mean by that?"

"You know what I meant." Danny stepped toward Kyle, his fists clenched.

Kyle didn't back down, the man only a few feet away. "Why are you here, *Danny Boy*? You afraid to tell the truth?"

"I ain't afraid of shit," Danny said.

"Then tell the truth. Why are you here?"

"I wasn't gonna do nothin'."

"You weren't gonna give it to her all night long? You weren't gonna make her come? What's wrong? Too many steroids?"

"Fuck you. I'm all natural. I would've given her the time of her life."

"You don't care that she's thirteen?"

"She invited *me*. It ain't my fault."

"It's against the law."

"I didn't do nothin'."

"You could be arrested for obscene internet contact with a child, attempting to entice a minor by computer, attempted unlawful sexual conduct with a minor, and intent to commit a felony."

Danny cocked his massive dome. "You a cop or somethin'?"

"No."

"What the fuck you gonna do about it then?" Danny puffed up his chest and stepped inches from Kyle's face, his breath heavy and acrid.

"She's thirteen, you sick piece of shit," Kyle said, still not backing down.

Danny Boy slammed Kyle against the wall, his forearm jammed in Kyle's throat. "I'll fuck you up, you little bitch."

Boots stepped into the kitchen, followed by a clicking sound.

Danny Boy fell to the floor, shrieking in pain, his body seizing as the police officer sent 1,200 volts of electricity through his body. Five officers crowded around the scene. With Danny Boy subdued, two officers turned Danny on his stomach. Another wrenched his hands behind his back, cuffed him, and read him his rights.

As he was led from the house, Danny Boy said over and over again, "I didn't do nothin'. I didn't do nothin'."

The cops were unmoved by his pleas.

An EMT entered the kitchen and approached Kyle. "You all right?"

Kyle rubbed his neck. "I'm good."

"You should probably have the doc take a look."

"OK."

Detective Fitzgerald waltzed into the kitchen. He rapped Kyle on the back. "Nice work, Kyle. We can add assault to this douchebag's charges."

"Thanks, Sean," Kyle replied with a nod.

Kyle left the kitchen for the garage. The two-car garage was actually a repurposed room with heat and AC, a collection of desks and computers, as well as a staging area for law enforcement. Twenty people could work comfortably in the space. Kyle approached a few young men working on computers, the confrontation with Danny Boy MMA on the mounted flat screen.

"How was the footage?" Kyle asked.

A young man adjusted his glasses and grinned. "Pure television gold."

CHAPTER 71

RIGHT HERE, RIGHT NOW

Kyle circled the lot, but it was full as usual. He drove across the street and parked his Honda Civic in the alternate lot. He hustled across the street to the three-story restaurant. A few flurries landed on his wool jacket. He pushed through the revolving door. Kyle looked around for his date. The restaurant was decorated with nonreligious holiday decor such as mini-lights, garland, and red bows. Well-to-do people bustled about, chatting and laughing and holding pagers. He couldn't find her. He felt panicky. *Where is she?* He thought about the many men he'd confronted. Was there another Big Bad Wolf lurking out there?

Soft hands slipped around his waist from behind, followed by a kiss on the cheek. Kyle smiled wide and turned around.

Kate grinned right back, wearing a long red pea coat and a scarf. Her grin disappeared at the sight of Kyle's neck. Her blue eyes were wide. "What happened to your neck?"

"Danny Boy MMA put me in a chokehold."

She frowned. "Does it hurt?"

"A little. It was great TV though."

"I think you've taken enough risks for a lifetime."

Kyle shrugged. "The guys were right there. I'll have to show you the footage of the guy getting tazed. The guy was enormous, and he dropped like a sack of potatoes."

"I'm glad you're OK."

"Me too." Kyle nodded, reflecting for a moment. "Have you been here long? I'm sorry I'm late."

"I just got here too, like, five minutes ago." Kate removed a restaurant pager from her pocket, holding it up. "It'll be a while."

A few people recognized Kyle and stopped to say thank-you, to shake his hand, to clap him on the back. Others nearby smiled as recognition dawned, giving him a head tip or a chin nod.

Kyle and Kate moved to the waiting area and sat side by side, their thighs touching. It was crowded, but they sat in the corner, talking and laughing, lost in each other.

Kate checked her watch. "We've been waiting over an hour. I should've known not to suggest dinner out on a Saturday night. I know you've had a busy week."

He put his hand on top of hers. "I'm right where I wanna be."

FOR THE READER

Dear Reader,

I'm thrilled that you took precious time from your life to read my novel. Thank you! I hope you found it entertaining, engaging, and thought-provoking. If so, please consider writing a positive review on Amazon and Goodreads. Five-star reviews have a huge impact on future sales. The review doesn't need to be long and detailed, if you're more of a reader than a writer. As an author and a small businessman competing against the big publishers, every reader, every review, and every referral is greatly appreciated.

If you're interested in receiving my novel *Against the Grain* **for free and/or reading my other titles for free or discounted, go to the following link:** http://www.PhilWBooks.com. You're probably thinking, *What's the catch?* There is no catch.

If you want to contact me, don't be bashful. I can be found at Phil@PhilWBooks.com. I do my best to respond to all emails.

Sincerely,
Phil M. Williams

AUTHOR'S NOTE

According to the study entitled "The Long-Term Sequelae of Child and Adolescent Abuse: A Longitudinal Community Study," 80 percent of twenty-one-year-olds who reported childhood abuse met the criteria for at least one psychological disorder.

As many as two-thirds of the people in treatment for drug abuse reported being abused or neglected as children.

Children who experience child abuse and neglect are about nine times more likely to become involved in criminal activity.

When a child is abused, he or she is not simply hurt in that moment. They are hurt for a lifetime.

GRATITUDE

I'd like to thank my wife. She's my first reader and always will be. Without her support and unwavering belief in my skill as an author, I'm not sure I would have embarked on this career. I love you, Denise.

I'd also like to thank my editors. My developmental editor, Caroline Smailes, did a fantastic job finding the holes in my plot and suggesting remedies. As always, my line editor, Denise Barker (not to be confused with my wife, Denise Williams), did a fantastic job making sure the manuscript was error-free. I love her comments and feedback.

Thank you to Deborah Bradseth of Tugboat Design for her excellent cover art and formatting. She's the consummate professional. I look forward to many more beautiful covers in the future.

Finally, thank you to my mother-in-law, Joy, for her expert medical advice.

Made in the USA
San Bernardino, CA
25 January 2020